Retrovival

Also by Douglas Thompson from Elsewhen Press

Entanglement
The Rhymer: an Heredyssey
Stray Pilot
'Bird Brains' in *Existence is Elsewhen*

Retrovival

DOUGLAS THOMPSON

This book is a work of fiction. All names, characters, places, governments, political parties, media organisations, research institutions, religious institutions and events are either a product of the author's fertile imagination or are used fictitiously. Any resemblance to actual events, organisations, activists, states, places or people (living, dead, or resurrected) is purely coincidental.

Al Jazeera is a trademark of Al Jazeera Media Network; CNN is a trademark of Cable News Network, Inc.; Glasgow University is a trademark of The University Court of the University of Glasgow; Star Trek is a trademark of CBS Studios, Inc. Use of trademarks has not been authorised, sponsored, or otherwise approved by the trademark owners.

*Now doth this man, who from the lowest depth
of the universe as far as here has seen
one after one the spiritual lives...*

*I, who never burned for my own seeing
more than I do for his, all of my prayers proffer to thee
that thou wouldst scatter from him
every cloud of his mortality.*

– Dante Alighieri
  The Divine Comedy, Paradiso, Canto XXXIII.

PROLOGUE

Two thousand years apart: two men dream the same dream. Both are soldiers, of a kind, paid by rulers far distant to patrol the boundaries of their vast estates. One is a Roman centurion, the other a border guard of the new Scottish Republic.

The centurion has been marching in his sandals and armour twenty miles a day through England for the last two months. Although England is not a name he would recognise of course, it will only emerge five centuries later after another civilisation invades, the Angles from Germany. England to him is merely southern Britannia, that which lies behind him, having arrived last night at the boundary Rome has built to wall off Caledonia, the domain of dangerous blue-painted savages to the north. The boundary is an impressive stone wall from coast to coast across the narrow waist of the long island of Britannia, and he is glad and proud to sleep in a barracks in its shadow, after so many days of travel and exertion. But in his dream, curiously, the wall has become one of glass rather than stone. Glass, the impressive new invention he has only so far seen in the windows of the most exotic palaces of the patrician classes. In his dream he finds himself walking uphill across green moorland to reach up his hand and run his fingers across the perfect surface of a wall of glass of almost infinite length and daunting height, struggling to find any joint-lines in its construction.

His counterpart, a border guard of the future, walks downhill within the same dream, expecting to find the metal chain-link fence with barbed wire top which has been a defining landmark of his adult life and a demarcation of his responsibility and jurisdiction. He too is surprised to find it replaced with implacable glass.

The two sight each other within each of their dreams,

and are astonished by their disparity of dress and complexion. One draws a sword and spear, the other a rifle. They both approach the glass wall from different sides and test it with their weapons, trying to find weaknesses, some way through. They shout at each other, whether in warning or greeting it is hard to say since neither recognise each other's language and the sound is attenuated by the thick transparent barrier.

To the Roman's astonishment, the border guard lifts his strange weapon to his shoulder and shoots projectiles at the wall, perhaps stones so small and fast as to be as invisible as the glass itself. The first two shots bounce off, but the third one creates a tiny hole far above his head.

To the border guard's surprise, the Roman reaches up with his spear and pushes its point into the hole and works on it until a fissure then snakes down across the glass, through which he can prise his sword in order to expand it. Working together with the strange opposing soldier, the border guard draws a bayonet of his own, and uses this and his rifle butt to help push the glass further apart.

To the Roman's alarm, long shards of glass break out and tumble down onto the uphill side of the boundary, one of which slices into the border guard's chest, wounding him fatally. The Centurion steps through the boundary on to the other side and walks up to stand over the guard for a moment, puzzling over his strange weapons, his camouflaged trousers and jacket, his bizarre uniform. He sees that a pool of blood is spreading under him. Then he is alarmed to notice that the man's flesh is turning brown and black like the skin of bruised fruit, decaying rapidly as if soon to expose the bone underneath. He looks down at his own arms and hands and thinks he can see them already darkening in a similar process. He cries out in alarm and spins around, and clinging to the strange logic of dreams: hopes to race back to his own side of the boundary. In the irrational and desperate belief that there he will be safe again. As if the glass wall has been containing two different atmospheres, two different worlds, across which any escapee will suffocate like a fish stranded out of water.

Both men cry out and wake up in a cold sweat, one in 2088, the other in 142 AD. One is comforted by his wife in the bedroom of their farmhouse, the other mocked by his fellow soldiers in their humble barracks. Both will forget their dream shortly afterwards, although certain events in their lives in the days to come may for just a moment evoke a resonance, an echo, a lost fragment of recollection of what they dreamt and what it might have signified.

~

I

Lachlan had hated the Sassens since he was a child. Now that Senator Drest had won the election he felt as if his time had come at last, his views and resentment vindicated. Lachlan's father had been a hunter too, in these bleak hilly borderlands, and had passed on to him all the skills that he and his wife Flora now used to put food on the table each week: deer and squirrel and occasional wild boar. He respected the deer and admired their beauty, strength and grace, and yet he felt no remorse when he shot and skinned and butchered them. He chose his targets carefully, understood the principles of conservation, always avoiding juveniles or pregnant mothers, choosing instead the males of a certain age whose glory days were probably gone and who he might be doing a favour anyway, letting their lives end with a bang rather than a long sordid decline as the young bucks progressively wounded them. Lachlan understood that he was part of nature.

So much for deer, but as for Sassens: Lachlan felt they should each know better than to enter border land and attempt to pierce the boundaries of his beloved and hard-won homeland. Back before independence, how they and their children had lorded it up when he was young: coming up here with their families and taking all the best jobs. Lachlan's own father had lost out on the promotion to senior lecturer that he should have got at the university, lost out to some loud smarmy Sassen upstart with a posh accent who'd gone to the right school. That was the saddest and most galling thing back then: that Lachlan's own people had been prejudiced against themselves, brought up to regard themselves as second-class citizens, eager to appoint a Sass whenever and wherever possible in the belief that they were some superior race that would always make a better job of whatever they did than someone who actually grew up and belonged here in the homeland.

Today Lachlan had been out on the moors and tracked and shot a stag, and was dragging it back down the valley on horseback, still the best mode of transport in this territory despite all the technology which roamed over and above it now. His government drone, provided to him as standard issue for a Tracker in the Border Defence Force, was only allowed to assist him in his 'domestic' business such as deer culling, when its autonomous border duties went quiet. This occurred around midday today, as Lachlan knew it would from experience, when most of the people smugglers and refugees had given up or gone to ground until darkness fell again. Tonight would be Lachlan's first all-night shift since last week and he found himself looking forward to it more than usual. It was good money but also, he felt, good, noble work, that his forefathers would have been proud of him for.

Back at the cottage, Lachlan found that Flora had the stock boiling already, must have glimpsed his figure with its spoil from the kitchen window even at great distance, rounding the head of the high pass. She was sharpening the knives, and they set about the deer carcass together in the shed with skill and alacrity born of long experience. They were accustomed to the rich brassy smell of blood and its constantly renewing and deepening stain upon the rough brown of their overalls, the good sight of it running in the ancient stone channels on the barn floor.

The radio was on when they sat down for dinner, as the sun was beginning to set behind the dense forest of pines in the foothills beyond their pasture. Drest was speaking, *President* Drest as they would now have to get used to calling her, expanding on her acceptance speech of last week and her many bold new plans for the homeland, how the property of wealthy Sassens was to be seized by the state at last, their bank accounts to be frozen. And the border skirmishes, the night incursions of refugees from their broken towns and cities to the south: this is where

Lachlan most pricked up his ears, even laying his knife and fork down, leaving his fresh venison steaming on the plate, while he stood up to turn up the volume.

No more chickening around then, a strong stance at last... Lachlan said when the news story finished and he switched it to some traditional music, not wanting to spoil his mood or his dinner with any of the other less important tittle-tattle of the world's comings and goings for the day. Flora had some news, she said, not unconnected with this. Her nephew and his wife and baby were selling their house down south and coming home, she said they'd told her today, inspired by Drest's victory, coming back across the border to resume their citizenship before any immigration clampdown the new administration might bring in could potentially complicate things. *Complicate?* Lachlan asked, helping himself to more carrots and turnips, *They're not Sass, why would they have any difficulty coming home to here?*

Well that's what I told them, and to quote your name at the border post if necessary, since I'm sure you'll be held in high esteem in official circles for the work you do, or will be, for the new regime. Lachlan nodded his head in silent agreement and in slow, secret, solemn pride. Flora reached around for her photograph of the young family that she kept on the kitchen window sill and beamed at it happily as if she was face-to-face with her home-come relatives already.

*

The night air was sharp and pleasingly chill when Lachlan stepped out a few hours later. A fifty percent likelihood of snow had been forecast for the night. He drove the first ten miles in his jeep to the remote ridge above Chatto, then released the drone from its place under cover in the boot and set it off to hover a thousand feet above him as he proceeded on foot. The moon, almost full, was rising up out of the lower lands to the south so that he might not even need his infra-red goggles until the cloud-cover thickened. He approached the edge of a vast pine forest that he knew well, the long lonely path through which he always enjoyed, sometimes sighting fox and deer along the way. When he emerged from its other side he knew he would have a full overview of the twenty mile stretch of border that had been assigned to him to patrol tonight.

Lachlan was not an ignorant, uneducated or uncreative man, whatever the prejudices towards him of city dwellers – those who he occasionally encountered when they ventured out to these parts in summer in search of relaxing holidays amid what they regarded as blissful emptiness, which in fact to Lachlan's eye was a place of business, always buzzing with unseen life. He had been a student once in his youth, in the great historic city sixty miles to the north, and had gone out with a girl who was at Art School, who had led him around various galleries and museums to share with him the source of her inspirations and aspirations.

One picture he had seen there often returned to his memory as he entered this and other similarly remote forests along border country. It had been by some German Romantic painter of the 19th century, of a French Napoleonic soldier standing alone looking into the edge of a vast German forest. Angela, that had been her name, had explained that the painting referred not just to Napoleon's ultimate failure to conquer Germany, but also to the defeat of the Romans two thousand years earlier in the same impenetrable forests beyond the frontier of the River Rhine. Some people had been likening Drest to Hitler recently, but Lachlan considered the analogy unfair. The homeland had been enslaved to others for centuries, it had never had any colonies and empires of its own, other than in alliance with its pompous, militaristic neighbour. We weren't about to conquer anyone, let alone the world, only to *Get our own house in order*, yes that was the phrase that President Drest had used. She was like an empress ushering in some golden era the homeland had hitherto always been denied until now. Now was its moment at last.

These were Lachlan's forthright, uplifting thoughts at least, when the drone network, his and the others all 'talking' to each other, picked up the first infra-red targets of the night. Two human traces, his visor read-out told him, when he paused to fold it down over his face, about as far from the electrified wire as he currently was, which was perfect timing. A third trace could also be seen downhill from them in the other direction, clearly a guide, a people trafficker who had got them to this point, perhaps placed some bypass device on the fence at a point he had directed them to. Lachlan's drone overhead had been engineered for complete silence, deadly as a barn owl if it needed to be, although Lachlan usually preferred to conserve its battery and fire off any shots himself.

Leaving the edge of the woods, just before the moon vanished behind clouds and he had to pull his full infra-red headset down, he caught sight of the gnarled and twisting roots of some of the much older trees that pre-dated the current plantation. Oak trees that probably carried the scars of bullets and swords from the skirmishes of previous centuries. Something about those roots made him shiver tonight, touching upon some buried memory perhaps. As he walked on it came to him. The burned-black bodies of women and children that he had witnessed at the aftermath of the massacre the Sassens had carried out in Freedom Square when the homeland resistance protested the attempt to suppress the independence vote. It had been a peaceful political demonstration, a party atmosphere almost, handmade banners swaying in the spring sunshine before the army had turned their tanks on them. Like wolves preying on sheep, foxes let loose in a hen house. That black day had marked the end of innocence, the start of the short and savage war. The memory was just what Lachlan needed at that moment, to set his pulse racing and his blood on the boil. He could see on his visor that the targets were running now, so he followed suit, aiming to reach the wire before them.

It was a simple trick that MacDaid had taught him, that he said he often used on his stretch twenty miles west. Lachlan whispered into his mouthpiece to tell the drone to power down this section of the fence and wait on his signal to re-charge at treble strength. The Sassens would think they'd lucked out or found their guide's bypass section, and rather than hang about might just plunge right in there, try to scale or cut the ten-feet-high barrier. Lachlan was a quarter of a mile from them but his telephoto-toggle meant he felt near enough to touch them. A man and a woman, husband and wife perhaps. He didn't think of them as human, but as lower than animals, particularly at moments like these. He whispered the code, E52, and the drone switched the power back on, with one target at the top of the wire the other half way down. They screamed and smoked in a brief flash of light then fell on the homeland side, which was always a relief to Lachlan. The drone could lift him to the other side if required, but it was against official protocols which meant he might need one of Geordie's pals to fiddle the software afterwards. Geordie, like MacDaid, could be trusted, was an old soldier too, in on the same racket as Lachlan. They didn't talk about it much when they met, no longer needed to. Men you had fought beside in the Independence War could be trusted unto death. If you talked about shit like this, the old team took care of you and you'd be found a month later with your tongue cut out in a ditch beside some lonely road miles from anywhere.

Officially... a word that Lachlan and the older guards laughed out of the side of their mouths at. Officially, you were supposed to arrest intruders like these, cuff them and escort them down to the nearest barracks, but nobody he knew did anymore, not with the smaller parties, the ones and the twos, the stragglers. The border force were overstretched these days anyway. The Sassen towns had been disintegrating into crime and starvation in the wake of the economic meltdown their once belligerent nation had brought upon itself with its flagrant defiance of international law, the atrocities it had sanctioned against Lachlan's people, the crippling UN sanctions imposed upon it in retaliation. Hell mend them. They should have stayed home and stewed in their own self-made disaster zone of a country that had turned its back on the rest of the civilised world. Roasted their own dogs on bonfires, as far as Lachlan was concerned. For what they had done to his race, his country, not just in the recent war but for centuries of arrogant oppression and colonial exploitation: for this they could never pay dearly enough for him. They had forfeited their right to be human by de-humanizing others. What goes around. History had tipped against them now.

Lachlan even had a code for what happened next, one that he had programmed into his drone. He and the Owlbot worked together like a farmer and his trusty sheepdog. *D42* he whispered, then *G19*. He'd been reading for some time before the election that Drest might be planning to strengthen the border fence, replace it with a solid wall of concrete or steel. For that reason, he and MacDaid and Geordie had agreed a sub-routine for the drone to follow that would ensure it dug a grave pit two hundred yards from the border line, just to be on the safe side, clear of any possible future foundation excavation or trial cores.

When Lachlan reached the foot of the fence he saw that the male target was sprawled unconscious face down in the mud, upper limbs twisted in an ungainly pose, legs tangled upside down in the barbed wire above. He drew his rifle and fired three muffled shots at close quarters, one to the head, two to the back near the heart. Then something startled him. An object broke free unexpectedly from the female and snagged half way down the fence. The woman opened her mouth and began to say something. How he resented the inconvenient historic fact that they spoke the same language as he did. This of course being yet another dimension of their villainy, how they had driven the language of his forefathers underground, tried to stamp out their culture.

He tried never to see the faces of the fugitives, let alone hear their voices speak. *Please...* was the only word she got out before Lachlan, almost reflexively, had fired a couple of shots into the centre of her spread-eagled form. He saw that her long hair had fallen loose anyway, covering up her face like a drawn curtain.

Then the bundle on the fence began to cry out. What he had thought at a distance had merely been a pack on her back had been, it seemed, a papoose, a baby carrier. The sound shocked Lachlan to his core. In a flash he was remembering the sound of his own daughter crying when she was newborn and he thought of her far away from all this in the city to the north, safe and unaware, blind to all this darkness. He raised his gun. The child writhed, stretched out its little hand, recoiling from the harshness it found, the barbed wire like strange festive holly. Then he was remembering that other birth, of his own son, who had died in the civil war, before even his seventeenth birthday, before he'd even kissed a girl. Where was **his** son, **his** family? – the children he might have fathered, were he not now beneath the ground for ten long years? Lachlan looked down at his own finger on the trigger, wondering why he had not yet fired. He found himself moving closer, against his will. His limbs shaking. The sound, he had to stop the sound. It made no sense. He didn't need to get any closer, so why was he doing so? Babies all look the same. It would only grow up and produce more, over and over, the endless proliferation of their kind. Sound could travel so far in these hills at night. He had to stop it, terminate the unanticipated situation. He fired.

But the silence that came then was not what he expected. Not the silence of the hills and the moors that he thought he knew. His legs gave out under him and he knelt, sat down in the mud and stared into the distance to the west, where a patch of cloud was clearing and he could dimly see a twinkling of stars. It was the silence of the death of his own child, his own death, the laughing grin of a skull at all humanity, the ultimate, monstrous joke. He was a beetle, an insect, and nothing could stop the boot that was crushing us all. Truly, the devil walked upon the earth. His mother would be ashamed of him. This fact flooded in and alarmed his mind so suddenly that he fled from the thought, knew that he had to expel it at all costs. He staggered to his feet again and mechanically, with an enormous weariness in his limbs, resumed his task of cleaning up the mess that had been created.

Again he felt ashamed, that he could not cut the mother and child down from the wire himself, as he might usually have done, but had to instruct the drone to do it for him. It would not be as careful and dexterous as him. Less *respectful*, yes that was the word he admitted to himself, reluctantly. Small fragments of flesh and blood left on the wire for the rain or snow or the birds to clean away. He had two Hessian sacks with him, the child would share one with the mother. As the Owlbot whirred its little blades in the chill night air above him, Lachlan worked beneath it like its servant, never looking up, heaving one body after the other into the bags and tethering them up so that the drone could lift them in short flights to the disposal site. He dimmed his infra-red vision so as to see as little as possible of what his hands held. There were no reds, only black and white. No blood, only dry and wet, cold and lukewarm. The child's body felt like a lifeless doll, nothing more, and again he unwillingly remembered his own daughter and a doll he had once mended for her. He imagined the mocking laughter of Satan burning the back of his neck again as if to ask: why he could not repair this doll?

When the drone had backfilled the perfect six-foot square of dirt, Lachlan sat down on the mossy ground near it, with his back against an old tree, and lit himself a cigarette to try to stop the shaking that had taken hold in his whole body. Snow had begun falling from the night sky high above, in increasingly large flakes, which would be a blessing, covering up his tracks and traces and the square of disturbed ground itself. It might even stay frozen now for weeks after this. The drone came down and rested on the ground facing him at close quarters, folding its limbs like a faithful dog. In the light of the LCD screen of its interface, he now saw that both he and it were spattered with blood, which the fresh snow might yet erase. An old soldier had once told him that there were only two ways to dull the traumatic memories of atrocities you'd witnessed. The first was to live through enough decades of peace afterwards for the memories to fade through overuse, forcing yourself to picture them every day. The second was to crowd out and overwrite those memories with fresh ones of other atrocities, ones in which you avenged the first set. The soldier had said he didn't have time for the first method, and he'd been right. He'd heard some months later that he died in an ambush the week after their conversation.

Lachlan spoke to the drone. He knew it could only respond with silent dispassionate words on its glowing display, and something about this felt consoling at this moment, as if talking to a cold, dispassionate God, who dealt only in the hard currency of facts. *Owlbot 87b... erase your memory of this evening.*

Event Log Blanked As Requested... came the glib reply a moment later, letters dancing in demonic procession across the sickly green screen.

Erase sub-routines D42 and G19... he further instructed it. From now on, he decided, he would play all this straight. Cover, at the very least, in the unlikely event there should ever be investigations. MacDaid would think he'd gone soft, but this was the explanation he would spit back at him and the topic would never be discussed again. He was getting too old for this job. When would this sick lurching in his stomach subside? It was like the first hunt his father took him on as a child, his horror of cutting the deer open, the smell as its innards had slurped out. His father and uncle had laughed at him then for his childlike squeamishness and he had vowed never again to harbour such weakness. No one had warned him that life might be a circle like this rather than a straight line. –

That he might weaken with age instead of strengthening, and return to the girlishness of a child. Maybe old people were just like children again, right down to the nappies. A thought came to Lachlan, of something Geordie had told him once, that the drones had protocols to protect their operators. Reaching the nadir of his private despair he addressed the machine again out of curiosity: *Owlbot 87b, raise and prime your weapon.* Its lights flickered for a second then it raised its mechanical arm and spun its barrel in his face. *Shoot me in the head...* he said, then waited, trying to overwrite and mask the sickness in his stomach with a new one. But it didn't seem to work. Was he no longer even afraid to die? *What are you waiting for then? Why can't you do it? Lost your nerve?* –he taunted it.

Unable To Harm Fellow Homeland Defence Operative... came the answer at last. Grimly, he laughed out loud. So that was it then, the joke Geordie wanted him to see. He was recognised by a robot as its brother, a cold metal machine. He got to his feet and dusted himself down, preparing for the long walk back down the hillside through the deep forest. A few minutes later the drone received a signal to join its fellows on another hunt further east and they parted company for the night, its compact rectilinear form unfolding its wings like a hellish bat and setting off undaunted into the flurry of weather overhead, its tiny red eyes glowing.

Walking alone back down the long track through the woods, Lachlan switched his headlamp on as the snow fell in thick flakes, its endless motion slow and hypnotic. He wondered at all the branches and fronds around him and reaching far above, arching over at times as the vaults of some enormous cathedral. The light on his helmet lit everything from below like a marvel as he moved through it, as if to remind him that there was no escape from his own view of the world and his own role and responsibility within it. Did he create this world by revealing it as he moved through it like this, like the captain of a ship? Or did it somehow create him, make his every action inevitable? What was the difference between a robot of metal and one of flesh? Glimpsing pairs of lights in the woods he switched the lamp off for five minutes and knelt down to watch a lone grey wolf crossing his path, stalking a deer it had seen on the other side. He could have shot either of them, but instead he felt a strange impulse to hail the wolf, address it as he would some fellow woodsman, share with it the food in his pocket, let it lick in curiosity all the blood off his hands. The wolf had no choice either.

*

Returning home as the first dim glow of dawn was starting to emerge all around the horizon, Lachlan found himself half-heartedly preparing stories to tell Flora to account for the excessive blood on his uniform. He would have to say it was from some wild animal he had shot, but since he had no meat with him would also have to say that it had only feigned death then wriggled away injured from his grasp and escaped before he could get a shot off. As it was, no such explanations proved necessary, since she did not even notice his clothes before he had removed them and taken them to the laundry room. Flora was too engrossed in putting up Christmas decorations, having heard the unexpected good news while Lachlan was away that her nephew had decided to come home even earlier than expected and intended to be dropping by their house late afternoon. Not having many visitors these days in their rural isolation, they usually left decorations until as late as possible, when in-laws and children might be coming round. *Why the change of plan?* Lachlan asked. *I thought they weren't coming for another two weeks at least?*

He was but they heard that new rules might class their baby as Sassen because he was born there, —Flora answered from above from where she stood on a chair, her head lost among the gaudy heaven of green, red and gold coloured crepe and tinsel *...So Gregor said they were taking no chances, were going to go by some secret* *route over the border a friend of his knows rather than an official checkpoint and the sooner the better...*

What? Lachlan whispered, his voice gone unexpectedly hoarse. *What age did you say their child was?* His back was turned to her, and looking down at his hands, still shaking very slightly, he saw that he was absentmindedly holding a hand-made painted figure he had lifted up from the kitchen table, of the baby Jesus in his cot. It was from the little nativity scene that his great grandfather had carved back before the First World War, a beautiful thing that had been handed down in the family ever since. He recalled that the infant had once even had painted eyes and lips, as was the usual tradition, but saw that now the colour had faded, as if the child was asleep. The heirloom could only grow more strange and valuable over time, provided it was cherished by each generation.

~

II

In the spring of 2089 a hand emerges from the mud of Balmore marsh, black with age, its fingers clutching skyward. A farmer's ditch-digging drone has been cutting a line across the bog in an attempt to drain and reclaim it as the wheat field it was in his father's time, before global warming began raising water tables. When the device strikes something untoward it immediately recoils as it is programmed to, folding its arms like a disgruntled farm-hand on strike, or a sheep dog called to sit down. Its discreet red warning lights coincide with a signal being sent directly to the police and to the Scottish Government's archaeology section *The Tacitus Project*.

The farmer kneels down and puzzles over the error codes listed in his manual for a few minutes, before understanding what the machine's shutdown probably signifies. Through ignorance or impatience, he breaks the recommended protocols and gets a spade to gently take away a little more of the dark peat around the hand. He suspects it's just a fluke and trick of the eye, that it can't be human, perhaps just a piece of ancient tree branch, so dark and distorted is the form. But the gleam of moisture is already rapidly evaporating from the surface, revealing a browner colour and texture that strikes a chord of primordial revulsion to make him shiver. He sees now that it is not just a human hand but an arm also, connected to whatever still lies hidden beneath the ground.

By the time he is arriving home at the farmhouse door fifteen minutes later, the police are already coming down in an air car. They then follow him back out to the fields, as his wife watches anxiously from a gap in her still-drawn curtains. It is early morning. She is left gazing south across the patchwork of hedgerowed fields in the direction of Glasgow, but the city itself is hidden by a landlocked peninsula, a long green ridge of hill that crosses the waist of lowland Scotland here like a belt from coast to coast, east to west. She knows the crest of it carries the Forth and Clyde Canal, now a domain of water-lilies and ducks and pleasure barges rather than the vital freight artery the Georgians built. It also carries the buried traces of the Antonine Wall, built over two thousand years ago as the northerly boundary of the Roman Empire.

*

The view from the lecture room is across the rooftops of the city's west end, a bricolage of slate roof, stone chimneys and church spires interspersed with mature trees showing their first green leaves and blossom. Professor Ailee Kenzie is talking to her students at Glasgow University at the time when she receives the message from Tacitus. She usually ignores all messages, her phone on mute during lectures, but notes from the corner of one eye the importance of the correspondent. She might reflect for years afterwards on the coincidental topicality of the lecture subject she is giving at the moment of the call:

*...Some of you may have the mistaken belief that archaeology is a dry, stuffy subject. You may even have been teased by your friends and family about it. Indeed, some of you may conceivably even have chosen the subject in the hope that it **will** be a little boring and enable you to pursue a quiet life of whole days spent brushing grains of sand off shards of clay pots in wooden huts in obscure moorland locations in Shetland and Siberia. Your colleague will be a sandal-wearing Vegan called Nigel from Hemel Hempstead with a straggly white beard and a penchant for Reiki and healing crystals. If you think any of this or anything like that then I am here to tell you that you are going to be surprised, pleasantly I hope. The field of archaeology has been radically transformed in the last thirty years by technological breakthroughs that your parents and*

grandparents might have regarded as the domain of science fiction. That's the exciting bit, the new bit. But what is not new, but may be news to you unless you've studied history closely (which is something you're also going to have to do of course...), well, the news is this: that nothing is more political than archaeology. So if any of you have come here to escape politics, then you won't succeed. If you are going to be an archaeologist at all, a successful one certainly, then politics is going to find you sooner or later, whether you want it to or not...

After the lecture Ailee is too busy reading the text from Tacitus to pay due respect and attention to the words of one of her students, a shy young woman called Sarah Watson who stands next to her and stutters a complaint about the 'Hemel Hempstead' lines. *I may lodge a complaint about that to the head of faculty, Professor Kenzie. I'm sorry but frankly I thought that was a cheap laugh, a sly piece of anti-Englishism, slipped in below the radar. Don't you think there's enough of that going on at the moment..?*

Ailee is too deep in thought to respond more thoughtfully than a mumbled *That's just fine, you do that...* which enrages the girl further until she turns around and storms out of the room.

*

The Tacitus Project arrive on site two hours later and are able to dismiss the police after a few minutes discussion and a call to the President's office. The Balmore marsh site is apparently not a crime scene for the simple reason that the 'victim' died two thousand years ago. Tacitus arrive in the way that they usually do: in the form of an elliptical archaeo-pod that hovers over the site then slowly lowers down to about a metre above it where its graviton-drive can hold it indefinitely, maintaining a safe distance above the surface to be studied without touching or damaging it. Ground-penetrating radar then surveys an area equivalent to the footprint of the pod, about five metres diameter. Ailee joins the team, her air-car docking at starboard as the first scan results are emerging on screen.

Inside the pristine white interior, the pod operator Bruce Moffat shouts hello to her, raising his coffee in greeting, tipping his head towards the drinks machine by way of an invitation for her to join him. She's met Bruce on previous occasions and isn't surprised to see his fingers are already whirring on his keyboard, his attention absorbed by a stream of numerical and geometrical data on the glass data-screen in front of him. He introduces her to his assistant seated next to him, one Sonja Delvaux, who looks young, perhaps a foreign exchange student, the angle of her head indicating dutiful attention to the screen but probably as yet limited understanding.

What have we got then? Ailee asks inevitably, sitting down to face Sonja with a disarming smile, while addressing her question sideways to Bruce.

Complete body, bog drowning victim, hand and arm exposed to air within the last few hours, condition deteriorating as you'd expect of the exposed parts at least. The rest of the body looks in better shape from the scans but we better lift the whole thing soon. Next ten minutes maybe, if that's okay with you?

Yes, if you've cleared permissions from Strang. How's the skull look, the all-important head?

Good, but that near the surface the chances are the brain matter might be mostly blown.

Blown... Ailee repeats, smiling wryly again at Sonja. She remembers now how Bruce always drops in these unscientific phrases although he surely knows better. *What's the chemical composition of the surrounding ground-matter?*

Unusual, as it happens. We might be in luck this time. Extreme acidity, very oxygen-depleted. Been a very deep bog for a very long time.

First time? Ailee asks Sonja in a lowered voice.

Sonja opens her mouth to answer, but before she can, Bruce says over her shoulder: *First time for all of us, if this is what I think it is. Could be the best since Tollund*

Man, except now we have better know-how, won't be turning him into a leather handbag for museum display.

Sonja and Ailee find themselves laughing almost involuntarily at that, face to face, breaking the ice, Ailee reaching out to shake her hand, a gesture the young don't seem to use much anymore. *Yes...* Ailee says, to the question she imagines her asking, *he is usually this irreverent. That's why they call me in I think, to keep an eye on him.*

An hour later a large cuboid of dripping marsh soil is slowly hoisted into the archaeo-pod. *It's like an enormous slice of black forest gateau, isn't it?* Sonja gasps, making Ailee laugh.

Or Halloween cake maybe, like they used to do it, with little trinkets inside for your kids to choke on. This one's got a whole person in it. Fuck, I hope they never dig me up like this, just to find out where my clothes were made and what I had for dinner.

Before Bruce flicks the switch to seal the smoothly sliding glass screens around it, the pungent smell of bog fills the room like an ancient mist invading from another world. *The smell of time travel, eh?* Bruce looks over his shoulder, exultantly.

Funny it should be your nose first, to receive a message from deep time, eh? Ailee remarks to Sonja. *It will be all our other senses next.*

*

Arriving home that evening, to her cottage in the hills five miles north, Ailee's air car lowers down over the long grass, blowing it in rotating drifts like the waves of a green sea. Her dog Plato comes bouncing out to meet her, released from the house by her daughter Iona. His wet black nose, the texture of his soft black fur, remind her for a moment with a shiver of what she has left behind at Balmore.

Iona's sister Onya is back up from England for a long weekend, so Ailee expects a party atmosphere as she enters the cottage, maybe even a hug, but sees instead that the girls are glued to the video wall, the sound turned up loud. *What's going on?* She shouts half-heartedly, taking her coat off, doubting she'll be heard.

Drest is invading England, Mum. She says we're taking back Berwick-upon-Tweed and the Cheviot Hills, as a buffer zone to protect us from English unrest.

What the hell? Are you kidding me on? –Ailee asks, shaking the rain out of her anorak.

She says it's only temporary, precautionary, but no one believes her. Apparently the UN are meeting in emergency session. –Onya chips in.

She's a fascist, a racist! Ailee stands in the living room doorway, hands on hips in exaggeration, as if pronouncing motherly judgement on the entire world for a moment. *Scotland doesn't elect people like that as leaders.*

No? Well Scotland did, Mum. Three months ago. Iona replies.

Murphy's law... Onya sighs, *anything that can go wrong, will. Democracy's gone wrong, folks.*

*

Over the dinner table later, she asks her daughters what they think Drest stands for, what her 'reign' is going to be like. Iona, a student of politics and history, is the most alarmist. *It's like the rise of Hitler, Mum, or Donald Trump's disastrously divisive effect in disuniting the United States. There's been a very clear pattern to these last few months, and we've seen it all before, a textbook case. The passing of laws designed to fall foul of the judicial system so as to turn the public against the courts...* Iona lines up her cutlery as she speaks, a piece of silver for each step. *Next will be reforms to neuter the courts in the name of satisfying public opinion, and on it goes.*

What can we do? Ailee asks the room, turning her head from one child to the other.

Resist, of course. As people always do and always have. Onya answers.

But how well was the Scottish constitution written? Can it withstand its first major challenge? Iona posits.

Ailee turns her head from Iona to hear Onya's reply: *In the construction industry they have something called destructive testing I believe, for new material components.*

How much did the people who opposed Hitler, even those who tried to assassinate him, ultimately achieve though? –Iona responds. *There's another strategy. An even braver and more cunning and dangerous one. Go work for the dictator. For years. Become their trusted friend and closest confidante. **Then** kill them.*

I can see you've been thinking hard about this. Ailee interjects. *Maybe you should offer your services as a political strategist to Team Drest.*

Iona laughs. *No chance I'm afraid. My Socialist Party membership is on the public record.*

What about you Onya? You still a soldier of fortune? How are things over the border?

Pretty bleak I'm afraid, Mum. But all good experience for my post-grad. Water and sanitation projects in refugee camps for displaced English people. The Brummies continue to thump the Geordies while the Scousers and Mancunians get in the way. Same old, same old. I'm safe though, they keep us well away from the conflict zones.

Good. Well let me tell you about my day then. Remember when I had to go to Norway for two months to investigate that bog body? Then to Russia a few years later for that mammoth in the permafrost? Well today they found something a bit closer to home for me.

Tell us more, Mum, sounds exciting. Just how close to home are we talking? They digging up Tibbles in the back garden?

Not quite that close, yet. You two are always clowning around so much. I never get to say anything serious. Balmore Marsh. You know, near Baldernock. Got to keep it hush-hush for now though.

Is it a woolly elephant, Mum?

No, not this time, dear. It's got an arm and hand whatever it is, a man or a woman.
Attached to what?
The rest of the body, which we haven't thawed out yet.
Arm and hand raised then ?
Like this?
Yes, how did you guess?
Were they hailing a taxi?
Or signalling Heil Hitler?
Enough. Ailee stands up raising her hands in mock despair. *I'm away off to bed early to tell Plato about it. At least he listens to me.*

*

In Ailee's dreams that night, Plato and the black soil of the marsh become confused and intertwined, and she wakes up in a sweat at 6am, filled with revulsion at the idea that every black surface or texture around her might be full of micro organisms waiting patiently to spring into life. In a moment's lucidity before she steps into the shower it hits her that it's not death that's truly frightening, but life.

*

As Ailee is about to leave the house she gets a call from Ed Strang, director of Tacitus' Scotland operation, a sure sign that the previous day's discovery has been raised a level in terms of importance. *Good morning Ailee, I want you to take a slight detour to pick someone up on your way to the site. He's a former professor of Roman Antiquities at York University.*
Former? —she asks, trying to put her coat on one-handed.
He freelances now. Trevor Watling, perhaps you've heard of him. We're hiring him as an advisor to you. His knowledge of Roman Britain is way up there apparently.
Up there... Ailee repeats absent-mindedly, as she exits the house and throws her kit bag into the air car.
One of the best, top ten at least. We've shown him the

first scans from last night and some of the numbers, in confidence of course, he believes we may have a Roman legionary on our hands.

Ailee pauses, sighs and gazes out across the countryside falling away towards where a few towerblocks peek above the far horizon.

Ailee, are you still there?

Ailee feels a little annoyed, since she will have to unload one of her bags from the air-car to clear a seat for him, and was hoping to get to the site as early as possible.

Strang's 'slight detour' turns out to involve going down into the city, to the south side of the river. But once she is speeding through the air over the historical centre of Glasgow, she finds herself enchanted by all the history below her, surprised to realise how long it's been since she wandered around down there.

*

Ailee's car lowers down onto the grass of Queen's Park recreation ground then she makes her way on foot towards where her phone tells her Trevor's house is located nearby. She likes the name of the street: Queen Mary Avenue, reminding her of the sad but essential piece of Scottish history that the entire district is named after. Trevor's house is a run-down Victorian stone villa in what estate agents tactfully call a transitional area. In the driveway she sees bright plastic toys: a child's bicycle, football. She hears voices from the back garden.

When the door opens, Ailee is surprised by Trevor's appearance. *Ailee Kenzie, right? What's wrong?*

Ailee pauses, unable to counteract a slight involuntary widening of her eyes at Trevor's torn jeans and T-shirt. *You're not what I expected.*

No? Why?

Something about your name.

What's wrong with my name?

Trevor Watling. A professor. Somehow it sounds old and stuffy, like you wear a suit or corduroys. Ailee smiles too late to signal that she's trying to be humorous.

Isn't that racism? You're a professor too, aren't you? Trevor scowls.

Racism!? What? Why?! Are you crazy? Ailee counters in frustration, running her fingers through her hair.

My name sounds English so then you add on all those other negative connotations to it. Anti-Englishism is somehow the one kind of racism still acceptable in Scotland, isn't it?

Ailee steps back, wide-eyed. *Well wow. You're a bit touchy.*

Wouldn't you be, after a night like last night?

Last night? How do you mean, were you out drinking or something?

The invasion, dummy, hello? Frau obergruppenführer Drest annexing the Sudetenland last night? How long until she burns down the Reichstag?

Oh it's not that bad, is it? That's all just politics. She isn't any real threat to anyone is she?

You don't think so? Easy for you to say, a true blue Scot I presume. How long until she permanently closes the border then starts sending people like me home? As they talk, Trevor puts on his jacket, throws a bag over his shoulder.

A long time. Never, ever, I hope, and hope that you're entirely wrong and paranoid. Ailee turns to go. *But what's so bad about going back to England anyway?*

You kidding? Do you watch the news? It's an economic basket case these days. Bread queues, civil war, race riots. You lot did the right thing, getting out when you did, rejoining the EU. He closes the front door behind him and catches up as they begin walking along the pavement, Ailee leading the way.

You lot? She asks over her shoulder.

The Scots. The Scotch... as we ignorant Sassenachs like to say.

Ailee pauses as they wait to cross the road, wary of ground traffic. *We appear to be off to rather a bad start, Trevor. Shouldn't we be talking about your assignment? Like why Strang has asked you to come on board?*

I speak Latin and can think like an ancient Roman, I suppose.

So?

Haven't they told you yet? They paged me at 3am, no less. Looks like they've got a Roman soldier up there at Litana. You'll see when we get there.

They hurry across the road together and enter the park.

Strang did mention that this morning, yes. I was there last night and all we had was a big chunk of black bog with a leathery human arm sticking out of it. Litana?

Oh, Bearsden to you. You see? Already I am your link to the ancient world, to a time when our ancestors, yours more than mine I'm afraid, were still painting themselves blue and sacrificing goats to Cernunnos.

Ailee unlocks her air-car and they clamber in each side. She turns to look at him, smiling. *Kids?*

Sorry?

Those toys in your driveway, the sounds from your garden. Your kids?

Trevor frowns. *Not mine. My wife's sister's, over visiting. Nephews and nieces.*

Strapped in? Ready for lift-off then? I'm a very good pilot, famous last words. Here we go then.

Trevor marvels at how rapidly the park dwindles from something around them to something resembling an aerial photograph far below. *I guess the birds do this every day, but I can't say I ever get used to it.*

Most birds don't go straight up, to be fair, must be more like just running fast to them. With wings. Do you get sick?

Not if I keep looking at everything, keep my brain posted on what the hell is going on.

Good. Four eyes are better than two. Bird strikes and neds firing rockets are never much fun. Ailee laughs and Trevor looks at her.

You love this don't you? You look exhilarated. Like you're inhaling helium or something. He unconsciously ducks as they zip past a tall church spire.

Ever done that? Helium? She asks.

No. Should I have?

A friend of mine and I did it a few times in a bar we worked in as students, when the boss was away. You'd take a huff of helium then your voice would sound like Mickey Mouse for the next five minutes. It sure gave the customers a jolt when you asked them 'What'll you have?' three octaves above C.

Trevor laughs, throwing his head back.

That's a fine laugh you have there, Trevor, a guffaw even. Laughs were the best bit actually. A high-pitched helium laugh is one of the funniest things you can ever hear. Especially if it wears off half way, turns into a burp and breaks back down to middle C again.

Trevor marvels at the glittering waters of the Clyde now passing underneath them. *Just don't break down and take us down to the middle sea here, will you?*

Ha. I'll try not to.

*

The first person they meet after docking against the archaeo-pod is Sonja, white as a bed sheet and quite possibly on her way to the toilet to throw up. *You okay?* Ailee asks.

Mind. Blown... Sonja mouths, wide-eyed before vanishing through a sliding doorway.

A coffee in a paper-cup is thrust into Ailee's hand as she turns the corner into the main space, which she promptly drops onto the floor, burning Trevor's toes. *Jesus Christ...*

Over fifty percent of the black cuboid of wet earth has melted away overnight, beginning to reveal the crumpled and contorted figure of a man suspended in space inside the glass cage, numerous tubes and rods supporting him and beginning to pump fluids back into his cranial orifices.

Morning, Ailee, Bruce calls over to her, as he moves between control screens, a couple of new assistants endeavouring not to get in his way. *We're homing in on his brain tissue now, starting to charge it with SHG.*

GBH? –Trevor asks Ailee, but Sonja, returning from the toilet, answers before she can.

SHG. SynthaHemoGlobin. Artificial blood that can be controlled remotely at the molecular level, but that can also adapt and modulate itself. Smart Blood, it's also sometimes called. I'm Sonja by the way.

Trevor, Trevor Watling, he replies, while mopping the floor with his handkerchief, standing to shake her hand, and simultaneously organising Ailee another coffee. *Now I understand why these vehicles are all curves and no corners, easy to wipe up stains. Coffee or blood or whatever.*

This is a lot more than a vehicle, Trev. Ailee laughs, *and we've got a little floor robot that can do that mopping for you.*

Ailee, we've sampled his DNA. –Bruce shouts over his shoulder. *From his skin and a fragment of the hair on his head. Can you run an analysis on it? Tell us where this guy was born? His likely age at death? Health and history of disease. Strang will be here soon, apparently, we've gone to the top of his priority list as of this morning.*

*

By the time Ed Strang's air-car docks, Ailee has identified that the bog body's racial origin is from the south of England.

Not a Roman soldier then? Damn, how bad luck is that? Ed exclaims, striding in as the door hisses shut behind him.

Good morning, or afternoon rather, Ed. Ailee stands up. *But Professor Watling was just telling us about Auxiliaries. Ed, this is Trevor Watling. Trevor: Ed Strang.*

Welcome aboard the good ship Burke and Hare. Ed shakes his hand. *Auxiliaries?*

Statistically, it's just as likely you'd find one here as a Roman soldier actually, and not necessarily any less interesting... –Trevor explains. *They were sort of half way between slaves and Roman citizens, volunteers not conscripts, usually drawn from other provinces so that they weren't going up against their own people. It's thought that at certain times and places, auxiliaries made up at least half of the Roman fighting force. This was probably one of those times and places.*

I see. Ed nods. *Depends on your perspective then I suppose. We know plenty about Rome from all their records, but precious little about our own ancestors on the ground, the poor painted savages.*

Yes, Ailee agrees enthusiastically. *You could argue that the mind of an Iron age servant of Rome would be a greater breakthrough in historical knowledge.*

Ah, sorry to be pedantic... Trevor breaks in. *But the moment he was Romanised he ceased to be an iron-age man. That's how the definition works. And we keep saying man. Was he male? Do we know that? Bruce?*

Yup. –Bruce shouts back. *I can confirm he has a ding dong.*

Ailee notices that everyone laughs apart from Trevor.

Right then. Strang claps his hands. *How long until the subject is ready for Retrovival?*

I'd say another 36 hours, Mister Strang. Bruce answers, taking his headphones off and sitting back with a sigh, and turning around to look at everyone in the gleaming white pod. *We're soaking the brain matter now, like a big fat prune. Then we'll see what we've got in there.*

*

What's wrong? Ailee asks Trevor later, as she's flying him home to the south side after dark. The city lights below are mesmerising, but would be unintelligible without the computer terrain mesh playing on the screen between the two occupants.

I don't know. I'm sorry. Trevor rubs his face, runs his hands through his hair. *You're obviously used to this game. But I find it all a bit weird, a bit...*

What? Ailee glances over at him, his face eerily uplit in the cockpit display.

I don't know. Distasteful. Poor taste. I'm every bit as devout an atheist as you, Ailee. But this is a dead body, a dead man, and we're laughing about his genitals. There you go, you're laughing again. I'm serious.

He's been dead two thousand years, Trevor. He doesn't know. Or care.

No. I know that. But don't you think maybe we should? Should what?

Care. Respect the dead more. If we don't respect the dead, how can we be sure we respect life, respect ourselves? And if we don't do that, then god knows what we're capable of. Next stop Auschwitz.

Ailee nods. *That's a bit heavy, Trevor. But I'm not mocking you. It's something that happens in a medical environment too. Certainly among the nurses. People make morbid jokes to relieve their tension and embarrassment. They let off steam.*

By saying the opposite of how they feel?

Sure. Nothing more human than that. Ailee begins the descent towards Queen's Park.

Or more stupid... Trevor muses.

~

III

The media drones wheel overheard like starling murmurations, ricocheting their blades of sound across the genteel stone terraces of Edinburgh's 19th century New Town. President Fiona Drest walks from the darkness of Bute House into the blazing white light and noise of the crowd gathered outside in Charlotte Square. The unbelievable has finally happened, her hour come round at last. Nobody had believed she could do it. The first far-right President of Scotland has arrived.

A reporter turns back towards her live feed, addressing an estimated five million viewers: *The square is filled to the brim with chanting crowds, both the green square of grass inside and the cobbled roads around it. Although in a city centre as compact as Edinburgh that still isn't a vast number of people, the cynics will say, but it is enough. Even if Drest's support is less than 50% of the voters of Scotland, it was still sufficient to get her elected, and given the kind of people who support her: perhaps enough to drown out the sound of everyone else for five years...*

Drest climbs the small makeshift white podium and raises her hands for the crowd to be silent. Her speech begins:

We are here today to commemorate Scotland's independence day, a national holiday for the last sixty years. We're also here to celebrate the first three months of Scotland's first term of government under the Saorsa Party, a party of national dignity, committed to ridding our country of the last vestiges of colonial English rule. The Act of Union of 1705 and the Battle of Culloden of 1745 sounded the death knell on Scotland's nationhood and ushered in three centuries of suppression of our culture. A period in which English people insinuated themselves into our society as an elite ruling class controlling property and wealth. We were to be the slaves in this scenario, the barbarians, the second-class citizens, the peasants. To rise above this wretched state, a Scots man or woman had to go to the right schools and learn to pass themselves off as English by changing their accent and outlook. Become a turncoat in other words, a lickspittle. And let's face it, a parcel o' rogues, as Robert Burns put it, we were never short of knaves willing to take up that role and turn their backs on their own people, on their own class. Class was what it was all about, the system beloved of the English and the British Empire, which supposes that there are different kinds of people, different kinds of blood, superior and inferior. Friends, fellow Scots, I am here to tell you that from today there will only be one kind of blood in our country: Scottish blood. And that those who have preyed on us by exploiting our resources and keeping the ill-gotten gains for themselves, these have been the vampires, which we have taken too long to rid ourselves of since our day of independence. I speak of course of bankers, hedge-fund managers, landowners, landed gentry, everyone whose mindset, whose way of thinking and talking and behaving reeks of one thing clear to all of us, and which if we are honest makes any true Scot twist his lip in disgust and contempt. That thing is Englishness…

Drest steps back as if at the prow of a storm-tossed galleon as the crowd go berserk and waves of applause and yelled adulation come rolling back across the square at her.

…Yes, Englishness. It has been like a cancer in our society for three centuries and now at last under Saorsa we are driving it out. All we have to do is look south to see what Englishness really means, what the English have done and are still doing to themselves and each other when they follow through their vile creed to its inevitable conclusion. Unjust societies, and there is nothing more unjust after all than the English class system, – these will always eventually dissolve into civil disorder and civil war. The myth of a god-given right to

be upper, middle or lower class will always degenerate into resentment, jealousy and violence as the poverty of the masses and the decadent wealth of those in charge become irreconcilable and then go to loggerheads. The Englishman will always seek to exploit his fellow man, will always compete against him, seek to make himself better than others, to do someone else down, to laugh at someone else's poverty, the English Tory way. Our cherished Scottish ideals of equality and fair play and social justice, are all anathema to the English Tory, and yet we allowed ourselves to be ruled by them like a herd of poor dumb sheep for far too long. The Scots have been too kind, too compliant, too sweirt, too feart of a fight. This is our country now, long since, and the last vestiges of English rule and domination must finally be driven out...

Jesus... Kirsty Denholm shakes her head on the ground at the edge of the square, turning to her colleagues in the press pack. *I think I might have heard enough. This train is going to hell, as a famous man once said.*

Do you know who actually said that? A young man in a black suit from a rival media group asks her.

Someone the Nazis ended up doing in, I think. Enlighten me, go on. –Kirsty answers quietly, keeping her eye on Drest.

Actually I was just asking. I don't remember either. Ben Woolf, by the way, pleased to meet you. Kirsty smiles and shakes his hand.

Well I do remember... –An older man cuts in, a rotund figure in braces as red as his florid complexion. *Want this old timer to enlighten you bright young things? Tam Fairley, ye ken me, and ah know both your faces aff the telly. It was a man called Franz Jägerstätter, an Austrian farmer and Catholic church officer, an ordinary humble man. History remembers him for a prophetic dream he said he had, in which a wonderful train came around the mountain, to which all the children of the village ran towards to jump on board. Then a voice out of nowhere said 'This train is going to hell'. Unlike so many of his fellows, Franz refused to fight as a soldier in Hitler's army, because he saw that Nazism was a satanic cult. He was beheaded for his trouble. Is that where we're at now, do you think?*

Maybe not quite yet, if we do our jobs right, –Kirsty answers. *But listen up, she's talking about her damned invasion now...*

Many of you may be wondering why, if we are in the business of ridding ourselves of Englishness, why the Scottish army are, as of last week, occupying Northumberland on my orders, and on the approval of the Scottish parliament. Those of you who know your history may not be quite so surprised, may know that Northumberland was part of Scotland in the 12th and 13th centuries.

For only 78 years... come on, get real... Kirsty snorts out loud to the other journalists.

...And that the border town of Berwick-upon-Tweed was a Scottish port until 1746, repeatedly seized by the English for its strategic significance, once as prosperous and populated as Edinburgh, whose inhabitants were massacred to the last man, woman and child by the English in 1296.

Ancient history, numbers contested... Kirsty says aloud.

Opinion polls show that the majority of the inhabitants of Northumberland are still of Scottish descent and wish to become part of Scotland...

Fabricated statistics, again contested... Kirsty says to Ben and Tam in frustration.

...But if any of you need more modern history and reminders, then we need go no further back than the Freedom Square slaughter of two thousand innocent independence protestors in Glasgow by the British Army in 2029. A war crime, under international law for which the culprits have never been brought to justice. We have unfinished business with the north of England, that we can best solve by bringing the majority of the region under our control, setting the River Tyne and Hadrian's Wall as our new southerly border. The people in this

region have been suffering the effects of interminable civil wars for the last 50 years. Our tanks have been welcomed with open arms, our soldiers garlanded with flowers, toasted for bringing these people peace at last under a strong and benign Scottish government.

Newcastle is on fire, for fuck's sake, woman, they'll fight you to the last man, building to building. –Tam speaks up behind them, his voice equally drowned by the crowd.

...Scotland is a bigger place today, with a bigger place in the world. We can all hold our heads up high and march towards a brighter future as we put our house in order!

Ah... the old catch phrase. Putting our house in order. Who'd have thought that it involved sticking on an extension, and stealing part of someone else's house? But only Kirsty can hear these last of her own words, as the crowd go berserk chanting 'House In Order'. Drest bows and leaves the podium as it is showered with white roses whose petals fill the air and drench the square with their cloyingly sweet fragrance.

*

The journalists stand ordering pints in the ancient wood-panelled interior of the Rampant Lion Bar after they've each filed their stories. Kirsty wants to know what each make of what they've just witnessed. *What next then do you think, folks?*

Carpet bombing of Newcastle... Tam Fairley ventures, ensconcing himself on a bar stool which scarcely looks up to the job.

Oh come off it, Tam, that's going too far, you're not going to print that are you? Ben laughs.

Maybe not, but it will happen soon enough anyhoo. Tack it frae an auld yin. And tack a look across the room. Look at yon young loons over there, frae the Daily and the Mirror, they ken all their readers are bampots, they'll be printing stuff tae encourage it a', wait and see. 'Cos their readers lap it up and they know it. They're like drug dealers, feeding their hof-wit junkies wi' their daily fix o' racist bile. Scape goat syndrome it's cried, as auld as the hills. Kick the English to make yersels feel better.

To distract... Ben slips a word in edgeways.

...From our own economic problems, Kirsty takes over. *Sixty years after independence, why is there still poverty in this resource-rich country, still drugs and alcoholism?*

Aye, but that's her argument, you see... Tam leans in closer, *that's what's so cunning about yon bitch. That it's somehow still the English's fault for a' these things. And by the time folks cotton on that it isnae true, she'll have killt hof o' them and bunged the other hof in concentration camps.*

Well, those of us who get to write opinion pieces for our employers, must use our platform to warn of these dangers then, right?

Damned right we will... Ben agrees.

Tam sighs. *Aye, but it's a gey queer sight us media sounding like the left-wingers these days. When I was a lad it was much the opposite, I can tell you. We're the canary in the coalmine noo, when we were the fly in the ointment back in the day.*

You remember pre-independence days, Tam? Ben encourages him.

Only jist, but aye. The media were a' in the pay o' London, spouting doom and gloom aboot hoo shite the Scots wur and couldnae ston oan oor ain twa feet. Now look at us.

Maybe this is the central problem then... Kirsty muses aloud. *How to win nationhood with magnanimity, how not to yield to bitterness and vengeance.*

You know I'm Jewish? Ben answers, and the others half nod. *Well, I'll say this before anyone else does then. The foundation of Israel after World War Two should have been a beautiful and just thing, but it was an opportunity missed. Poison, bad faith and bad conscience were there at the start, greed, distrust, theft, dishonesty, and look where it led. To decades of violence, excuses for terrorism all around the world. I had higher hopes for Scotland than that.*

You know what I've always loved about the Jews... Kirsty answers.

*Yeah? –*Ben seems surprised.

That you have been a stateless people like the Scots, scattered all over the world. Often geniuses who worked harder than the host nation they found themselves in.

Yes, Ben nods. *Israel's foundation brought the possibility of nationalism and territorial jingoism to a people who had been denied it for thousands of years. It was like giving alcohol to a child.*

For the Scots... Kirsty continues, *it was the loss of the Darien colony and Act of Union shortly thereafter that denied us nationalism. That and the Highland clearances made us internationalists migrating to foreign shores. I'm glad we're independent, but I lament the loss of that modesty, that unconsciously internationalist outlook that we enjoyed before.*

*Aye, you might be onto something there, lass. –*Tam nods. *And something else: we were underdogs, with sympathy for all the other underdogs aroond the world. What are we noo though? Top dogs? Baying hounds, slavering at the mooth? It disnae sit weel, diz it?*

Oh, there's a story by the way, Ben adds. *I assume you know it already or I'd be a fool sharing my scoop. But Drest isn't her real name. It's a made up moniker, a nom de guerre it now looks like, a bit like Stalin, man of steel. She changed it by deed poll I think. Drest was an ancient king of the Picts. That's how barmy she is. Who the hell names themselves after a ninth century Pictish ruler?*

*

Two days later Kirsty Denholm is singing to herself on her morning drive to work along a picturesque rural road to the north of Stirling. The floodplain of the River Teith, the Wallace Monument, Stirling Castle itself: all are laid out below her like stage scenery with veils of mist separating the layers of woods and hills. She suddenly notices flashing blue lights in her wing mirror and pulls over. The two policemen accuse her of driving slightly over the speed limit. To her surprise, the constable doesn't show any leniency, nor suggest an on-the-spot fine, but instead insists that she accompany him to the police station. This turns out to be a very large regional headquarters on the outskirts of Stirling: a hulking piece of neo-modernism that broods over the green land it occupies, seemingly hovering on tree-like stilts that belie its brutal weight. Inside she is led past reception and taken through a series of increasingly secluded doors until she is asked to wait outside the office of the Chief Constable. A minute later he emerges and politely invites her inside to join him. The room is modestly but comfortably furnished in a vaguely old-fashioned style at odds with the modern architecture. The room strikes Kirsty as having the feel of an inner sanctum, a refuge from the wicked world of crime.

Chief Constable? Wait a minute, I know your face from the television. Head of Police Scotland, aren't you? She exclaims then immediately feels foolish.

Well, that's what Chief Constable means. He smiles patiently. *I also know your face from the telly, as it happens. News Caledonia.*

Snap, touché then, and all that. This is all a bit heavyweight for a supposed speeding offence, isn't it? And a very marginal one, I might add, I can only have been a mile-an-hour over if anything.

I'm surprised you drive a ground car, actually, Miss Denholm. I imagined journalists get paid fancier salaries than that.

I don't have much of a head for heights, Constable, Chief I mean, call me old-fashioned...

And what can I call you?

Sorry?

My name is Charles Doohan. You can call me Charlie. And there was no traffic offence, by the way, I've had you called in here for another reason.

Really? Kirsty. My name's Kirsty, and now I'm all ears. A bit cloak and dagger all this. Charlie Mike Four. Sorry, couldn't resist it. I make bad jokes when I'm nervous.

Understood. Kirsty stands up and has to suppress the bizarre urge to click her heels together and salute.

My secretary will see you out discreetly, to make sure you pass a minimum of enquiring eyes. Thank you for hearing me out. Let's shake hands on this as we part shall we? I'm putting a lot of trust in you. I don't take this moment lightly, and neither should you. You may need my protection at some point just as I may need yours.

*

After an afternoon at the Scottish parliament, Fiona Drest returns home like any other married woman and working mother, to her husband and two young children. Her daughters clutch her legs in joy, her husband showers her with praise. The family have draped Scottish flags over some of the paintings on the walls of Robert Adam's A-Listed interior which they found too redolent of a British past, and added framed photographs of more modern achievements, bridges and stadiums, striking images of West Highland landscapes in which the terror of nature dwarfs man. Patriotism is the defining emotion of the household, profound pride in their country.

After putting her kids to bed, Drest sits with her husband at the tri-partite windows overlooking Charlotte Square in the moonlight and starlight, drinking sherry together. *Doesn't it worry you, Fiona...* Roddy ventures, *–these sanctions the UN are talking about imposing unless we give back Northumberland?*

The Americans will veto it, as will several of the Europeans. Drest folds her arms as she thinks deeply. *England made a lot of enemies sixty years ago and has made more than a few since, with the last vestiges of their arrogant imperial delusions of grandeur. The world might not like what we've done, but they like the English even less. They value trade with us too much, a stable modern democracy. Some of them probably even secretly wish we'd take over all of England and impose peace and order on it.*

Oh please, God, tell me you're not contemplating that?

Roddy, what do you take me for? That's the mistake Bonnie Prince Charlie made, marching all the way to Derby. She waves a hand as if to gesture to the oil painting of Prince Charles Edward Stuart on the wall behind her. *We couldn't care less about the mess England's in, we only want back what's ours.*

As long as the loss of life stays low, maybe... Roddy continues. *But can we really take everything north of the Tyne? An urban environment like Newcastle, hand to hand fighting potentially. Wouldn't it be wiser to draw the line somewhere a safe distance north of there, say ten miles out?*

Maybe, time will tell. We have our own people on the Tyne as you know, partisans, undercover, special forces, have had for decades. Everything has to look as if the majority of the local people want it, whether that's the case or not. Ethnic division. Divide and conquer, just like the bastards used to do to us. Drest gazes at the streetlights through the cut-glass of her sherry for a moment, relishing the flavour.

Roddy takes his spectacles off and rubs them with his handkerchief, squints to check the glass is clear before replacing them. *People are frightened, Fiona. Scotland's never gone to war really, not since the Canongate Uprising that is, which was short and sharp and spontaneous, from the grassroots up. But something like this, decreed from the top, doesn't it reek of imperialism?*

Drest snorts. A bitter smile at the corners of her lips. *Not with the technological superiority we have, Roddy. It's all drones and robots these days, not fresh-faced boys out of school for cannon-fodder. Or not many of them at least.*

You don't mind me questioning you, even after a hard day, a big day?

Not at all, love. She takes his hand. *You're like a voice in my head. I value your doubts, your cross-examinations, they prepare me for what's out there every day, the opposition, the naysayers.*

Retrovival

Listen to me, Fiona, by all means. But never listen to them. You're a star, on the right course, leading the way. You're making Scottish history every day. The new chapters of this young book of a new nation.

Mummy... Their daughter Isla stands in the doorway in her dressing gown. *Will you sing me back to sleep? I had a bad dream and it frightened me.*

Drest hands her drink to Roddy, goes to pick Isla up, takes her on her lap and dries her eyes.

I dreamt there were machines in the sky... Isla snivels, *—black metal machines like teapots and motor bikes, and they all rained down red fire that ran along the gutters and drains. All the cats and dogs caught fire and a man stepped out of the hall cupboard dressed as a policeman. He had clockwork mice in his pocket, and he held one out to me... I took it and it ran up my arm and then I woke up screaming! But you didn't hear me, Mummy. This old house is so huge, Mummy, it scares me. I think it's haunted. I cried out and nobody heard me, not even you.*

~

IV

On her way over from Copenhagen, Val Breshkov, CEO of Retrovival is invited to 'call in' on the new President Drest, landing her air car in the grounds of the Holyrood parliament. She's been here before to meet previous incumbents, and each time the aerial view reminds her subliminally of something she must have seen once in Denmark: the carcass of a beached whale, the blubber rotting, some of its bones showing through. The overhead door closes behind her as she walks across the serene green terraces towards the entrance portico, leaving her two assistants pacing around the car on their mobile phones.

Congratulations on your election as President, Mrs Drest... Val begins, shaking hands with her on the broad garden-lobby stairs within.

Bit late for that isn't it? Three months is a long time in politics. Drest answers, turning around and signalling for Val to follow her. *Fiona, just call me Fiona, Val. I've heard a lot about you, secretive as you are. I used to think Val stood for Valentin, as did many others. Now we know you're Valentina, a woman, good to see so many women in powerful positions these days, isn't it?*

Yes, of course, although...

Drest leads her down a long corridor towards her private office. *You don't approve of my politics, perhaps? Keeping the English immigrants out, giving jobs to indigenous Scots?*

I am a Ukrainian of Russian descent resident in Denmark with a European Union passport, so local politics here are of limited interest to me.

Drest eyes Val carefully as they sit down either side of her desk. *Of limited, but not none?*

Needless to say, as an archaeologist, I know my history.

Ahh... Drest chuckles to herself. *Then I think we understand each other. Your country had to fight for its independence from Russia just as we Scots had to fight for ours from England, or the United Kingdom as they used to try to mollify us by calling it. Would you like some coffee, tea, water?*

No thanks. You talk as if it was yesterday. Those battles are long over, surely?

Maybe for us, but not for England it seems. Their internecine wars constantly threaten to spill over and destabilise us, undo the progress the Scottish Republic has made in the last sixty years.

With respect, Mrs President, what relevance has this to me?

Drest raises her eyebrow, sits back in her chair, breathes deep. *I'm told it wasn't a Roman you found this week. A little disappointing?*

Val shrugs. *It is still very interesting. And who knows, we may find other bodies in the bog as we go on studying there.*

Is that possible, likely?

Why are you so interested in us finding a Roman, can I ask?

Our history was written by the Romans, and then by the English, Valentina. We've long suspected that it's been suppressed and distorted in every way. Was Mons Graupius really a Roman victory or a strategic retreat by the Picts into their mother forest? And why was the Antonine Wall abandoned only eight years after its completion? I'll bet there's a story of heroic local resistance there, the Picts overrunning the wall.

We? Who are 'we'?

The Scottish people of course.

And you hope that I can prove your story right for you? Uncover a new legend of heroic Scottish victory?

Now it's Drest's turn to shrug. *Why not? Tacitus was the son in law of Agricola, governor of Roman Britain, so hardly impartial. And yet our archaeological unit is named after him. A little unfortunate, don't you think?*

I see you know your history too. Tacitus and Julius Caesar are all we have to go on, apart from what we dig up now. You do not approve of the previous government's name for its efforts? What would you change it to?

Oh, I don't know, what's in a name? Calgacus would be the obvious choice, our great leader at Mons Graupius, who said 'they make a desert and call it peace' and all that. Or maybe you'll find out something, the name of the local leader who attacked the wall. How's the brain looking... of the body you've turned up? Thinking you'll be able to read it like they did with that mammoth in Siberia last year? A movie from inside a beast's head is one thing, but words and thoughts from inside a human being would be something else, wouldn't it?

Yes, that would be making history, ground-breaking. And we live in hope. Although we are constrained by the Rossan convention, you know.

Remind me of the terms of that, would you?

Val stands up and paces to the window restlessly, gazes down into the irregularly shaped courtyard below. *Heartbeat, basically. We can re-blood a brain but we cannot restart a heart.*

Why ever not? Drest spins in her chair to look up at Val's back, to follow her gaze as if looking into an uncertain future.

I suppose... she begins hesitatingly, *the traditionalists say at least, that the heart would take us into Frankenstein territory, resuscitation, resurrection.*

On a body two thousand years dead? Do you approve of that protocol?

Val pauses, sighs, thinks carefully before answering. Turns back to face the room. *I can't say that I do, on the whole, no.*

Drest folds her arms over her chest, ruminating. *Well, maybe I can do something about that for you.*

Val returns her stare and sits down. *It is international law.*

Still... Drest draws a dismissive hand across the air

between them. *Let's ponder it, until we talk again. In the meantime, keep up the good work, Valentina. Good luck with the dig. Now if you'll excuse me, I have to prepare this week's address to the parliament.*

Val smiles politely and prepares to leave, before catching Drest's parting remark: *Oh and Valentina... I'm so glad you were born a woman, a real one. Not one of those transitioned people.*

Breshkov scowls involuntarily as she turns and makes her way down the steps from the President's office as the door closes behind her.

Outside in the daylight again, Val breathes the April air deeply, looks down at her own reflection in the still ornamental ponds and doesn't recognize herself for a moment. She takes out her phone. *Well?* Her wife asks, face appearing on screen.

What an odious woman... Val whispers, glancing over her shoulder at the security guards, *I'll tell you about it later once I'm safely out of here.*

*

Picking Trevor up again at his villa on the south side, Ailee is surprised to notice graffiti spray-painted across his windows and door. *What the hell?* She exclaims as he opens the door, *–this is a listed building isn't it? Don't the neds have any respect around here?*

Respect for buildings is the least of it, Ailee, Trevor answers as he pulls a jumper on, *it's respect for people you want to be worrying about. Have you read what it says yet?*

As Ailee steps back to look again, Trevor is called back inside and Ailee hears him shouting angrily at someone behind the door. She sees the graffiti reads *English Sass Cunt Go Home.*

When Trevor re-emerges he slams the door behind him as female shouting continues inside. *Is everything alright?* Ailee decides to ask quietly as they walk to the park.

Not really no. You read our little epistle from the

neighbourhood youth then? It's not the first time of course, but it feels more threatening now, what with everything in the news. Judith blames me for us having moved here, even though it wasn't my idea, not solely mine at least. Christ, Ailee we've been here ten years, we're not refugees, not Vietnamese boat people, I mean we look and talk the same as anyone else don't we?

Racist idiots will always find someone to pick on, Trevor. If it wasn't the English it would be left-handed people or witches, like it was in the middle-ages. She catches his arm before crossing the road, a fast lorry speeding by.

But this isn't meant to be the middle ages, Ailee. Is society going backwards, is that what we're looking at? Can civilisation just reverse gear and head back to the monkeys?

Monkeys have a modest carbon footprint and don't trash their natural environment, Trevor. We could do worse.

But seriously, seriously, Ailee... Trevor looks at her as they sit down and strap themselves in to the air car. *I don't know how long my marriage is going to last at this rate. Surely Drest will protect all the English people that are needed up here, won't she?*

I don't know. Ailee sighs, starting the engine. *I hope she doesn't get to deport anyone at all, that all her stupid new laws get quashed by the courts.*

Maybe the Jews in Germany had conversations like this... Trevor sighs dolefully as the park dwindles to a green square beneath them. *It will never happen, they'll spare the most influential of us, that sort of thing.*

Ailee puts on her mirror glasses to deflect the morning sun. *Look at the project we're working on, Trevor. If there's any kind of elite then we must be part of it. If there's any elite list of folks to be saved from President Nazi-knickers then I'll make sure you're on it with me, I promise.*

*

Val Breshkov's air car docks beside the Tacitus archaeo-pod moored over the Balmore bog site. Her two assistants carry in various pieces of technical equipment and begin to set up shop. *So, what do we have then? —*she asks, breezing out of the air lock.

Good morning, Val. Ed Strang greets her. *We've been feeding SHG to the brain, it's responding well. You can see the figures here. What do you think? Could it respond to your process?*

My **process**, *eh? Retrovival is a patented technique as you probably know...* Val pauses as if noticing everyone else in the room for the first time. *Oh hello everyone. I'll need you all to sign NDAs before we fire up. Is everyone OK with that?*

Various heads nod. The bog body now appears entirely recognisable, suspended in space within the glass cage. *Like turning a raisin back into a grape, isn't it? —*Val laughs *...sorry, that joke still makes me laugh, especially when I am twitchy before a gig. Game on then? Everyone sitting comfortably?*

All eight seating positions around the archaeo-pod are now taken with each participant facing in towards the suspended bog body. Each seat also has a glass screen suspended in front of it, running with data feeds.

Val takes her seat and begins typing furiously. *Initiating electrical current. Bruce, how many volts are you registering at your side on the EEG?*

*50mV, Mrs Breshkov, —*Bruce answers.

*Increase slowly to 70mV please. By slowly I mean take ten minutes. Deirdra, Jeff, —*she calls out to her assistants, *How are we looking for blood oxygen, sodium and potassium levels?*

25 percent optimum, rising 2 percent a minute.

We may need some stem-cell injections, the tissue in the left lobe is looking weak...

*

Half an hour later, Bruce breaks the silence in the room: *I'm getting something, we have a signal, switching to on-*

screen feed. The darkened archaeo-pod blinks suddenly into life and then goes dark again. Then erupts, then again, then dark. Like an old-fashioned cine projector in reverse, something resembling old fragmented colour film gradually stabilises and begins to flow on the projector wall to the side of the suspended body.

Do not worry, it is all being recorded, digitised, converted into numbers! Val shouts over her shoulder like a manic organist to a bewildered congregation. *We will each be watching this a thousand times over no doubt, over the coming weeks. Anyone like to put headphones on, olfactory and touch sensors? Sometimes smells will be the first and strongest thing to come through.*

*What's a smell like backwards? –*Sonja asks.

This catches Breshkov's attention, who turns sideways to eye Sonja for a moment. *Backwards, eh? You've been doing your homework, young lady. I did not know that had been published yet. The data will always come through backwards when we first S and R. That is Stimulate and Retrieve I should explain. It is hard to predict what we are going to find first. Sometimes it tends to be the last few minutes of experience that a living creature enjoys, if enjoy is the right word, other times it might be a random memory, from childhood perhaps. We believe that extreme stress, the presence of endorphin and adrenalin heighten the memory-making... oh Jesus... did everyone see that? Oh, Christ.*

The screen shows an axe flying up from the ground to lodge into a tunic, a blood stained stomach, which then heals then the axe flies backwards out of the stomach and flies off out of view. Ailee cries out in pain, taking her headphones off.

Oops, so sorry, should have warned you, Professor Kenzie, Val crosses the room to place her hand on Ailee's shoulder. *You might want to hold the sensors at arm's length when physical pain is in the offing. A pain backwards is still pain unfortunately, not euphoria, although at least this way around it ends in well-being, unlike in the forward replay.*

The screen goes blank again for ten seconds, then leaps back into action, as Val turns the dial and scans across different areas of the hippocampus.

Woah! What was that? Sounds enter the room, echoes across the walls, with the peculiar sucking effect of backwards waveforms but recognisable as human shouts, animal braying, some kind of harsh musical instruments even. *Did you see that? There it comes again, we must pause it later. That looked like the wall to me. Did everyone, anyone else see that? Timber stockade thing on top of a turf wall?*

*My God, are we actually looking at the wall of Antoninus Pius, in the flesh? –*Trevor gasps. *It must be around 150 AD. This is unbelievable.*

Ed Strang stands up and paces over to point at the main screen, breaking his silence: *What was that? Anyone? Confused fragments coming through. Like jigsaw pieces we'll need to analyse later. It looked like the wall again, or a different or earlier part of it, under construction. And what's this? Water?*

Baths, the baths at Litana... Trevor answers in awe, *his morning routine no doubt. You hear all those chattering noises? That will be Latin when we reverse it, banter and gossip of the day, absolute gold dust.*

Right, Bruce... Val cuts in, *power down when I say so, we are in danger of overheating. We need to rest for about 45 minutes before repeating, trying another pass. I know it seems harrowing or ghoulish, but his dying moments are probably the most valuable to us.*

Why's that? Trevor asks.

Do you want to tell him, Professor Kenzie? Ed ventures.

Because that's where we'll find clues, if there are any, to whether anyone else went down into this bog and if so where, Ailee answers Trevor.

Especially if this was a violent attack, as this now certainly seems to look like... Ed continues. *If this wasn't some isolated mishap, a man getting stuck in mud, then the chances of others dying at the same time become high.*

Mr Strang's looking for a Roman legionary or centurion... Bruce explains.

Aren't we all? Val turns to face the room, beaming. *Greater knowledge, literacy, orders from his general, the governor, that sort of thing. That would be the motherlode, to actually tap into the mind of the Roman emperor, if only indirectly.*

*

You don't have to keep doing this, Ailee... Trevor says as he and Ailee cross the sky above Glasgow city centre again at sunset. *–running me home and picking me up.*

Strang's instructions, Trevor... and besides I'm starting to enjoy our conversations.

Trevor gazes down at the River Clyde, its surface tranquil enough for him to look for their own fleeting image, two distant people seated inside a buzzing technological insect. *Maybe I should re-phrase that then. Soon you won't have to keep doing this, since that wasn't a Roman legionary after all.*

That... *as you call it,* **that** *is surely just as interesting, maybe more so, an auxiliary, a Briton working for the Romans.* –Ailee replies, checking her altimeter and opting to lower down early to get a better look at the passing buildings.

That... You're feeling uncomfortable too then, about the way everyone seems to be expected to treat that man hanging there like a slab of butcher's meat?

I didn't say that. I'm a scientist as well as a historian. The auxiliary soldier, the man, is dead.

Well, maybe that's the difference between us right there then. I'm a historian and linguist. I don't have that cold dispassionate side that you and the others seem to delight in.

Delight in? The auxiliary is 2000 years dead, Trevor. This is like an Egyptian mummy, a Danish bog body, Ötzi the Iceman.

We're supposed to keep telling ourselves that, no doubt, Ailee, but do you really believe it? Ötzi the Iceman was controversial enough I seem to recall. Italy and Austria had a right old barney over him. That technology your friends are using, isn't it the devil's work?

What? The devil's what? What are you, a Luddite? A superstitionist? A traditionalist?

Luddites get a bad name, Ailee. As a historian you should know that. A church spire whistles past Trevor's left side, and he clutches his seat tighter. *Do you have to fly so low? Aren't you worried about old cables, flagpoles and stuff?*

The car tracks all that by echolocation, would swerve us automatically.

Sounds even more dangerous.

Luddites. Not my period of specialisation perhaps. Ailee shrugs.

Well let me lecture you for a moment, then. They did not hate machines. They were simply opposed to machines being used to lower the wages and impoverish the lives of ordinary people. And for that, they were hanged. So it wasn't really machines that the state was defending, it was the rich and the privileged and their right to abuse the poor. Or abuse the dead, in our current example.

History written by the victors, eh? So who's the rich in this scenario, Val Breshkov?

Governments and their media lap dogs. A cliché of course, but true in this instance. History not just written but turned into an everyday slur against Luddites, a lie, to be repeated by generations to come, every day, in every-day speech. Like dancing on the graves of the innocent.

The air car comes down to rest again in Queen's Park. Ailee puts her hand on Trevor's knee. *Oh Trev. Lighten up. Pandora's Box and all that. Once something's invented it can never be uninvented. People just have to adjust to it. Humanity's moral odyssey can't be blamed on the gadgets, it's an ongoing project from the caves to the stars.*

You're right. Must be this day job that's doing it, eh?

Messing around with boats. Messing around with bog bodies.

Ailee smiles broadly at him as Trevor climbs down from the car. *You agree that he's dead then, our ancient Briton?*

For now, yes. But will he stay that way, I wonder?

It's just his brain we're probing, Trevor, the rest of his body is off-limits as the Rossan convention stipulates. No heartbeat no life. Listen, we could both do with some cheering up. These investigative passes by Breshkov are going to take a few days before we start analysing them, are you free tomorrow morning?

Trevor puts his hands in his pockets, looks down at the ground then up at the emergent stars. *Maybe, why?*

We could try a VRKO programme together.

I've heard of them but always kept clear of them.

You're kidding? They're the reason we're doing this. The reason there's money in this industry. Humanity's vast appetite for entertainment, immersive historical enactments. What do you say I pick you up at ten?

Trevor nods his head and backs away as Ailee restarts the motor and lifts back up. He turns to wave up to her and she flashes her lights in silent goodbye.

~

V

Right, Trevor. –Ailee exclaims on his doorstep. *I said I'd pick you up, but it turns out I lied, unknowingly. It turns out we can actually just walk there in three minutes. How cool is that?*

Trevor looks dishevelled as if just out of bed. *Good, I could do without another flight in your jitterbug today. I was just having some toast. You want to come in for coffee for five minutes while I finish getting ready? Judith is away at work anyway.*

Ailee follows him through to his kitchen and dining room at the rear of the property. The interior is shabby but distinguished, like ex-royalty, down on its luck. *Lovely...* Ailee remarks, admiring the elaborate cornices and architraves. *Is that an original fireplace there?*

Yes, Georgian or Victorian I think, though we never light it because the flue isn't lined and the chimney was taken down years ago. Nice to light candles there over Christmas though, – that's about the sum total of its usefulness.

The best things in architecture aren't always useful, though.

Oh yeah, where did you hear that? Trevor asks over his shoulder as he scrapes butter onto his near-burnt toast. *You want any of this?*

No thanks. Ailee answers absentmindedly, still looking around at the room's timeworn original features. *My eldest daughter studied architecture. In fact it's her who's put me on to this VR program I've downloaded for us.*

It's something architectural then?

Ailee nods. *I'll bet you didn't know there used to be an architectural masterpiece two blocks away from here, did you?*

I thought you said we were going to try VRKO, like a battle or a key moment in history we can participate in?

Well it's all of that too in a way, trust me. Maybe the RK can stand for architectural sometimes, rather than archaeological, eh? She notices he seems distracted. *Is everything alright, Trevor?*

Big fight last night. Tried to blot it out with beer. Mistake. Trevor hands Ailee a mug of coffee and goes to stand at the window looking out to the green lawn and tangled rose bushes of his back garden, deep in thought. The visible steam from his drink unwinds upwards until Ailee comes and stands next to him in silence, coffee in hand likewise.

What are we looking at? She asks eventually.

The future... he answers absentmindedly, as if still asleep, as if in a dream.

*

Ten minutes later they walk together to the bottom of Queen Mary Avenue. *Just look at this rubbish brick tenement here, late 20th century probably. This site used to be filled with a masterpiece, a fantastic church by Glasgow's finest architect, a man who influenced Frank Lloyd Wright in America. Alexander 'Greek' Thomson. His Queen's Park church, destroyed by German incendiary bombs in 1943.*

Really? Trevor rubs the stubble on his chin. *It was right here? I never knew. I've seen a few of his buildings that survive. He was pretty original wasn't he? Almost as good as Mackintosh.*

I just knew you'd say that. –Ailee snorts. *Spoken like a tourist. He was better than Mackintosh, Trevor. Born about fifty years earlier, even more radical and influential, an innovator. Or so the voice over will tell you if we put these headsets on. Here, let me help you.*

But I can't see a thing.

Of course you can, I've switched it on for you.

No, I mean I can't see where I'm going, my feet in front of me, the pavement, lamposts. I'm scared I'll walk into something.

That's the whole idea. Here, take my hand. This entire

area is pedestrianised and the park over there behind the brick rubbish has a scaffold in it with two stairs and a gallery that align with those inside the simulation. See, now how's that?

They cross the road, Trevor as tentatively as an old age pensioner. *Wow. What a building. It's so real. Blonde sandstone.*

It was probably muckier than that in real life after a few years what with all the smoke around back then, but this would be how the architect first saw it. And there he is.

What? Trevor spins around inside his headset, stunned.

That big guy with the beard standing outside in period costume with the horse and hansom cab waiting for him. He's talking to the church minister. That's Thomson himself. We can come back and talk to him afterwards, it's allowed. I feel like your mum here, holding your hand.

Trevor and Ailee wander around outside the beautiful church, admiring its wrought iron and patterned glass, its bizarre but bizarrely successful fusion of styles: a dome that seems from India or Angkor Wat, pylons that seem from ancient Egypt, geometric ornamentation from Greece, proportions that seem Roman. Wandering inside they find a play of light and shadow so intense that it affects them both like music. Trevor jumps when they find the architect himself walking behind them. *I am profoundly religious you see...* the man intones in a deep bass baritone, making the hairs on Trevor's neck twitch. *To me, light is sacrament, a living symbol of God's grace, except more than a symbol, light **is** God, his very presence. So I use it as one should use a sacred thing. I let it pour from above at select moments, sparingly, to draw you on, or for a moment of revelation, like this one: like manna from heaven.*

Trevor swears he can feel the big man's outsized hand patting his shoulder to give him friendly encouragement as he and Ailee walk into the main auditorium itself. The use of painted colour on the walls and ceilings, strong reds and blues, gold and greens, dumbfounds the senses after the austere monochrome exterior. Light pours down from the frosted and stencilled glass of the regular succession of clerestory windows high above. He feels Ailee squeeze his hand tighter as they climb up into the gallery and walk around between the long red-painted hardwood pews, marvelling at the supernaturally thin columns with their spinning capitals of acanthus leaves and harlequin strips, like celebrations of creation, circus tents frozen, transmuted from motion into the stillness of faith and peace. Even for the unreligious, it is a religious experience.

It's Jewish and Hebrew as well, isn't it? Trevor gasps. The screens and fretwork, like a synagogue. Why didn't I see it as that at first? It's so obvious now.

Of course! Thomson laughs from the other side of the gallery before waving them goodbye. *I was trying to rebuild the temple of Solomon, every time, every single time. Some kind of mystical paradigm, the ultimate balance and harmony. I never succeeded of course, but sometimes I almost felt I had come close, close, sometimes so close...* his voice trails off, repeating and getting quieter as if talking to himself, as he vanishes down the stairs.

Wait! Trevor calls after him, trying to follow until Ailee catches him, laughing, as he takes his headset off to find he is teetering on the edge of a steel scaffold in the middle of dismal grey tarmac carpark. *Shit, shit, that was awesome, Ailee. How can that not have been real? That was better than sex.*

Ailee laughs until she looks down to see Trevor is still holding her hand. *You can let go now if you like, you're safely back in our world! Glad you enjoyed it. It was my first time too. I must thank Onya for her excellent recommendation.*

*

When Ailee and Trevor arrive at the Balmore archaeo-pod they find Strang and Breshkov concluding their recordings gleaned from the auxiliary soldier's brain.

That's the body exhausted of memory traces now I'm afraid. Only about fifteen minutes worth all in all, but still... an extraordinary breakthrough. We've made history folks! –Strang claps his hands excitedly.

This had been done on animals before of course, Breshkov takes over, *but this is the first time Retrovival has had successful results on the body of a human being.*

Bravo. What now then? Ailee asks into the stunned silence.

We all sit down and watch the recordings. Probably for the first of a hundred times as we try to make sense of what we see and hear on them...

And smell... Sonya chips in.

And touch... Ailee adds.

And taste... I suppose I'm supposed to add. Trevor says, *although I ought to point out that it's a myth that there are only five senses. There are more.*

Like what? –Ed looks at him puzzled.

Feeling whether you are stationary or in motion. Whether you are upright or not, i.e. balance. Sensing high or low air pressure. Sensing where all your body parts are orientated. Sensing humidity. I could probably go on.

No. I mean yes, fine. Ailee cuts in. *But what I really meant was what happens next to the body of the auxiliary, whatever his name was.*

Ed nods his head. *Essentially, we're done with it here, on site at least. Over to the usual specialist labs and universities to study it in fine detail for the usual standard archaeological analysis, you know, stomach contents, pollen, radio carbon dating, genetic sequencing, comparison with local living descendants. Then eventually tasteful display to the public inside a temperature and humidity-controlled glass box in a museum, an award winning visitor centre designed by an award-winning international architect. That sort of thing. The usual drill.*

Trevor stands up and goes over to stand beneath the suspended body in its misted glass cage festooned with leads and tubes. He gazes up into the tanned skin, the eternally closed eyelids. *So this old body has now been used up by us like a dried raisin, a prune, and is to be discarded like a husk. Why does that haunt me, ladies and gentlemen?*

Breshkov shrugs. *It's what we do, professor. You'll get used to it.*

I'm not sure I ever want to... Trevor sighs. *Anyway, on with the show as they say.*

Strang dims the lights and the analysts rotate their chairs to face the screen on the opposite wall on which a flashing sequence of vignettes begins to play. On the third rendition, the viewers begin to call out for pauses and re-runs of specific segments as meaning is debated and deciphered.

Horses... it looks like his people trained horses from an early age. And see that? Stop, freeze that. That looks like huts, round houses, his home village perhaps. Note how there's no stone base, they just appear to be cones of densely woven willow, some of them covered in daub, the wealthier ones. We're looking at the lives of ancient Britons for the first time, it's like time travel. And the language, what do you make of it. Trevor, Ailee?

Latin and a form of a Brythonic Celtic tongue, a bit like Welsh to our ears. Ailee answers. *We'll get the computers on to it, but it may need more words than we have here.*

If only our man had been deeper in the bog and his posterior superior temporal lobe better preserved... Strang sighs.

What is all this then? Breshkov points to the screen. *Could these be the things that run through a man's brain when he knows he's dying? A fast back and forward across key moments in his life? His home village, his mother's face, the girl he loved?*

Or something more random? Ed reflects. *As if the brain is like an old vinyl record, 33 revs per minute, and we've broken off a black triangle of it like an arbitrary cross section or sample?*

Both and neither perhaps... Breshkov muses. *I mean we don't have enough information yet, excellent though these questions are. With a larger sample from a better preserved brain we might begin to say whether the information is random or specifically related to the closing moments of an organism's life. Our studies with ancient mammoths and bears did not resolve this question either.*

What we appear to still lack, despite these fascinating glimpses into the past, is a story. I mean the coherent story of who this man was and how he came to find himself sinking into this bog with his last breath.

Sonja speaks up. *My degree is in neuroscience. I would suggest that we have been limited by the way we have explored specific areas of the subject's brain in isolation. A living brain is not just a memory or language processing centre, it is all of these things and many more when all working together. The human personality or sentience if you will, is greater than the sum of its parts, a virtual event rather than purely physical real world event. Something essentially sublime and transcendental. You can't hope to recover that from a dead brain.*

I might take issue with some of the non-scientific terms you used there, Sonja, but nonetheless I'd say you're making a significant point, thank you. –Breshkov responds. *If we can find a subject with a more intact extent of brain matter then we should strive to revive and stimulate all its lobes simultaneously.*

And then what about the body? Trevor counters. *I'm just a linguist, but I know that a lot of the brain's functionality is related to the body that it controls. Even when we sleep, noises and smells affect the content of our dreams. Without those stimuli, might not a brain always remain, to borrow a computer term, offline?*

*

Kirsty Denholm of News Caledonia is invited to attend a press conference called by The Tacitus Project in the spectacular setting of Glasgow University's Bute Hall:

the centre of George Gilbert Scott's Gothic Revival late 19th century masterpiece of pointed arches and slender steel columns, all colourfully painted in the Catholic style of its patron, the Marquess of Bute. The courtyards and cloisters surrounding it evoke Scotland's ecclesiastical past with a fairytale atmosphere at odds with the violence and treachery of every minute of how the real thing went down. As her feet echo under the stone vaults of the cloisters, Kirsty hears a voice call out behind her, sending the echo of her name bouncing across a hundred curves and facets.

She sees it is **Ben Woolf**, and exclaims: *Thought I might see you here. The press release came at very short notice, don't you think? And very cryptic. It must be something big.*

A bog body is always big news, but the rumour is that Retrovival are involved. —Ben answers as he falls into step beside her, heading to the grand staircase to take them up to the hall above.

Val Breshkov? Controversial figure to be invoking unless it's something major.

Think she might be there in person? Ben muses.

Doubt it. That would be big news in itself. Kirsty laughs. *Lives the life of a recluse they say, like Howard Hughes or something. A patron of graverobbers all over the world, if you listen to the religious right wing.*

And do you? Listen to them? Ben asks.

No, and neither should your paper. That was a nasty little opinion piece you hosted last week about Drest's speech. I hope you weren't involved.

Me? No. That was all Lisa Andreoti herself, the editor entertains her as a kind of tame tiger to bait our readers. Ben answers defensively.

A dangerous game. Look what happened to Siegfried and Roy.

Who were they? Ben asks wide-eyed as they mount the giant stairs.

Las Vegas performers, big stars. Played with Siberian tigers on stage for forty years, until one day for no apparent reason one turned on Roy and bit through his neck and spine, in front of a horrified audience.

Nice. You should tell that little Aesop's fable to my editor some time, Kirsty. Maybe during an interview, I'm sure he'd like to hire you. He admires your work.

That's the worst news I've heard all week, Ben, I'd feel cleaner if he hated me.

See? That's the kind of dry humour he likes, right there. I wish I could be sassy like that in print. You doing anything for dinner tonight?

Who says I was joking? But I hope you are. I have a prior appointment I haven't invented yet... Kirsty's voice trails off suddenly as they enter the hallowed hush of the grandiose hall with its galleries and stained glass.

They take their seats and after a few minutes, the head of the University's faculty of archaeology calls the meeting to order: *Ladies and gentlemen of the press, thank you for coming along today. I will now hand you over to The Tacitus Project Scotland in the form of their two spokespersons today Professor Ailee Kenzie and Professor Trevor Watling.*

Thank you. Ailee stands up. *We're here today to announce the historic discovery of a bog body on a site to the north of Glasgow. We'll run you through some slides on the screen above us as we talk. As you can see this human body is in remarkably good condition, on a par with previous similar examples such as Lindow Man, Tollund Man and Ötzi the Iceman. The reason for this appears to be the exceptionally rare combination of elements and conditions present in the bog we have been studying.*

This discovery would be remarkable enough in its own right, but the work of Retrovival, who Tacitus invited to join the project, has led us to what we believe is a truly epoch-making breakthrough. Some of you who keep abreast of archaeological developments may be aware that Retrovival have over the last decade retrieved sequences of visual memories from the brains of mammoths and sabre-tooth tigers. Well for the first time in history, what we are going to play you next is a film retrieved from inside the brain of our Roman auxiliary soldier.

The audience watch in awed silence as sequences from inside the bog body's mind play on screen. Occasional gasps and whispers electrify the room, a few reporters hurry outside to make calls, sensing that a story is breaking of greater significance than they had anticipated. When the lights come up afterwards Ailee addresses the room again: *The fragments of language you heard spoken in those excerpts were probably incomprehensible to most of you. Professor Trevor Watling, one of the British Isles' foremost Latin Scholars will now explain something of what we can glean linguistically from the Retrovival sequences...*

Trevor stands up. *Our auxiliary soldier spoke Latin most of the time, as he would have been expected to of course in the Roman army. His pronunciation surprises us however, and seems to be shared with the senior officers who occasionally address him. Thus we suspect that we may not be looking at a regional accent, but at a general evolution of Latin away from how it was written, by a greater degree than we had hitherto expected. Put very simply, Latin eventually evolved into modern Italian, but what we are hearing here is a language further along the process of that transformation than we expected. Words are beginning to sound as if they end in vowels even though they still possess consonants in the written form.*

Trevor clears his throat, takes a drink of water and continues: *Furthermore, our subject also appears to speak his mother tongue occasionally, and as our genetic analyses have predicted, this sounds like a Brythonic dialect from the south of England. In layman's terms a form of an ancient Celtic tongue thought to have existed in numerous variants across pre-Roman Europe. To our ears it sounds closest to modern Welsh, but may not in fact be very close at all. We are in the process of enlisting the help of other linguists, computer applications and artificial intelligence in order to arrive hopefully at a translation application for this language, although we could do with a lot more vocabulary than we have so far gleaned.*

Any questions? Ailee turns over the conference to the room.

Kirsty Denholm, News Caledonia. Are you concerned about a potential backlash from religious communities here and around the world? I mean in the sense that these faith groups believe that the human soul departs upon death to migrate to some kind of heaven or afterlife. Does this discovery imply that no such afterlife exists? That we, whatever constitutes a person, are merely the product of the physical organ of the brain?

Ailee frowns and thinks to herself for a moment. *Well, I suppose I should say that we are at the dawn of a new age here, sorry to sound melodramatic about it. But what I mean is that societal discussion or series of discussions is going to be necessary over the weeks and months to come. I am not religious personally, so I can't vouch for how a person of faith might seek to explain our findings. But what I would say is that the central message of all religions strikes me as being one of love and peace and tolerance, and nothing we've done challenges that.*

Trevor cuts in ...*If I may, I would suggest that from a religious perspective if a soul can leave a body, why should it not return when that body is revived?*

But isn't that problematic, professor, with respect? – Ben pipes up. *Alarming even? You're only talking about having retrieved memories from dead brain tissue as I understand it. If you're talking about bringing people back to life then this really is a Frankenstein moment, and people should be justifiably concerned should they not, horrified even?*

Before Trevor can answer, Ailee cuts across an open-mouthed Trevor in order to terminate the line of enquiry: *–With respect, I don't think that's what Professor Watling was actually saying. As I've said, we are scientists and it's not our place to postulate how religious* *groups may choose to reconcile our findings with their faith. That is entirely up to them.*

*

After the press conference, Ailee and Trevor look at each other in relief and decide to look for a quiet pub somewhere in which to let off steam. *It's years since I have wandered around down here on foot...* Ailee laughs as Trevor leads her to the cobbled lanes parallel to Byres Road. *I've become used to viewing it from above and worrying vaguely about what's going on down there.*

We're all like beetles under a rock to you, eh? Ants and slaters creeping around caught up in our tiny wars.

Sounds like history. Ailee says, trotting to catch up with Trevor's strides. *Sounds like the view from outer space or the future.*

Maybe we could all benefit from the high view. –Trevor says pushing the pub's double doors open, their frosted glass throwing unexpected blades of light. The hubbub of talk from within rushes out to meet them. *What are you drinking?*

A bar... Ailee exclaims, *I'm standing at a real bar again.*

Yes, and no one's assaulting or insulting you. You're safe as houses. Street life gets a bad rap.

Do you think we're going to become household names soon then? Weel kent faces, as we say in Scots. –Ailee beams.

Christ, I hope not. Here, did I make a faux-pas with my answer to that religious question do you think?

Relax, Trevor. It got everyone thinking at least. Maybe it will get Breshkov thinking too.

Hey, English cunt! –Someone shouts from across the pub, and Ailee tenses.

I spoke too soon, Trevor mumbles, not turning around.

The voice comes again: *Sassanach, ah said. Whit makes ye think yer welcome in here, pal? Go hang oot wi some of yer ither soft pals.* An overweight drunken youth with a red face waddles up to bump into Trevor's back.

The barman has returned with the drinks now, but takes them off the bar top and says quietly to Ailee: *I'm sorry love, but I don't want any trouble, I think it would be best if you just leave.*

We've to leave? Trevor overhears him, incredulous. He calmly puts his wallet back into his pocket as Ailee strokes his arm, noticing his rising temper.

Hey, pussy, you heard the man. –The voice comes from behind again.

Ailee screams as Trevor spins around and kicks the lad's feet away from under him, twists his arm behind his back and runs him forward until his chin is resting on the surface of the bar, his face contorted, foam coming out his mouth. The barman appears stunned in a mixture of fear and anger.

Trevor pronounces his words through gritted teeth with forced calm and politeness: *This lad seems to be looking for his lost cat, said something about a pussy. Maybe you can put him straight for me, direct him to the lost and found.* With that he takes Ailee's hand and they leave while the lad collapses to the floor as his pals feign unconvincing attempts to block Trevor's foreboding exit.

Outside, Ailee persuades him to break into a run until they find a darkened alley and doorway to duck into. It begins to rain heavily, dampening the belligerent cries of confused pursuit behind them. Ailee looks out then back up into Trevor's eyes. She takes him in her arms and they kiss for the first time, the rhythm of the rain on the cobbles merging with the beating of each other's hearts.

*

Ailee gets a call from Strang at ten to midnight. *You asleep yet, Ailee?*

She cradles the phone against her shoulder, sitting up in bed. *Would it matter to you if I was, Ed?*

Oh... I'm sorry. Thought you were great on the telly today by the way. Now don't be sore. Thought you'd want to be first to know though.

Know what?

I think we have another body, or a position for one rather. Five metres away, due north-west. Piecing the auxiliary's fragmented memories together and cross-referencing them with topographical data, things that haven't changed, the Campsie Hills and so forth. It looks as if a centurion and his horse both went down in the bog a minute or so after our auxiliary did. Some kind of flight and pursuit was obviously underway, a desperate bid to get back to the wall by crossing the bog.

Pursued by who?

The blue-painted devils no doubt, you know, our great great great great grandparents, give or take a few hundred greats.

You've seen them? I mean, did the auxiliary see them?

Yes... a few glimpses. You don't tend to look back that much when you're running for your life to get away from something, I suppose.

Well, Queen Drest will love that. Our butch and terrifying ancestors making those puny Romans run away like a bunch of jessies.

Jessies, eh? A fine Glasgow term. Tell you what she'll like even more then, and you will too. At least one of the blue devils is female. As scary as any of the males of her tribe, she seems to be at the forefront of the chase.

Mmmm... that is exciting. Wait until the media get a hold of this.

Think you can sleep now, or do you want to come down and get a look at this?

I can sleep just fine, Ed. And so should you. Your good work can keep until tomorrow now. Ailee hangs up and turns around to find Trevor has woken up too. He is rolling a cigarette. *Is that grass I smell? You old hippie. I thought I was the one leading you astray.*

Never anywhere I'm not willing to go. When I woke I had this terror for a moment that your daughters had come back and caught us here.

Don't be daft. I told you, Onya has gone back to England and Iona is staying with a friend of hers in Edinburgh tonight.

Still. I better make myself scarce in the morning. Was that Strang? Anything interesting?

Very, actually. They've found another body in the bog. Ed thinks it's going to be a Centurion and his horse, intact.

Jesus... Trevor whistles. *This thing is going to be big, it could get out of hand in fact.*

What are you afraid of, Trevor?

Nothing really. Just that it might turn into a media frenzy. Right now in recently racist Scotland I'd rather keep a low profile, be a boring old English fart of an academic.

No, I mean, what are you afraid of generally, your whole life?

Oh right. One of those conversations is it? He takes a long draw on his joint and passes it to Ailee. *Funny you should say that, I was just about to have one of my recurring dreams again when Strang woke us. I've had this one all my life, more of a nightmare actually. I seem to be standing on a flat rooftop somewhere, a tall building I assume because I feel a bit scared. And there's a couple of people nearby asking me to take a run and jump from one building on to another one nearby. Maybe one of them has done it already and is waiting for me on the other rooftop, because I'm thinking this is easy and I should be able to do it. So I take a few steps back and I run and run and then I leap, except that suddenly the distance doesn't seem so little as I thought it was and I'm terrified that I'm not going to make it. Usually I just wake up screaming at that point, or wake myself up to snap out of it, or sometimes I get so close that I can see my fingers are just about to clutch the edge of the concrete coping as I slam into the facade... but I always wake up before that. What about you?*

Ailee sighs, blows a smoke ring and hands him back the joint. *You've never been a parent, have you? That's when your nightmares stop being about yourself. After my girls were born my fears were all about leaving babies behind, children getting lost or catching fire or some crazy shit. Even though they're both adults now, I suppose my terrors still run along similar lines. Our fears get smart it seems to me, like a game of chess they're always one step ahead.*

I dreamt about you the other night, you know... Trevor chuckles.

You did, really? Ailee looks at him wide-eyed. *Do tell.*

No... Trevor frowns, stubbing out his smoke.

Oh I see, Ailee slips into his arms. **That** *sort of a dream was it?*

Might have been. Look... Trevor points up at the window above them, a full moon visible in a gap in the curtains, soaring between night clouds. *This is the dream, right now. Maybe we are the dream. Maybe what I fear most now is waking up.*

*

Kirsty Denholm meets Charlie Doohan in the car park of a country pub by a beautiful wooded loch. They enter through the back door and are led through the kitchen, its stainless steel surfaces gleaming in the April light, a large pot of Scotch broth bubbling on the hob. *Friends of mine...* Charlie mumbles over his shoulder, as the chef waves to them, *we might even be the only ones in today, they're not yet geared up for the tourist season, still early in the year.*

When they are settled in a dark area of booth seating in the secluded back bar, Charlie takes a yellow folder from his brief case and pushes it across the table to Kirsty before the barman arrives to take their order.

How are your investigations going? Kirsty asks.

Charlie squints at the menu, looks for his glasses in his jacket pocket. *Not as well as I would like, frankly.*

I was at a press conference the other day, Charlie. Maybe you saw something about it in the news. An archaeological dig near Glasgow has managed to retrieve memories from inside the brain of a Roman soldier who died two thousand years ago.

Astounding. Disturbing, isn't it? The waiter brings a jug of water and Charlie studies the bottom of his glass, holding it up to the light.

Well, it occurs to me, what if the same technique could be used to help your investigation?

You mean on the brains of the English immigrant victims? That's just the problem, we haven't found any remains yet.

That's not what I meant necessarily. You said one of the murderers committed suicide. By what method may I ask?

Christ, that's pretty monstrous thinking. But I follow your line of reasoning. Hanging, he hanged himself.

That might be ideal.

Ideal? Charlie looks perplexed.

Yes, where a bullet to the head would decidedly not be. Was he buried or cremated though?

I'd need to check. Are you serious?

Totally. Why not? Kirsty shrugs.

This technology you're talking about has been used on mummified bodies, bog bodies, is that right? Never on a recently deceased human being. That would be desecration, grave-robbing, off the scale in terms of law breaking. And I'm a flaming policeman, remember.

Think about it though. Kirsty becomes animated. *The procedure could be used on a victim, but how much does a victim see or understand during their last moments? But a perpetrator? A perpetrator knows everything, does everything. And this one has already confessed so you said.*

I suppose, now that I consider it, that we do exhume bodies now and again to take DNA samples. Charlie ponders. *It's not really without precedent. I see what you mean, although I don't like it much... But how would we go about contacting these people, what are they called again...?*

Tacitus, and Retrovival who licence the technology to them. Tacitus work for the Scottish government, so they'd be hard to trust. But Retrovival are international on the other hand, led by someone called Val Breshkov who is somewhat camera shy, keeps herself out of the public eye. But I could contact the company, pose as a potential client I suppose, who's found some ancient remains.

Too deceptive, Kirsty, not a good way to start or win trust. I have authority, gravitas, that you wouldn't, and the press certainly don't. I think I've met this Breshkov person before, come to think of it. And might do so again soon in the normal course of my day job, through our friend Drest. Leave this with me.

Their drinks arrive, and they clink glasses. *The staff will probably think we're having an affair, Charlie.* Kirsty winks.

Hardly, that was my wife's nephew, and his dad's my brother-in-law. Charlie sighs. *They know it's business and that we're up to something way more serious than sex.*

~

VI

Ailee and Trevor arrive at the Balmore archaeopod to find Strang and Breshkov overseeing the lifting of the second bog body. Mist briefly fills the interior again before the dark cube of earth is sealed into its glass enclosure.

It's huge this time! Trevor exclaims, *was this guy a giant or something?*

Horse, Trevor. Strang answers drily. *There's a horse in there too. He's on horseback.*

An X-ray scan briefly illuminates the figure hidden within, animal and man contorted in their last agony as they struggle against the inexorable force of the bog sucking them down under their own weight. Various tubes and electrodes slowly penetrate the cube, heading for the subject's brain, as a solution of neutral pH detergent begins to wash away the earth from around the bodies. Ailee notices from the X-ray screen shot that one tube is targeted towards the centre of the body. *What is this?* she asks Breshkov, pointing at the screen.

The heart, Ailee. This looks like it could be the most intact brain we've ever found. We need to feed it with blood via the route it expects it from.

But if you start the heart, even by accident...

Yes, I know. International law.

Ailee winces, runs her hand through her hair. *Val... can we talk privately for a minute please, in the conference chamber or something?*

Sure, it is a bit tight in there, like taking a sauna together, but Ed and my assistants and the computers are practically on auto-pilot as you can see...

Ailee and Breshkov retire discreetly to the meeting room. Closing the glass door behind her, Ailee notices the babble of noise evaporates instantly behind the hermetic seal. She thinks carefully, looking down at her feet for a moment before continuing: *Val, if you re-start a human heart, I'm out of here, basically.*

You mean resign, or what is the contemporary phrase... 'grass' us all up to the authorities and the media? Breshkov sighs, leaning back in her chair.

Never the latter, but certainly the former. Ailee answers quietly, *If we bring a man back to life we are crossing the line, playing God, Doctor Frankenstein.*

Breshkov grimaces and runs her hands over her face. *That is not my intention, Ailee, you know that. I mean, what would we do with a resurrected Roman? All I want to do is to harvest the maximum amount of trace data left over in his brain.*

Strang knocks on the door. *Really sorry to interrupt, folks, but you want to take a look at the media reaction this morning. We're on CNN and Al Jazeera...*

Sonja draws black-out curtains across the centre of the pod to conceal the thawing centurion while everyone turns to face the screen at the rear. News reports reveal condemnation from sources as diverse as American evangelists, Islam's Grand Imam, Iran's Grand Ayatollah, the Pope and the Dalai Lama.

Dalai Lama? Strang snorts, *I thought he was a relaxed sort of dude.*

Interferes with reincarnation maybe... everyone's got their red lines... Sonja muses.

And their bête noires. Looks like we have just filled that universal job vacancy. –Breshkov remarks grimly.

Check this out... Bruce flicks across to a local channel. *There are protestors gathering outside an archaeopod in Falkirk. Police are cordoning the area off to force them back.*

Why the hell Falkirk? –Ailee laughs incredulously.

They must think we are there. There are 14 pods across the central belt at the moment. We were careful at the press conference not to reveal which one was us. Breshkov answers.

Excellent... Strang rubs his hands in glee. *We have attained a very useful decoy then, quite by accident.*

Weren't there clues to our whereabouts in the memory segments we released at the event? Trevor asks.

No. We kept out the segments with the Campsie Hills in them. No landmarks... Breshkov answers.

You cunning devil... Strang marvels. *But those are still our colleagues trapped in there, I better get them on the phone and check they're alright.*

They're not even there I reckon, Bruce answers, *look I have them on this App. That station has been stood down for the last month while carbon dating results are awaited on some pottery finds.*

Right... Strang flicks channels, *back to the Archbishop of Canterbury then.*

Who cares what he thinks? He's got a ravaged country to administer to... Bruce mutters.

In an interview, the Bishop is seated beside a morning news reader, his fingers caressing nervously the cross around his neck. *I have questions, I have to say,* he intones earnestly, *and severe misgivings regarding the morality of this and its spiritual implications.*

Do you think it should be stopped? A moratorium imposed? The interviewer asks him tensely.

Certainly, at least until, as I say, the spiritual ramifications have been considered and society as a whole has had a conversation about how it feels about this.

Do you think this potentially disproves religion, Your Grace? If consciousness is purely a physical phenomenon that can be mined like this, like coal or gold?

The Archbishop half laughs, without amusement, waves his hand dismissively as if swatting an invisible fly. *No, not at all. This dead Roman or Ancient Briton is not still alive of course. I would say that his soul is still absent from this earth. It's merely that his mind has left behind more traces than we had hitherto thought possible.*

There you go then... Strang sighs. *They'll all simmer down in time as they get used to it. This is Scotland anyway, we can do what we like.*

Ailee and Trevor look at each other. Ailee speaks to prevent Trevor doing so: *You're all starting to sound like Drest fans to me.*

Everyone groans or clucks in indignation. *I see I have got a request for a meeting from the head of Police Scotland anyway...* Breshkov says, taking out her phone. *Even if we manage to continue this low profile here, we better have the police ready to throw a cordon around us at the least sign of trouble.*

*

The sound of helicopters and fighter jets taking off is deafening, followed by the lesser heat and light of the graviton-drive of President Drest's hoverpod firing up. Army and Air force personnel criss-cross the runway of SAF Boulmer, until recently RAF Boulmer, England's most northerly air force station, now under Scottish control. As the pod ascends rapidly, Drest takes care not to look directly into the camera lens strategically placed to her left side to capture her in army fatigues alongside some appropriate top brass briefing her on the extent of territory below, which is now under her control. Alnwick, Morpeth, Ashington, Cramlington, the patchwork quilt of fields and towns roll by underneath for fifteen minutes, occasional fires and plumes of smoke still visible from skirmishes and pockets of resistance. Gradually the formidable mass of Tyneside comes into view. A top general proudly indicates to her how the white eyebrow of the Gateshead Millennium Bridge is jammed open, with Scottish Navy warships sailing up the Tyne, confident of no fire being returned from the areas to the south recently scoured and strafed into retreat. The voluptuous silver curves of the Gateshead Glasshouse are cruelly punctured as if Scottish artillery have been amusing themselves with target practice from the opposite river bank. Black wisps of smoke continue to issue from inside.

For the best photo opportunity, the pilot lands the pod on the A167, the high cast-iron flyover leading to the

Tyne Bridge itself. Drest exits the pod, other generals join her and they walk across the bridge. Hostile media outlets will later pair this scene with photographs of Hitler in front of the Eiffel Tower. The filigree green girders above throw dramatic shadows across the party as they progress towards the centre of the span, from where Drest gives an exultant speech to a privileged group of soldiers and a handful of carefully selected and 'embedded' reporters and cameramen:

Everything north of here is now Scotland. Scotland again, as it was in the twelfth and thirteenth centuries. But I want to stress that no one in these lands who has hitherto considered themselves English need be in the least afraid. Scotland is a just and generous country that values and protects all within its fold.

I am told that this wonderful structure on which we stand was designed by the same engineers responsible for Scotland's Forth Rail Bridge. Two great twentieth century icons, one painted red, one painted green. I am tempted to have this one painted red now too, but suspect that the media would have a field day, likening the colour to blood. There has been remarkably little blood spilt during this remarkable campaign, an almost bloodless coup de grâce to the failing state of North Northumberland. The internecine wars in this province are now over. Scottish law and order shall prevail.

Behind me, the River Tyne stretches inland to where Hadrian's wall meets it at Wallsend, the former Roman fort at Segedunum, all now also under Scottish control. The Romans left there in 400AD, abandoning what had been their boundary between Roman England and the so-called barbarians to the north. Now, nearly 1700 years later, I hereby declare that Hadrian's wall is once again the boundary between Scotland and England...

...Shit... Ailee's daughter Iona exclaims next to her mother on the sofa, watching television at home to the north of Glasgow. *That's her just annexed half of Carlisle at the drop of a hat.*

Or a slip of the tongue perhaps... Ailee muses. *I wonder if her generals even knew she was going to say that, or know what it implies. Look at their faces... proud or scared, what do you reckon?*

And on a technical note... Iona adds, consulting her phone, *I see it's the Forth* **Road** *Bridge that was designed by the same engineers. Her advisors couldn't even get that right.*

The least of her false facts I would imagine.

I'm *scared, Mum. I think we should all be.*

Plato comes running in from the porch and nuzzles his warm black snout against Iona's knees as if he had heard her. They both kneel to pet and reassure him. As they get up to make lunch together, the television behind continues to play images of Drest pinning medals onto the chests of soldiers, while political pundits and precision-wafflers the world over pore over maps, second-guessing what Scotland's outrageous new demagogue might be planning next.

*

Arriving again at Trevor's door, Ailee smiles broadly. *We have a bit of time to spare again today, Trev, I reckon. While the technical boys thaw our centurion on horseback out of the black forest gateau. Wanna try out another VRKO together?*

Why do I feel like you're trying to get me hooked on drugs, professor?

You can talk. Ailee laughs. *Now loosen up. I promise, Trev. No blood and guts, no shocks and horrors. Or not much anyway. No heads coming off at least.*

What is it then? Trevor asks over his shoulder as he gets his jacket on.

The Battle of Langside. Keeping it local again.

Sounds bloodthirsty to me, but I guess I can't claim to be above violence myself after last week's incident.

No trouble about that I hope? CCTV, police etcetera?

Not so far. All I did was bump his chin off the bar top after all. Apart from the heinous crime of being English.

He closes the door behind him.

Ailee reaches out to touch Trevor's fingertips but notices he recoils.

Let's go now then. Judith is working from home this morning. Trevor thrusts his hands into his pockets and silence takes over the space between them as they walk from his door towards Queen's Park. *Where do we start then?* He asks eventually to fill the void.

What? Ailee asks, revealing that she has been deep in thought. *Oh, right, up at the monument of course at Battlefield, but let's go through the park, it's a nicer route.*

Yes, I am going to leave her... in case you're wondering... he says quietly as they cross the wide green of the park, heading for the woods at the crest of the hill.

You're assuming I want you to, aren't you? Ailee answers and they both look at each other seriously, curiously, as they keep walking. Considering this harsh on reflection she reaches out her hand and this time he takes it. When they reach the wooded edge of the park they look down together at the Langside Battlefield memorial: a sixty foot high sandstone column with four eagles around the base and a rampant lion sitting atop its Corinthian capital. *Right, headsets on...* Ailee prompts him, taking them from the sterilising booth at the park gates and paying with her phone. *The monument's here because this is where the decisive moment of the battle ended, but the whole confrontation took place across a swathe of ground from here south towards Cathcart. You see that hill in the distance, highlighted in the terrain mesh, that's called Court Knowe. Mary's men took her there to watch the battle in safety until she saw her army had been beaten then she fled in despair. May the thirteenth, 1568. You know the background to all this, right?*

Hideously complicated and tragic as I recall it, but let me hear the simplified version by way of a refresher.

The voice-over is a bit dry and wordy, so I'll irreverently summarise for you, Trev, it will be much faster. Ailee takes a deep breath and puts her arm around his shoulder. *Henry The Eighth kept marrying women and discarding or killing them if they didn't bear him any children, since he was obsessed with having an heir. He was an arsehole that way, like most royalty. Well the Catholic church, who basically ruled the world at this point, regarded divorce as a sin, and without their blessing his credibility to be king was severely in question. So he solved this problem like a bull in a china shop by withdrawing his entire kingdom from Christendom, a bit like Brexit really. To hell with all his subjects who had been Catholics up to this point, they'd all have to become Anglicans like him, his new personal sect of Christianity with him as the head of the church of England. Plenty of people didn't want to go along with this, and had to become secret Catholics, whose covert desire was to overthrow Henry and have a Catholic monarch back on the throne. The rival nations of France and Spain quite fancied this idea too, and Henry became paranoid about plots to dethrone him, many of which were not just paranoia, to be fair. Mary Queen of Scots, very much still a Catholic, happened to be next in line to the throne after Henry The Eighth's children, of which there was ultimately only one: Queen Elizabeth the First of England. Understandably perhaps, Queen Elizabeth feared and hated Queen Mary because she was paranoid that Mary might want to depose her with the help of all the Catholics and make herself Queen of both Scotland and England. This paranoia was also not ill-founded. So here's the irony: many if not most people think this story is about England fighting against Scotland. A similar misunderstanding pertains about so-called Bonnie Prince Charlie, much later in 1745. In both cases it was nothing of the kind. Both Mary and Charles Edward Stuart 175 years later were trying to become the rulers of both Scotland and England, i.e. unite them, not separate them. Both were French Catholics hoping to return both Scotland and England to that faith. So the underlying cause of this battle was Catholic against Protestant, and to some extent men against women since many prudish Scots protestants couldn't stomach how Mary took male lovers and behaved in a way that we might classify today as simply being a modern woman equal with men. The ludicrous puritan bigot and sexist bastard John Knox had a role in this, but let's not sully our minds with him right now, this mess is black enough already.*

Trevor toggles the controls to fly past arrays of soldiers marching towards the battle, while Ailee continues her pre-amble into his ear: *So Mary has been deposed as Queen of Scots by the time of this battle, by a conspiracy of Scots noblemen, who have replaced her with her infant son James, and placed her half-brother James Stewart in charge, known as Regent Moray, as acting-king until the boy grows up. But Mary has escaped from the castle where she was held captive and is now leading an army of about 6500 men towards Dumbarton Castle from where she hopes to build up more support to re-take the Scottish crown. But her half-brother, with a smaller army of about 4000, is shadowing her and trying to find the right place to block her progress. That place turns out to be the tiny village of Langside, right here.* Ailee spins Trevor around to see the two versions of his surroundings, past and present. *Look how small it is in the simulation compared to what it is now. None of these tenements and churches and colleges were here then, not a thing, none of this urban sprawl from Glasgow city centre which has seeped out here and enveloped it in the five centuries since.*

Who'd have thought it? Trevor muses. *So quiet here now. And yet there's battles raging right now, probably as we speak, in Northumberland. Is history repeating itself?*

Well, perhaps... Ailee leads him by the hand further along the pedestrianised street to gaze down on the assembled flanks of Moray's men taking up position at the top of the hill. *But then as now everything is about tactics and experience, not about numbers of soldiers or supporters. Regent Moray and his men had a lot of recent war experience. Mary's army was led by the Earl of Argyll whose military experience was pretty much none, and at any rate he took ill just before the battle. He and Mary were cocksure, thought they had the larger army and could just push through by force of numbers. But Moray realised that Mary's army would have to march up the narrow main street of Langside, so hid lots of his musketeers in the gardens, ready to open fire when they came through. Look how narrow that street is in the simulation, it was known back then as 'the lang loan'. And that hill to the side of it is Clincart Hill, which Mary's men first used as a vantage point to view Moray's army at close quarters, and due to the topography couldn't see the full extent of the enemy's numbers. Now watch...*

Trevor jumps as explosions seemingly rock the air around him and cast-iron spheres whistle overhead and thud into the ground. *An exchange of canon fire from both sides!* Ailee claps her hands excitedly. *Watch how Mary's men begin to march up the lang loan but get fired on by the snipers. Her cavalry come down to support them, but the snipers turn and harass them simultaneously. The foot soldiers and cavalry gradually make it up towards Moray's hill where we're standing now but will become jammed against the enemy when everyone's pikes get stuck together.*

Trevor and Ailee walk around the melee, deafened by the shouts and jeers, the clashing sound of metal on metal. Sometimes assailants run right through them, or a spray of blood blinds them for a second. *Look at the length of those pikes...* Trevor marvels. *How strong do you need to be to even lift one?* The deadly-sharp blades at the head of the wooden shafts jam together like a metal hedgehog, sixty feet across, no one able to get at anyone else. Like a rugby scrum or tug-of-war men on both sides strain and push as the centre shifts back and forward.

They might as well hurl stones or insults at each other! Ailee laughs. *The pike shafts are so dense we could probably walk across them now, if we wanted to, except there's nothing to support us outside the simulation.*

Moray's right flank begins to lose ground and gets forced back. Ailee resumes her commentary for Trevor: *Look at that guy over there galloping around the outside on horseback. Before the age of mobile phones, Moray has the vital accessory of a scout on horseback to examine and report back on what he's seeing, on who is failing where. This scout has been given the authority by Moray to give orders on the spot, so he not only strengthens the formation's right flank but adds many reinforcements to it, attacking not just from the front but the side. Now watch. In a minute, Mary's men will panic and turn around and flee, while Moray's men follow and fire on them. They will kill about three hundred men this way until Moray tells them to stop out of mercy.*

Ailee and Trevor let the fleeing men and their pursuers run straight through them, then the musket balls fired after them, which through some weird kind of auto-suggestion seems to give them a tingling feeling as each shot enters and exits the body. Trevor and Ailee stand for a while, zooming in and out of the slaughter of Mary's fleeing men, before Moray on horseback to their left raises a hand and trumpets sound for hostilities to cease. They walk down the street and step over bodies that aren't there. Apologise as they bump into occasional passers-by who are.

Ailee takes their headsets off. *And there you are. Bob's your uncle. The reason why the street you live in is called Queen Mary Avenue. The entire history of Scotland and England transformed in only forty five minutes of disaster or glory depending on whose side you might have been on at the time.*

Pretty good... Trevor whistles. *But what was the point of it all?*

Sister or half-brother on the throne, Protestant or Catholic.

But Scotland still has both denominations, as does England, why the hell did they care so much?

Ailee steps out of the way of a passing shopper, noticing that most people seem to be ignoring them, assuming they're tourists. Trevor and she continue down hill. *The Protestants thought the Catholic church had become corrupted and materialist, the Catholics thought the Protestants were fanatical heretics. People really believed in Heaven and Hell, the fate of their souls after death. Religion was the only show in town to give you hope in a miserable and frightening world.*

Maybe science is the sop that has replaced it since as a source of peace of mind for most people... Trevor muses.

Good point, yes. Ailee nods her head.

And they pray by upgrading their phones or downloading pointless updates! Trevor laughs.

But Mary got what she wanted, in a way. Ailee continues. *Even though after the battle Queen Elizabeth kept her in various English prisons for two decades before having her beheaded. Mary's son eventually became king of Scotland* **and** *England, because Queen Elizabeth died childless. Mary's personal motto, sewn into her clothing was 'In my end is my beginning' you know. And so it proved. Not that even that settled anything of course. Her son was deposed in time by William of Orange, the next king, and that was the final end of Catholic rule in Britain.*

Your knowledge of history is impressive of course. But why are you telling me all this right now, Ailee? Trevor asks.

Ailee looks downcast for a moment. *I thought you'd find it interesting.* She thinks for a bit then resumes with vigour: *Or maybe because I want you to understand that the thugs who harass you and paint slogans on your door don't know their history, and how dangerous not knowing our history can be, because people fill the void almost without realising it. – Fill it unconsciously with all sorts of vague garbage, made up stuff to feed their own agenda of xenophobia and blaming everyone but themselves for their own problems. Scotland's real battles have more often than not, been with itself, against its own treachery and self-loathing, rather than with the English. When Robert Burns said 'such a parcel of rogues in a nation' he was referring to us, not you. And look at Drest. She's just another Scot trying to conquer England, and for some reason everyone seems to think she's the first to try it. But she's one of a long line, who'll fail like all the rest. Maybe the answer to the world's problems is just for us all to sit on our own arses and leave other people's countries alone.*

Maybe I shouldn't have come here then... Trevor says quietly. *Maybe I should go back.*

Ailee takes both his hands. *Look. There are millions of English people here, ya dafty, it's hard to tell Scots and English apart, their accents fuse, particularly in Edinburgh. I'm speaking English for fuck's sake, the only language I or my parents or grandparents had. We're the same people, long since. Just as we were before the Romans came and built their walls, part of a pan-European Celtic culture. The Vikings and the Saxons and the Irish arrived later to complicate everything and good thing too. But all that matters is governance. Scotland and England are distinct national entities, just like Germany and Austria. Only a fool like Hitler would try to unite them now. Governance, politics. Drest is just playing the classic populist demagogue's trick of scape-goating an immigrant minority in order to appeal to the basest instincts in the stupidest voters. She's drunk on power, an incurable addiction, and in the end that will kill her. It always does.*

I prefer my own period I think. The Romans. That must be why I went down that road way back at university. Everything was clearer with them. What they were fighting for, their technological advantage over their opponents, their cultural superiority. But this... Trevor raises his hand, echoing the concluding gesture of Moray's: *this was just a load of equally-matched people killing each other over nothing, the fine print of their religion, or worse than nothing; the hunger for power of some deranged monarchs.*

Sounds no different to today to me, if you switch monarchs for leaders.

Well, quite. You've made your point then. Fancy a drink after all that carnage?

What, a pub?

No, I think a cafe would be safer. Coffee and cake with pensioners who won't try to beat the shit out of me for my Yorkshire accent...

*

When Ailee returns to her house in the evening, she finds a pile of newspapers on the kitchen table as Plato pants and snuffs around at her feet. *What's this?* she calls out to Iona watching television in the next room. *I didn't think anyone bought newspapers any longer.*

Well they still make them... Iona answers, *for walking on while redecorating, or wiping your bottom with when all the loo roll runs out. I suppose I bought them as a curiosity, as souvenirs to record my mother becoming a household name, but it seems I got more than I bargained for. Look...* she folds them out one after the other.

WHY IS ENGLISHMAN PRESENTING SCOTS PAST?

SASS PROF MUSCLES IN ON RKO DIG

Ailee gasps in horror, her hand to her mouth. *Oh that's terrible. Disgusting. The racist shitbags. Poor Trevor.* Tears form in her eyes, which Iona notices with interest.

Are you and he... you know, Mum?

What? She looks up at her daughter wild-eyed for a moment. *Oh don't be so childish. He's just such a lovely man, kind, decent. He doesn't deserve any of this. I don't know where this country's going.*

Well, I think I know... sighs Iona as she turns around to return to the television. *And I think I know where you and Trevor are going too.*

What? What's that supposed to mean? She calls after her, but feels too timid to repeat it loudly.

~

VII

In Edinburgh, at the President's residence at Bute House, Flora Graham, widow of Lachlan Graham, stands in line to receive a medal on behalf of her late husband. Next to her stand Lachlan's friends, fellow members of the Scottish Border Defence Force including Hugh McDaid and Geordie Armstrong.

Kirsty Denholm, standing among the press pack held back behind rope cordons, surreptitiously checks McDaid and Armstrong's names and faces against those in a printout in her pocket, of files given to her by Charlie Doohan. Key figures in the border atrocities. She nudges her photographer to make sure he gets multiple shots of Drest and Lachlan's widow shaking hands, and of all the other SBDF personnel present.

Drest moves slowly up the line pinning medals to chests of the Border Trackers, exchanging a few patriotic and nationalist pleasantries with each. She pauses for a notably longer time with Flora Graham, turning her shoulder slightly to try to evade the lip readers. *I'm so sorry for your loss, Mrs Graham. I'm told your husband Lachlan was a great patriot who did more than anyone to secure the borders of our glorious nation.*

You should tell everyone that, Mrs President, Flora almost whispers, almost curtseying, *the police have been sniffing around lately, like they'd like to dishonour his memory.*

For just a minute, Flora sees a seed of doubt and even fear in Drest's eyes, before she begins to turn away and Flora hangs onto her hand for just a second too long, endangering the careful choreography.

Ben Woolf catches Kirsty Denholm's eye as he looks on intently, registering something unusual in her attention that arouses his curiosity.

*

Kirsty and Ben go for lunch afterwards at a restaurant nearby, and Ben asks her shortly after they sit down: *What story are you working on right now then, something big?*

Mmm… Kirsty averts her eyes from his, asking for the menu. *I wouldn't like to say. Frightfully hush-hush don't you know.*

I see, Ben flexes his knuckles, releasing a cracking sound like electricity discharging. *You know what I think?*

No. I haven't the slightest idea. Do I want to know?

Let me put it this way then, Kirsty. I have a theory and I want you to hear it.

Well I'm all ears, like a rabbit in the proverbial.

I think you're following something big, a political scandal with the potential to damage this administration, and that it has something to do with the soldiers who Drest has been decorating recently.

Now what makes you think that, Ben?

A hunch. Intuition. My spider-sense is tingling.

Oh come off it. You're a hack not Mystic Meg. No super hero. Your special powers don't extend beyond bribery and phone tapping.

Ha! Very good. The waiter puts down a bottle of mineral water and Ben pours for both of them. *Very well then. I was watching you closely back in there.*

You're married with two children.

Not like that for pity's sake. Give me a break. I was watching how you were watching Drest with those soldiers and that widow, and you were like a cat on a hot tin roof. Agitated, nudging your cameraman, checking your notes like they were a recipe for nuclear fission.

Kirsty's mobile phone rings and she curses, apologises and stands up. *Sorry, Ben, I better take this outside, it's too noisy and the signal's not great. Just order me the Lobster and a glass of Chardonnay, I'll be back in two minutes I promise.*

Left alone, Ben can't help but notice the bright white

gleam of Kirsty's notes, ten to twenty folded pages sticking out enticingly from the top of the handbag she has left behind on her seat. The single ceiling spotlight trained on their dark leather booth and banquette seating seems almost to be angled specifically to highlight the white papers, like an actor on stage about to launch into soliloquy. – Or a flash of knickers glimpsed at the top of a short skirt and an impossibly long pair of stockinged legs. He can't help himself. He takes a quick look around, then keeping an eye on the door: reaches over to remove the notes and casually but rapidly photograph them with his phone.

Out on the street, Kirsty is talking to Charlie Doohan on her mobile while using her powder mirror and the much larger mirror behind the bar to give herself a covert view of Ben left back in the booth. *You were right...* she whispers. *He's reaching over and ogling the scoop. He's even got his phone out now, snapping away. Lapping it up. How did you know? An old copper eh? Human nature, I get it. Right. Time to dash back in noisily and enjoy making him blush then. You sure you want to play it like this? I hope you know what you're doing...*

*

Drest and her husband relax upstairs at Bute House after dinner, wine glasses in hand, after the children have gone to bed. The room is dark, lit only by candles flickering in the breeze from the open window. The historic oil portraits on the walls seem at home in this light, the predominant blacks of their backgrounds almost reaching out to come alive and fuse with the room. Robert Burns, Robert Adam, Neil and Donald Gow with their violin and double bass, each seem to pause and lean their heads from their canvases to lend an inquisitive ear.

Are you sure that was wise, Fiona? Roddy ventures. *Giving medals to those border defence guys? You saw the police report suggesting some of them have been involved in extra-judicial killings? What if the media ever get a hold of that?*

How would they? Drest frowns. *We're in charge of investigating it or not, or SI7 are rather, whose loyalty we can rely on.*

Yes, perhaps... Roddy ponders. *But the police have been leaky as a sieve in the past. Under previous administrations. I'm not sure I trust that Doohan bloke in charge.*

Why not? Drest swills her wineglass around in her hand, takes a sip then leans her head back, gazing at the crystal chandelier glimmering above.

There's something shifty about him. I've watched the look in his eyes closely at meetings recently. He seems alarmed by some of the things you say, uncomfortable.

How old is he anyway? Drest stands up, paces to the window, parts the voile curtains slightly.

Not sure exactly, I could check. Roddy says over his shoulder, still facing her now empty chair. *Early retirement you're thinking?*

What if he doesn't want to? Loves his work and all that jazz.

Roddy laughs. *There's always ways and means of persuasion, isn't there? Nobody on this earth is squeaky clean, and even if they were then that would be so rare as to be yet another form of weakness...*

You're like a Samuel Beckett play sometimes, Roddy. Drest returns to her seat, smiling. *My wing man. So bleak and dry. Like you've been married to all the Scots leaders since Kenneth MacAlpin.*

I'd rather be Samuel than Thomas. Beckett.

Very good. Drest chuckles. *A joke for history buffs. Bang on trend as they say. More Walsingham than Darnley. I'll get SI7 to open a file on Doohan then. With the express purpose of designing a humane retirement plan.*

*

Arriving at the Balmore archaeopod, Trevor and Ailee are shocked by the spectacle of the body of the centurion and his horse now fully cleared of residual earth. Even the red-dyed horsehairs of his helmet crest are almost clean now, the bronze of his helmet green with verdigris and occasional lustre of gold. Soldier and horse hang at one end of the pod interior in a manner that reminds Trevor of cattle carcasses in a butcher's shop. The horse remains a desiccated and shrivelled black husk, but the centurion's skin has now returned to a tanned pale brown, much closer to the appearance of a living body than anyone present expected or feels entirely comfortable with.

As before with the auxiliary soldier, Strang, Bruce and Breshkov and her assistants initiate the feed of Smart Blood to the centurion's brain, and after fifteen minutes the first fragments of visual sequence begin flicking into life on the wall screen behind and on each of the team's monitors. The archaeopod's computers use artificial intelligence to rapidly group, patch and re-assemble the backwards data feed into sections of coherent content.

The team see what Caius sees, hear what he hears, feel what he feels: A few rapid flick-throughs of his childhood in Etruria, intense sunlight on blonde dust, the dark green of cypress trees, hillsides terraced with grape vines, sandals clip-clopping across cool marble, crimson curtains blowing in the breeze. The smell of figs, apricots, red wine in brass goblets. The sound of distant bells, a glimpse of blue sky with clouds like boats, tales told of elephants and naval battles. Then school days, chalk on tablets, running to catch up with his elder brother, his sister laughing at him in a bright courtyard of olive trees, flicking at bees buzzing around her, her blonde hair braided like the baskets in the market. Then military training. Endless fighting with wooden weapons, archery, horse-racing, falling, wrestling, running, competing with his friends. The terror of his instructors, lashes. Bathhouses and comradeship. Pride, armour, insignia. Hunting wild boar and deer, his hands bathed in blood. Girls in flowing dresses in pastel shades, carrying water jugs on their shoulders, whose dark eyes enchant him from the shade of colonnades he marches past, always in formation.

Then somehow to here: Britannia, Caledonia. Via sickening passage in wooden galleons, ports filled with traders from across the empire, wagons stacked with produce and slaves. Strange smells, raised voices, cacophony of light and sound. Then the endless roads his hobnailed *caligae* clatter down on, a deafening noise with an entire legion over cobbles. Battle formation, shields raised as if a cohort can become one being of a hundred limbs, the tortoise, *testudo*. Pilum spears thrusting, gladius blade slashing. Picking up the corpses like debris afterwards. Strange blue twisting tattoos on the dead or wounded flesh. Barbarians with their alien gods. – Hating him and his red-robed brothers for nothing it seems, the way it's always been, wedded to their darkness and ignorance. Unable to grasp Rome's supreme advantages: utter discipline, men working together as an intelligent machine. Superior knowledge, science and engineering, mathematics and geometry. Just as he was taught: the savage cannot learn until his blinding pride is broken. Broken like rocks. Pilum, gladius, shield, endless clash of metal on wood, metal on metal, on flesh, on bone. Rome, all powerful, all he has ever known.

Now the walls. Crossing the old stone one at the island's slim waist, then marched further north to begin the new one. A great honour. He writes home to his parents. A centurion now, promoted for heroism against the *Selgovae*. A hundred men under his command. His skill is in surveying, peering through the brass dodecahedrons the size of a fist, each glowing gold in the sun, fixing them to tripods as he measures out each mile that snakes up and down across the virgin terrain. Tribesmen passing uninterestedly at first, even friendly, trading. Two winters pass, more bitterly cold than Caius has ever known. A frontier under thick snow for weeks on end. Wine and grain in short supply, the impoverished Caledonian soil. Then the first raids begin, always at night. Sorties, skirmishes, just minor vandalism at first. The barbarians can see now what the wall will become, that it will succeed, what its purpose will be. Movement is still free between Caledonia and *Valentia*, the tribes talk to each other, conspire, draw plans. Roman spies bring back cryptic rumours.

Caius is called away south each year to quell attacks from behind, those in Valentia nervous about becoming hemmed in. His comrades continue his work on the wall, but always he returns to see its progress and is put to work, marching new recruits along its length on daily patrols, watching the masons carving each milestone, teams celebrating, amphorae of wine raised, goats and chickens sacrificed to thank the gods. But increasingly he feels the many eyes watching from the tangled wilderness beyond. At night torches are lit all along the ramparts, bonfires at each way station, trumpet alarms sounded, black smoke signals by day.

Caius is assigned to learn more about the adversaries. *Damnonii*, – he learns they are called, begins to learn their language from traders, prisoners and slaves, more of which are being taken as his legion begins punitive raids into their territory. One night his friend and teacher Marcus Claudius receives a barbarian spear through his neck and dies in his arms…

Suddenly Trevor's mobile phone rings, making everyone jump. He curses, apologises profusely as he takes off his headphones and goes to the meeting room to take the call in private. A minute later he emerges and whispers to Ailee that he has to go, asking her to explain to Breshkov that he's had a domestic emergency, telling her that Judith says that racist vandals have thrown bricks through their window, he has to go to meet the police and calm her down.

When the last coherent fragment has been collated and played by the computer Breshkov asks Bruce to power down to give the centurion's brain a rest for an hour before another pass. She gestures for Ailee to join her in the meeting room where Ailee passes on the message from Trevor. *Actually, Ailee, I was going to ask you for a word in private anyway.* –Breshkov answers. *I can see you and Trevor are quite close, and I wondered what you think might be the best way to pass on the contentious news to him.*

What news? Ailee frowns.

I know you hate Drest. We all hate her. But I had to meet with her in Edinburgh yesterday. She says she doesn't want Trevor involved in any more Tacitus press conferences.

Ailee sharply intakes her breath. *The bitch. Did she dare say why? His unbearable Englishness perchance?*

Breshkov smiles grimly. *You know politicians. They never say what they really mean. She was kind enough to say he seems like an asset to our team, but that she was 'under pressure' not to aggravate the right wing of her party.*

Ha! What right wing? Ailee exclaims. *She IS the right wing of her party, the rightest part of the rightest thing since Hitler. Except it's wrong. If you know what I mean. Shit, I bet that would have worked better in Latin.*

Well, what can I say, Ailee? Breshkov sighs. *I agree with you, but if you say things like that about these kind of people then you play into their hands, allow them to paint* **you** *as the extremist.*

So we have to remain silent then?

Well I have to at least. Breshkov nods. *It comes with my job. People don't let me dig around in their countries if I'm in a habit of pontificating on their politics.*

I'm tempted to refuse to take part in the next press conference myself, in protest, in solidarity. Ailee folds her arms in anger.

It's likely to be quite an event, Ailee. Do you really want to give up your place at the forefront of history out of protest? Stay on board would be my advice. Don't let Drest win by hobbling you as well. Find ways to bite your tongue and make your views known later. Don't let her take from you what's rightfully yours. Trevor will still be on the team in the background. He might even be happier with that. Ask him.

I suppose I'll have to...

Now Breshkov's mobile phone rings. *Sorry...* she says, seeing it is a call from Charlie Doohan. *This one is important and confidential, I need to take it. Do you mind if I'm terribly rude and usher you outside for a moment?*

Charlie? Breshkov answers quietly as the soundproof door slides shut behind her. *I got the note you passed me at yesterday's meeting. Can we talk? Not now? I see. You'll send someone else. Less conspicuous, I see. Let's agree it, get your man to meet me here at the Balmore archaeopod itself. Best place I can think of. Yes, but out of hours. 5am. I'll make sure I'm the only one here. How will I know your guy is legit? A password. Really? You're serious? Isn't that a bit John le Carré? Let me think now...*

*

Returning home, Ailee finds that Onya is back from England again, and that both she and Iona have laid out a fresh set of newspaper 'souvenirs' on the kitchen table for her delectation:

TRICKY TREV CHEATING ON WIFE

ENGLISH TREV DOES DIRTY WITH ALE

Ailee chokes, her hands over her face and mouth, as if braced to wretch. *Ale? –*she finally manages to say. *What are they talking about?*

ALE as in Ailee I think... Onya answers. *Welcome home, Mum.*

What, why? All they saved was two letters... Ailee mutters distractedly.

I thought it was quite clever actually. Same game as RKO, but that's not the main point is it? Iona asks.

No? What is?

Oh, come on. You have been seeing this guy, haven't you, Mum? Onya confronts her.

But he's my colleague, I have to...

Come off it, Mum, we're not daft. Iona crows. *You're involved with him, aren't you? Luvvy duvvy, kissy wissy?*

What if I was? So what? Ailee looks around at her progeny, startled. *It's nobody else's business. I'm a single woman these days, divorcee, what's it to you two?*

We just don't want you to get hurt, Mum, to make a fool of yourself. This guy is married, right? Onya insinuates, seemingly leading the inquisition.

Yes. Ailee blushes.

But I'll bet he's told you a load of bollocks about how he intends to leave her any day now, how their relationship's in a terrible mess. –Iona takes her turn to put the boot in, bad cop, worse cop.

Well, he has I suppose, but it happens to be true.

Oh Mum, can't you see you're being naive? Onya groans. *Men, like that, ageing lotharios, two-timing creeps, they always say things like that to get women into bed. It's a story as old as the hills.*

Ailee's eyes catch fire with fury: *Oh right, I see, so now all of a sudden you two are the most wise and most experienced pair of women-of-the-world on the planet are you? I wiped your bottoms for fuck's sake, bought you your first bras. You're a pair of daft wee lassies to me.*

Mum, come on...

*No, you come on. And don't you dare call Trevor a lothario or a creep, don't you dare disrespect my dear friend. He's a good, decent man. A brave man. What do you know about him or me? Amn't I allowed a little love in my life after all these years? After bringing you two up? You're adults now, I've done my bit, but it's just not enough is it? You still want a piece of my soul from now until eternity! Do you know what it's like to be a mother? To put your career on hold, to see your youth and beauty go down the toilet as you turn into a fleshy barrage balloon for nine months at a time? Amn't I entitled to a little bit of happiness? A little bit of love? Trevor sees me, you know that? Actually **sees** me. As a woman, a girl. Not as a big fat invisible food provider, and money-stumper-upper, not as a **mum**.*

Iona raises her hands, shrugging, retreating from the

room: *Calm down, Mum. I'm sorry we raised this now. We were just worried about you, that's all.*

Well you know what? Ailee spits back at them bitterly. *Don't be. Your mother's a big girl, she can handle herself, thank you very much. You know who you should be worried about? Trevor, and people like him. English people being harassed and victimised through no fault of their own. Marriages do fail, girls, as I know all too well. Marriages fail and people do split up and start relationships with other people. It happens every week, every day, it's not like I invented it.*

No, we get that, Mum. Sorry. –Onya almost whispers, trying to lower the tension. *We didn't mean to upset you so much. I can see you care about him a lot already. I just hope he feels the same way about you, that's all.*

As the girls leave the room, Ailee kneels and embraces Plato who wags his tail and licks the tears from her face, wondering to herself in a moment of despair if animals are a sounder emotional investment than children.

*

I feel bad about this... Ailee says, ducking out of the rain as Trevor opens the door for her on the south side. *Coming here when Judith's away.* She notices the plywood over the window of the living room. *At least the press can't take photographs through that. You've not got the window replaced yet then?*

Not until the CCTV cameras arrive next week, or else the yobs might do it again. She nearly didn't go to her conference, you know... Trevor answers, over his shoulder as she follows him down the hall ...*because of the window, but I told her we have to live our lives normally, not allow ourselves to be intimidated by the thugs. But is this living our lives normally I ask myself?*

What?

He turns around and kisses and embraces her at the kitchen sink. *Snogging you in the kitchen. Cheating on my wife.*

I know, I know. She gazes over his shoulder. *I feel...*

conflicted... in the same way. I try to tell myself not to do this, I told myself not to come here tonight, but...

But? Trevor pulls back and looks into her eyes, hands on her shoulders.

*It was hopeless. I feel as if, as if... we're battling something bigger than ourselves, a force too strong to resist. I feel... overthrown. Subverted. Degraded but exalted at the same time. **Exalted**, what a word.*

They resume kissing more passionately, until Trevor leads her by the hand and they go upstairs.

*

An hour later, they sit up in Trevor's guest room as he rolls a cigarette.

What a day that was today. Ailee reflects. *Could you believe it? The memories in the centurion's head...*

Trevor blows out smoke and sighs. *And the colour of his skin. He looked like he could wake up and walk right out of there. You still not think this technology is the devil's work?*

Every day, says the little primitive cave woman inside me.

How much more data did you glean after I left? He passes the roll-up to Ailee who takes a draw then passes it back.

Quite a bit. We think we've even established what his full name was, through hearing people in the memory segments call him it. Caius Septimus Flavius. But we could do with your help tomorrow to work out the substance of a lot of the other conversations stored in his head.

Will there be further material left tomorrow? Is Breshkov confident of many more passes before she's exhausted the brain? —Before she can throw it away like a used-up prune?

Ouch! Touchy touchy, Trev'. Ailee chuckles. *You sound bitter, not exhilarated at one of the greatest scientific breakthroughs in history.*

Well Hiroshima was a scientific breakthrough too. I

suppose I would have played the party pooper at that one as well, while my face fell off.

Take it easy. What's eating you so much? Ailee takes the roll-up back. *Talk it through with me.*

Trevor brings his knees up to his chin and thinks hard. *You know... I hated seeing that guy strung up there today. It reminded me of my father's butcher's shop.*

What? An academic like you? Are you having me on? I didn't know you were a butcher's boy. You never mentioned that. There can't be many of them left now in our brave new vegan world.

This was Yorkshire, remember. Trevor snorts. *A time zone all its own. All the gammon queuing up for their pies and steaks. Dad wanted me to take over from him one day. Made me watch him gutting and chopping things from an early age. I hated it. And he beat my mother every so often. I kind of thought it was normal as a young kid, assumed other kids' mothers got beaten too. Children accept everything, they adapt. But it leaves a scar. I hate violence, male violence particularly. The way it draws you in.*

Ailee turns to sit on the edge of the bed. Goes over to the window to gaze down at the streets below, then thinks of the orange streetlight making her visible from outside and withdraws. Trevor decides to change the subject:

I've been meaning to ask. What happened to your marriage? You don't talk about it much. Is the children's father still around, still alive?

Ailee returns to his side and he puts his arm around her. She leans against him and stares into space, remembering. *We drifted apart. Then separated. His name was Mike.* **Was.** *Because he died about two years ago. Cancer, you know. He saw the kids every second weekend, particularly when they were younger. It was quite sudden, as far as we could gather. An unpleasant surprise to say the least, as much to him as to the rest of us, little warning, quite far advanced. It had started in his liver, but spread to his bones.*

But why had you separated? Trevor repeats.

I don't know. He changed. People do. But he became more domineering, less tolerant over time. Began to remind me too much of my father, who although not literally a butcher like yours, was certainly a butcher of dreams. Classic lowland Scottish manic depressive. Nothing good would ever come of anything because the whole system is set against you, that sort of thing. Scottish independence broke him I think because he couldn't cope with anything so optimistic. It contradicted his expectational paradigm. Perversely, it's maybe disproving his pessimism that has driven me all these years, the urge to succeed and disprove his low expectations of me.

A career girl, eh? What a foul phrase. We don't hear much of career boys do we?

I think Mike was jealous of my career, although he always denied it, the mere suggestion drove him mad. It's that old male breadwinner thing. When we first met I was just a student working as a nurse, he was a structural engineer. It was the change in my status that seemed to cause problems for him.

Trevor runs his hands through the locks of her hair, wondering at the contents of her head, all the unreachable memories locked up inside. *I've sometimes wondered if all relationships between men and women are a power struggle. If arguments are where the power balance gets tested and re-set if necessary.*

That's a scarily primitive way of looking at it.

Yes, but we're still scarily primitive creatures in so many ways. Maybe if you and Mike had met when you both had good careers then you might have worked out.

Ailee frowns and sits up. *Or more likely... then we wouldn't have met at all. He wouldn't have wanted a woman who was his equal, a threat to his self-esteem somehow.*

So.. Trevor claps his hands, – *we're both on the run in a way, from male stereotypes, overbearing father figures aren't we? Maybe we should be big fans of Drest.*

Ailee shakes her head. *Surely that boil was lanced*

long-ago. Margaret Thatcher, Golda Meir, Indira Gandhi, Sheikh Hasina, Aung San Suu Kyi. Women leaders make just as good mass murderers as men.

*Do they impersonate men when they do evil? –*Trevor ponders.

*That would be too puerile a let-out clause surely. –*Ailee answers. *Look at Boudica, butchering Londoners, sewing women's breasts over their mouths. History as ever, contains all the uncomfortable truths we don't want to face. Gender becomes irrelevant when you attain sufficient power, like a mask thrown aside to reveal the old familiar demon underneath: a person so drunk and deranged that they want to rule over others. Maybe the people who don't seek office, are precisely the ones we should seek out to assume it.*

*And derange and debauch them in the process? –*Trevor asks.

*Probably, then cast them aside. But at least we'd have got a decent decade out of them. –*Ailee giggles.

Maybe it will happen some day, like some kind of science fiction future lottery thing. Jeff the toilet cleaner made emperor of the free world. Tom the foreman-joiner asked to run the UN... Trevor chuckles.

You're laughing at me now, Ailee complains.

Me? Never, darling. I get what you mean. Jesus was a carpenter. The meek shall inherit the earth and all that.

And what about our centurion? He's inherited an unexpected place in a museum of the future I suppose.

Or have we inherited him? Trevor muses. *An unconventional heirloom.*

Ailee ponders this for a minute. *Some tribes in Indonesia dig their relatives up each year and bring them in to sit at the dinner table with them. Some historians postulate that our ancestors here may have done the same.*

Maybe the iron-age sacrifices, the bog bodies found garrotted and so forth weren't being punished at all, but promoted to immortality, like mummifying Pharaoh. Trevor takes a swig of water from a bottle on the bedside cabinet then passes it to Ailee. *Are you cold?* He notices goosebumps on her skin.

No. I'm fine. Ailee shakes her head, pulling the covers up, continuing their train of thought: *Or signing yourself up for cryogenic freezing like some nutcases in America. There was a time when I'd have said we'll never know what our ancestors were thinking back then. But it's beginning to look like some day soon we just might.*

These bodies of ours, eh? Trevor reflects as he caresses Ailee's thighs. *They'll be a long time dead after this. All we can do is make the most of them now. I'm warming to this subject.*

They kiss, embrace and roll over together.

*

An hour later, Ailee's mobile phone lights up on the bedside cabinet with an urgent message from Breshkov. She and Trevor ignore it as they are otherwise engaged. They ignore another similar message another hour later when they are in the depths of sleep.

~

VIII

Centurion Caius Flavius of the Twentieth Legion wakes up to find himself expelling black water from his lungs onto the polished floor of an unfamiliar villa. He has a vague but horrifying memory of fleeing Damnonii barbarians with several of his legionaries after a botched prisoner exchange. Of trying to take a shortcut back to the Antonine Wall but getting sucked into the mud of a bog, struggling desperately, but weighed down by armour, of everything going black and cold, then nothing. It seems only a few moments ago.

He sees that he is lying on the floor of a bright white room in a pool of dirt and shattered fragments of glass. He associates glass with potters and the making of fine vessels, but the materials in the room seem inconsistent with this or with any craft or trade he is familiar with. Then he realises with a jolt that his horse Rhamus is still underneath him, but strangely shrivelled, turned black as a prune, its eyes dull as stones. The animal was alive and neighing in panic only a few breaths ago, but now is just a desiccated corpse. What kind of witchcraft have the savages performed on him? Perhaps the druid priest that guards their stone altar cast a spell. His secret fear of the Brythonic Gods grips him for a moment, – that he is not wanted in this land, their impenetrable domain of rain-soaked forests. Then he disciplines himself as he would one of his own men. A soldier of the world's greatest civilisation, he must uphold the honour of Rome and rejoin his legion. But where is he? Which side of the Wall?

At this point a man in very strange clothing enters the room, re-enters it, Caius senses, as if he was here before Caius woke up, was somehow part of the event that triggered his release. The man's eyes widen in horror and he shouts wildly in a language Caius has never heard before until a companion, similarly attired, enters the room to join him. One of them then advances towards him, and Caius finds his sword and unsheathes it, with more difficulty than he expects, too slowly in fact to pull it free before this stranger has got close enough to touch him. The feeling of the hand on his shoulder shocks him and he thrusts his sword in one rapid movement into the barbarian's stomach. The man falls to his knees and Caius struggles to his feet, leaning momentarily on the falling man and the wall to his left, which he finds is made of another unfamiliar material, like an incredibly smooth plaster. He advances shakily towards the other stranger now, commanding them in Latin to surrender, but finds his progress momentarily impeded by various obscure wires that have been connected through tiny holes in his helmet to his neck and scalp, which he breaks free from with a single swipe of his hand, releasing a small spray of his own blood. Now the other savage is screaming hysterically like a child, and Caius pursues them around a doorway to see the wretch climbing down a ladder through a hatch in the floor then vanishing.

Caius's body aches all over, his head throbs, so he takes his time now. Kneeling to check all is clear first, he then follows the route of the fugitive down the ladder and finds he is standing in a green field, a little water-logged, and that the building he has been inside was somehow hovering above the field like a ship. This puzzles then astounds him. He walks out and paces around the craft then checks underneath it again. A ship at anchor, that somehow floats on air. The men did not seem to understand Latin, and yet they or their fellows possess such craftsmanship and skill to build this marvel. Their language was not Damnonii, nor Pictish akin to Scythian, he knows the sound of both. Were they Greek? The Greeks built marvels, talking statues and metal astrolabes. He's heard Greek spoken, but nor was that the sound of their tongue. Egyptian, Persian? No way to know. And it would probably make no sense for them to be here without the knowledge of Rome. He puts his hand to his head, takes his helmet off and runs his fingers through his hair. Just how long has he been asleep?

Checking the angle of the sun and the bark of a nearby birch tree, Caius confirms what he thinks is north and south. He sees there is what looks like a whitewashed residential villa, which should not be there, about two hundred paces north, surrounded by hedging. To the south he thinks he recognises the ridge that holds the Wall of Antoninus Pius, but the topography seems altered, the pattern of land use and vegetation all different from his recollection. Most disturbingly: the line of defensive timber stockade along its crest is no longer visible as it should be at this elevation. Thus he surmises he is more or less in the same location as the marsh in which he sank. But the land has somehow changed in the blink of an eye, as if he has slept for a very long time.

Caius resolves not to go near the house, since it may contain more of the tribe whose members he has just routed. The fugitive will probably be gathering reinforcements from his fellows, so Caius needs to leave soon. Then in the distance he thinks he sees something familiar. His heart lifts in hope. A horse, horses, two, three, at rest, tethered in a field. He squints his eyes, sees they have no saddles. And where there are horses there must be drinking water. He aches with thirst. Normally he would listen for the sound of a stream, but he realises now that there is sound everywhere in this landscape, unfamiliar quiet rumbles and swishings in the distance from every direction. He rubs his cheek, feels the knuckles of his fingers, tries to check that he is not caught inside some weird dream.

Back inside the hovering white chamber, he retrieves the saddle from his dead horse, using his knife where necessary, puzzled and disgusted by the black slime that Rhamus seems to be dissolving into. Passing the dead barbarian, he notices with confusion how pale his skin is and how little muscle there is on the man's body. He appeared middle-aged and in good health and yet his limbs are spindly as a child's or an old man's. Whom has he killed? Somebody's apothecary or witch doctor? Druids perhaps. It makes little sense. Outside again this time he notices another detail that disturbs him. Underneath the white ship there is a dark rectangle in the ground with ragged grass around its edges. It's like a grave, about the size and location of he and Rhamus, and there are a few others scattered around, cordoned off with some kind of red ribbons. The other locations are approximately where he remembers some of his legionaries struggling in the bog with him. He shivers suddenly from head to toe, and sets off at a pace, hunched slightly, keeping low to the ground, clinging to lines of hedging where he finds them forming boundaries across the fields.

When he reaches the stream he lies face down and pushes his face out across the water to drink it deep, then fills his leather canteen with more. He is confused to see how badly the leather of the canteen has decayed, has now sprung multiple leaks. Likewise the colour of his own skin seems weirdly darkened. There are brambles on the hedgerows and he feeds on these greedily, now suddenly realising how hungry he is. He makes his way up towards where the Wall should be by scrambling through thick tangles of bushes and trees, a pocket of vegetation more like what he is familiar with, what he recalls covering most of the landscape beyond this Roman frontier line. Looking out south from the copse, he finds no Wall of Antoninus Pius, but two other things instead, both amazing to him. A deep and wide canal has been dug approximately where the Wall should be, and it has clearly been there for a long time since it is overgrown with water lilies and mature trees whose leaves hang low over the water. He assumes this impressive piece of engineering is Roman in authorship and feels a small flood of pride to calm his confusion. Over to the east beyond it however, perhaps four hundred paces way, there is some other communication route running perpendicular to it, on which large shining metal objects are running to and fro, glinting in the sun, emitting some of the strange sounds that he has been noticing since he first found himself awake again.

When he reaches the horses, he feels another pang of relief and familiarity. Caius knows about horses. These are beautiful and healthy animals, varying in appearance, one with slightly exotic markings, cross-bred perhaps with studs from lands unfamiliar to him. They are beautiful to look at, slim like naked young women, but then again, similar to the pale white men he met; in that he notes how underdeveloped their muscle tone is. And why are they here, anyway? Not being ridden by soldiers or traders, or pulling carts? Were those carts he saw on that road-like route bridging over the canal? But those had no horses pulling them. Caius whispers to the best horse, calms it, saddles up then leads it up onto the path beside the canal then mounts it and begins to ride it west towards Litana. He feels almost content, at peace, for the first time today, with clear purpose and the familiar motion of a good horse under him, hooves clattering firmly on what he believes is still Roman territory, despite the strange changes it has apparently undergone. Looking to the north, the familiar ridge line of the Campsie hills confirms to him that he must be nearly back at his fort, that all may yet be well, that he may be able to report back to his commander before nightfall. Peace seems to reign here. Perhaps unknown to him another wall has been built further north into Caledonia to impose Roman order, hence this one has been put to other use.

Then something comes towards him along the canal path that startles and confuses him, but not his horse; who seems used to the apparition. It is a man, pale-skinned again, but moving as fast as if on a horse, but using instead a pair of fragile wheels balanced inside a frame of thin metal bars. Caius stops to let his horse rest, then looks back at the spectacle. Then another one comes and passes from the other direction, then another. One of them even shouts something at him, which sounds friendly, although again in an unfamiliar tongue. Next comes somebody running. A Roman citizen, Caius presumes, so advanced does this canal seem. This citizen appears to be an unaccompanied woman, although dressed as a man in leggings and tunic, and actually raises her hand in salutation to Caius and smiles and speaks the same unknown words of greeting, followed by some others, as she passes. She seems appreciative and respectful of his military attire. *Salve!* —Caius finds himself calling back to her, and the woman half-turns as she runs on, seemingly puzzled by Caius' words, but laughing anyway. He wonders why she is running, since everything seems calm and she was not being pursued by a wild animal or a barbarian. She is likely the wife or concubine of a wealthy patrician, otherwise he might even be tempted to pursue her himself!

From time to time Caius has been noticing slow-moving glinting objects crossing the sky high above him, and now one of them comes into closer view, emitting a heavy drone like war trumpets. He flinches, but notices that his horse again seems unconcerned. How strange to find himself consoled by a mute animal in the face of danger. But he has always loved them, such noble creatures, no language barrier there. The object in the sky is like some huge metal war engine, with stiff wings like a toy bird. It seems to be gliding down to land somewhere to the south-west, well within Roman territory south of the Clota estuary. He is impressed again by what he assumes is Roman engineering and designed to be an intimidating display of Imperial power.

The birds are singing, the bees and insects buzzing in the undergrowth. Caius is in good spirits until he begins to notice to his surprise that the canal is gradually curving southwards, and thus will soon apparently part ways completely with the route of the once great Wall of Antoninus Pius. Standing up in the saddle he thinks he can dimly make out the route of the Wall as a faded green scar across the fields, leading to Litana. He will have to leave the canalside therefore, and make his way over open ground now. Litana looks a good deal more developed a settlement than he remembers it, but that is not in itself bad news at all. Before Caius leaves the canal, he comes upon a citizen fishing in it and notices various ducks in the water and remembers his hunger again. Dismounting and tying his horse, he is surprised to see the fisherman flee in terror as Caius dives into the water to catch a duck for his repast. This is good luck as it turns out however, since the careless man leaves a fresh trout in his abandoned knapsack, which Caius is also able to cook over the small fire that he lights himself by the waterside.

*

Upon reaching what he had thought was Litana, Caius becomes confused and unhappy again, fearful even. There is another carriageway of shining metal wagons hurtling by at speed there, crossing perpendicular to where he remembers the Wall being, and this time he sees that he will have no choice but to cross it. The horse seems to like it as little up-close as he does, so he ties the animal next to a stream, making sure it has plenty of fodder, then sets off on foot. He takes his helmet off and carries it under his arm, as is his custom in the presence of civilians and when not marching in ceremonial parade, and tries his best to appear relaxed and confident in an environment which so teems with weird and uncanny things. The roadway and footways are almost bouncy underfoot, made in what appears to be a black amalgam of stones and mortar or resin. He kneels to examine and smell it, impressed with its ingenuity. A little trumpet sound comes from a metal post at the roadside and the river of wagons comes to a halt. He sees citizens crossing so follows suit. The carriages are astounding up close with no visible construction-seams and glass surfaces through which he can make out seated passengers some of whom seem to look back at him as if he is the marvel rather than they.

Fences are everywhere, borders in timber and metal, and carefully clipped hedge. It is almost as if his beloved

Antonine Wall which he and his legionaries laboured for twelve long years to build, has not vanished but migrated into a thousand smaller walls and palisades. As if Litana is now the meeting place of many tiny personal empires, each jealously guarded by aspirant emperors. He passes some of these townsfolk on the pavements as he tries to make his way uphill to where he remembers his barracks being, trying to keep his chin held high as befits a soldier of Rome. They wear a surprising range of styles and colours of clothes, lacking any coherent order. He is unsure of the class of each of these people. All appear well fed and dressed, thus probably wealthy. Disturbingly, they remind him again of the first two men he saw this morning, one of whom he slew in fright, and he wonders if he might have inadvertently broken a law and killed a notable Roman citizen in error.

Nearing the top of the hill, Caius finds no barracks where he knows there ought to be one, but instead a whole array of strange civic buildings whose purposes are opaque to him, some as much as three storeys tall and well-built in good sandstone. Again he manages to smile amid his homesickness and confusion, pleased and impressed by the arches and classical pediments some of them boast, the careful craftsmanship of their architecture. He hopes to meet the masons and find out what corner of the empire they have brought their skills from. Then an open door catches his eye, and he ventures off the street and up a path into a building that looks different from the others. Something about it attracts him. Is there a smell, or an echo, or a quality of light within it? Or an essence more subtle, a silence, a sense of the sacred? Although it has something like a sharp pyramid of stone above it, rather than a portico and columns, he immediately feels sure this is a temple. His hopes are confirmed when he enters and approaches an altar inside and finds the familiar word 'PAX' inscribed there on pennons and coloured glass. He looks around for a priestess but can see no one for the moment. He lights a candle and adds it to the others, comforted by this small act of solidarity and fraternity with the other citizenry here, which since he sees so greatly outnumber him, he hopes will accept him and soon help him on his way.

Caius is looking up at the colourful glass window-frieze and puzzling over the depictions of crucifixion there, when a voice speaks at his side. A priestess has indeed come to attend him, and although her attire is strange it does not seem wholly unfamiliar to him. Beautiful white silk vestments, full-length cloak and mantle, with two decorated gold bands that come from her shoulders to join into a kind of central scarf that runs down to her feet. A silver chain around her neck carries a symbol almost obscure to him, but which awakes a vague memory which he can't quite place. She speaks to him in the same strange language he has been hearing all day, and he responds respectfully in the only language he knows with confidence: Latin. She cocks her head as if puzzled by him, especially by his clothing, to which she keeps gesturing as if asking him a question. It occurs to him that he does not know what god or goddess this temple is dedicated to, that perhaps he has caused offence by entering it in military uniform. Unable to understand each other effectively, she emphasises a word that sounds like 'Vestry' and gestures for him to follow her through a door to a small room attached to the temple, and there she holds out to him a book filled with words that to his delight he can read. She nods her head too, and begins to speak to him in very slow and stilted Latin. She asks him: *Quo Vadis?* Where are you going? *Quid est teum nōmen?* What is your name? *Unde venistis?* Where have you come from?

The priestess presses a white button on the wall and a yellow light like a tiny sun begins to glow on the ceiling above them. She notices he is shivering and leans down to press another button and a red glow of heat begins to emanate from a white metal brazier at their feet, and yet the fire within it is not made of flames but some strange divine light that she seems able to control. He tries to tell her that he needs to return to his barracks, his garrison and report to his commander Sextus Calpurnius. She asks him if he is a traveller, a leisure traveller from another country like Gaul or Germania. He gestures to his uniform, taken aback. Again they are misunderstanding each other.

She presses another button and a square of light appears on a table in front of them, like a magical mirror, a window that shows a changing view of other territories and peoples and worlds. He is truly in awe of her powers now. Her fingers tap at the little font in front of the magic window and words appear in the window in Latin. She takes down another book from her shelves and folds out a map of the whole empire in front of him, except that there are kingdoms on it that he has never seen depicted before. He points to where he was born, and where they are now, in Caledonia, although she calls it by another name. He points to Rome, and she shows him something in the glowing window that he struggles to understand. When he does understand after a few minutes it overwhelms him completely. A great city that she calls Roma, but which is full of strange new buildings and hurtling metal carriages. He sees the Forum there, the Circus Maximus, the Flavian Colosseum, but all in ruins, the Forum temples desecrated, reduced to broken fragments. He watches images of citizens of both genders, dressed in coloured short trousers and sleeveless and buttonless tunics wandering freely through sacred sites of temples without reverence, and the priestess points to them and repeats a word unfamiliar to him, that sounds like *Too-Rist*. Then she turns and taps him on his metal breastplate and repeats the word as if suggesting or asking if it applies to him. He shakes his head, confused and downcast by what she has shown him.

Quid est hoc anno? What year is this? –He finally thinks to ask. She makes a number appear on the glowing mirror that is more than a thousand years ahead of the one in which he last left his barracks. He shakes his head, and repeats the name of the emperor Antoninus, until he thinks perhaps she understands. She tells him in Latin that the calendar has changed since then. She writes the numerals for 146, points to the Antonine Wall on the map, then asks him back what year he thinks it is. He is amazed that she doesn't know. It is 1120 of course. Her numerals are not like his own. She needs to translate them so makes him write the number on a white sheet of parchment. The perfection of that sheet and the glass quill she hands him to write with are also a source of wonder to him. She takes a few moments to translate his numerals then adds to them the sum of 910 to create a new number that is two thousand years further ahead. He doesn't understand.

The priestess is kind. She leads him out of the temple, takes his hand to guide him carefully across the noisy river of metal carriages then beckons him to follow her further across some open ground covered in the black road-resin until they stand amid a strange set of broken and blackened stones, almost none of which protrude more than a foot or two out of the ground. The centurion and the priestess stand together in the middle of this formation, and she turns him around, indicating that he should take in the overall shape that the stones make on the ground. They seem like ruins, the foundation of something. She leads him to a plaque at the edge of the formation with a drawing on them, an architectural plan, and he stares at it for a long time. When he finally understands, she has to support him to stop him from collapsing, and then they sit down together on the stones themselves and he begins to sob like a child, until after a while she places her arm around his shoulder.

They sit together, as he and his friend Lucius did, only yesterday morning it seems, in this bathhouse, their bodies warm and exhilarated, exchanging stories and news, about to progress laughing, as they always did, into the cold pool after the steam room. He had looked up and seen the stone vaults curving overhead above the plaster frescoes, not quite the grandeur of Rome, but the best the men themselves had been able to muster from the varied skills among the legions, and a matter of modest pride.

He sees now, even now, that the stones show the sign of burning, of intentional destruction. *Qui ad ignem? Aliquem ad hoc?* Who burned this down? –He asks her.

You did, she answers, struggling with her basic Latin, *The Romans, as you retreated.*

Retreated, withdrew...*Recedere, Recetum...* he repeats her words slowly, in disbelief. *Then we lost.*

She shakes her head, and he is surprised to see that there are tears in her eyes also, perhaps in involuntary empathy with him. She tries to think of a word, but can find only one, holding up the cross around her neck as she says it, her eyes imploring him to understand: *Resurrectio.*

He stands up, remembering that symbol now. Some crazy cult from Judea that had been spreading underground, even in Rome itself they said. It seemed to be about weakness to him, from what scraps he'd heard, giving in to your enemies. He couldn't understand the attraction. They said of the man, their prophet, the most ridiculous thing: that he had risen from the dead. Then Caius remembers with a shiver the black rectangle in the grass this morning. He is standing up now, wavering, looking at the priestess in uncertainty, when he notices in the distance behind her that two white metal carriages have stopped on the road and soldiers in sinister black uniforms are emerging from them, strange weapons drawn, amassing into a phalanx, preparing to march towards him. To capture him no doubt and subject him to justice.

The priestess stands up and shouts at him as he backs away: *Recedere! Fuge!*

He turns and runs.

Caius leaps over fences, scrambles over walls, cuts his way through hedging as he takes the shortest route he can foresee back to where he left his horse. In a few of the gardens he runs past startled citizens sitting sunning themselves or bent over pruning their shrubs. The adults recoil in fear. But in one case some charming young children run towards him waving toy swords over their heads, one even sporting a little red cloak and plumed helmet. Incredibly, this makes him smile. When he reaches the busy carriageway again, he has no time to pause so dares to weave his way out between the fast-moving objects, some of them blaring angry trumpets at him, a few even skidding to a screeching halt. He rolls athletically down the unkempt grass embankment and un-tethers his horse where he left it under the bridge. Then sets off at a gallop heading east to get back out into open country.

The peculiarly flat and closely-clipped field of green grass that he crossed earlier now has some curiously-dressed citizens on it, some walking, others in little lightweight chariots carrying an array of oddly specialised weapons. Their trousers bear a kind of colourful pattern of intertwined horizontal and vertical lines that he recalls the Damnonii wearing. Could they be barbarians, tolerated so close to the frontier? Some of them shout at him now, waving their fists in the air, seemingly enraged at the damage his horse's hooves might do to their carefully groomed field. He notices small white projectiles on the ground and one of them even has the audacity to swing his hammer and fire these white balls towards him at considerable speed, whizzing just by his left ear. Reluctant to be waylaid but unable to suppress his affront at this, he charges towards the man and his companion, who turn and flee in panic. Remembering his *Pilum* strapped to his saddle, he takes it out, balances it up with his right hand, expertly poised high above his shoulder and launches it at the back of his assailant as he overtakes him at the gallop. Slowing his horse and turning around and coming back, he knows he ought to finish the wretch off where he now lies face down twitching in the turf, but simply retrieves the spear and resumes his course southwards and uphill back towards the canal.

Back on the tow-path he finds himself less welcome this time, as the increased speed he is driving his horse at causes the walking and running citizens, and particularly those on the wheeled balancing frames, to run themselves out of his way and into the long grass verges in alarm. He takes this as a sign of respect rather than them doubting his formidable skills at horsemanship. His mare and he even leap right over a panicked elderly woman whose wheel frame collapses under her as she dithers in fright. He senses that the curving route of the canal must lead to something further south, a greater concentration of civilisation, some higher authority he can appeal to, who will properly recognise his Roman military credentials.

Gradually he passes fewer people on the canalside as if they are being somehow forewarned up ahead to stay out of his way. And among the flying metal objects in the sky, a new kind appears, black with two sets of whirring wings like a bee, which seems to be taking an unhealthy interest in him. It follows his course closely and even begins to swoop lower over him, trying to frighten his horse perhaps, but he has calmed and guided such animals through worse tumults than this before, battles with bloodthirsty savages blowing their deafening war horns. He sees he is coming to a junction in the canal, a kind of triangular basin, with tunnels running under it. Thinking fast, he rides down under one tunnel where the metal bee cannot see them, then calms his horse and carefully stuffs its ears with a pulp of wet leaves and saliva, a trick he learned in Gaul. When he re-emerges this has also enabled him to cross to the other side of the water so he can gallop south again on the opposite tow-path, as he knows he needs to do in order to reach the thing he sees beginning to take shape ahead through the gaps in the trees. The height of the mature trees on this stretch seems to worry the mechanical bee, as it has to lift higher away above him, keeping its distance in the sky as if scared to snag its wings on branches.

When he finally reaches the edge of the city, for this is what Caius now finds it truly is, he is filled with awe. As large in extent as any Rome, a vast conurbation stretches from east to west and up to the southerly horizon. He remembers a tiny Damnonii hamlet here on the river

Clota which the Romans sought to absorb into the empire a generation ago. Somehow trade and military conquests staged from here must have made it wealthy and prosperous beyond the dreams of any barbarian. But the metal bee has not left him. A booming metallic voice is sounding from it now, trying to order him to do something in a language he doesn't understand. *Latine Loqui!* –He shouts back at it in vain anger, but knows it cannot hear him above the sound of its own wings.

But now Caius sees that he has reached an insurmountable problem. The canal seems to end here, turning into a wide basin for barges to unload from, although now no trade or transport seems to take place here. To enter the city he must leave the waterway and head south and downhill into the midst of it. He sees blue lights flashing and hears screaming noises like mechanical witches, the white chariots that he saw in Litana arriving and the same black-uniformed soldiers emerging. He strokes his horse's neck and trains its eyes on the very tall metal fence and sloping embankment beneath him. – Makes it take several steps backwards, braces for a few seconds. Then guides it into a rapidly accelerating gallop followed by daredevil leap into the air, then plunging and skidding down the grass slope until landing on firm black gravel below. The soldiers who had been ambling slowly towards him, thinking they had him trapped, are now trapped themselves at a higher level than he, all scrambling back to their carriages in order to take the long way around to pursue him. He laughs wildly, kissing the mare for its skill, then they resume their gallop southwards.

Entering the dense citadel of tall buildings, the greatest hazard becomes the metal carriages of ordinary civilians, whose speed and chaos the mare recoils from in distress. But oddly the soldiers seem to offer assistance here, calling the river of wagons to a halt wherever they can, trying to clear any street that Caius and his horse venture into. Reaching the brow of a hill, Caius glimpses something so unexpectedly familiar that it makes his heart soar. Less than a quarter-mile downhill he sees a broad civic square with a very tall ceremonial Doric column at its centre with a statue of some classical hero on top of it. Not unlike Trajan's column in Rome, surely this must be the legislative heart of this metropolis. But before he rides downhill towards it, he looks east along another street and sees at the end of it a black stone pyramid, tall and sharp like the one in Litana, which he takes to represent a major temple.

In the civic square he finds many statues, of heroes and gods unfamiliar to him, as well as crowds of noisy citizens being cordoned away from him by the black-uniformed soldiers, who are now deploying into large formations in order to try to block his escape into all the surrounding avenues. He now even sees some on horseback, and is delighted at the thought of competition with them, since they look stiff and poorly-trained to him judging by their postures. From the edge of this square he sees a large classical temple that pleases him greatly, with vast fluted Corinthian columns forming its portico of broad steps, clearly modelled on the great temples in Rome, although he recalls no plans to construct such a thing here during his lifetime. The equestrian statue on a pedestal in front of it makes him laugh, as he sees the citizenry have mocked the military general it commemorates with a colourful cone on his head. Caius had secretly hoped that he might be promoted to the rank of a general himself one day, and now sees the folly of that and all other earthly hopes.

Now the soldiers obviously think they have him hemmed in, so he turns and delights in charging them and leaping right over their heads, twice, over two different phalanxes, before galloping out of their clutches, north-east and uphill, to find the temple he saw earlier. He knows now that he cannot hold out forever, that they will capture him soon, but wishes to find their greatest spiritual edifice, to surrender himself at a fine temple where he can seek the clemency of whatever gods now rule this land. But when he gets there he finds its door is almost blocked, by a male priest rather than a priestess, who wears a black uniform disturbingly similar to the pursuing soldiers. Nonetheless, he dismounts and kneels before this holy man, whose frightened and frightening facial expression and demeanour then melts into an odd kind of recognition and acceptance. The priest steps aside and allows Caius to view the temple's beautiful interior, just for a few minutes but it is enough to soothe and restock his soul.

Anxious to do right by this horse that has served him so well, and conscious of the wall of black uniforms that now swarm the temple precinct behind him, he leads the mare downhill and across a handsome stone bridge into a magical realm that he recognises immediately as a graveyard, a carefully landscaped conical hill full of the stone tombs of this city's greatest citizens, many decorated with Roman and Grecian artistic forms which make him feel at home. He sets the mare free, bidding it farewell at the entrance, leaving it all the hill to graze on, then proceeds on foot up the winding paths towards the top of the mound, looking over his shoulder, wondering why the soldiers, although they outnumber him so greatly, seem so slow to follow him and reluctant to actually engage him in close combat.

On his way up the meandering paths he encounters three beggars in ragged clothes, staggering drunk from a bottle of wine that one of them carries, and this is a scene familiar to Caius as one that has doubtless scarcely changed across the ages in the neglected districts of any number of forgotten cities of the world. The cackling old men seem to mock his uniform, laughing and falling around, trying to mimic his movements and appearance. One of them looms in close and even tries to take his helmet off, while another paws at his chest. In a single fluid movement he draws his sword and swipes his assailant's head off, so that it flies into the air and falls in one long arc downwards to the slopes below, as the body it leaves behind collapses in the darkest of comedy. One of the remaining beggars flees in strange silence, while the other whimpers, vomits and faints on the spot, almost simultaneously. Caius marches on.

At the top of the hill, this necropolis, city of the dead as he now sees it is, after having passed so many tombs some of whose inscriptions he can read, Caius sits down on the steps of one particularly fine mausoleum. He is miserable but strangely content in his sadness, to have found at last the perfect place to end his strange odyssey. He forces himself to confront again the memory of the open grave he saw this morning on the marsh, and to accept that somehow it must have been his own. This must be the afterlife. Not the Elysian Fields as he had always hoped, but something worse perhaps, some kind of eternal punishment.

As if to magically answer this thought however, he now hears a voice speaking softly next to him, and speaking almost fluent Latin. Caius looks up and is sure he must be dead now or truly in a dream. The man sits only ten feet away from him, on the steps of another tomb. Facing outwards as he is, towards the huge city spread out below, but at an angle perpendicular to him, as if addressing him only diffidently and obliquely. He looks old with longish locks of white hair, his face craggy, his blue eyes locked on the horizon where the colours of sunset are now beginning to appear. *That bridge you crossed...* –the man says in Latin, *the locals call it The Bridge Of Sighs. There used to be a river that ran under it, called the Molendinar Burn, but now it is just a roadway that runs far beneath it in the gully.*

Like the River Styx... Caius answers him.

The man laughs, clearly relishing his reference. *Yes, so you have crossed to the afterlife here then, the Fields of Elysium where the good in life were granted the ultimate reward: that of forgetfulness when they drank the waters of Lethe.*

Are you a god? He asks the man, realising as he speaks that he now feels an enormous physical weariness creeping over him.

Again the man laughs, as perhaps only a god would do.

No, not at all. I am a scholar of Latin and of Roman history. I know all about you and the world you have come from.

The light is dimming now, but Caius sees that the man is wearing a white blanket as a kind of cloak, and that now he is standing up and handing a similar robe to Caius. He takes it gratefully, and wraps it around himself to stave off the growing chill of evening. *Who woke me up? Why have I been brought back to life?*

By accident we think. Can you believe that? And not by me or my colleagues, but by would-be grave-robbers. You would have had such things too in your time, yes? The Egyptians certainly had, tomb robbers I mean. They probably thought you were some exotic mummified corpse that they could steal this morning and sell in secret to some immoral trade magnate. Are you understanding me, Caius? My accent may sound strange to you. Latin has been a dead language here for centuries. You've been showing us how it was actually pronounced.

Yes, Caius answers. *I understand your words but not how you can have so much knowledge unless you are one of the gods. You even know my name. Why was I not a corpse? I noticed that my horse Rhamus had become one.*

At this point a second figure appears between them, and the old man stands and hands her a white blanket too. She sits on the steps of another tomb opposite him, so that the three of them form a composition whose symmetry is mystical and pleasing to Caius. He too has momentarily risen to his feet to greet the new arrival, and now he kneels when he recognises her. She is the priestess he met this morning in Litana, who showed him such kindness and urged him to flee in order to preserve his liberty and life. She is dressed differently now, in demure black, but comes close to him and makes an unfamiliar gesture with her hands in front of his face and chest, which he understands represents some kind of blessing or absolution.

The old scholar resumes his dialogue. *We asked her along because we thought she might help calm you,*

Caius. You are the rarest thing on Earth right now, the first man who has ever been brought back to life.

The priestess coughs at this, and the scholar looks up and laughs. *Oh, excuse me, apart from Lazarus and Jesus of Nazareth, allegedly. But even they were not under the ground for two thousand years. Caius, do you know what an elephant is?*

Caius searches his memory. *Yes, I've seen paintings of them. A Carthaginian enemy of Rome, general Hannibal son of Hamilcar, marched his army over the Alps with some, but reputedly they died in the months afterwards from shock.*

Good, well, there was another much more ancient kind of elephant in the world once, called a Mammoth, which was covered in long hair, had long tusks and lived in the ice-cold regions of the world. The last of them died out about six thousand years ago.

Then how can you know such things existed? Caius asks, drowsily.

Sometimes because of fossils, traces in ancient rock, but that doesn't matter very much now. The point is that in some very cold northerly regions far beyond the known frontiers of your Roman empire, we have been finding mammoths for the last hundred years, and been digging them up from where they fell into the ice and have been preserved there ever since, in some cases almost perfectly. Myself and many other scholars, or what you might call engineers, engineers of the living body, they have been trying to find a way to access the brains of those dead animals and find out what they experienced in life, what they saw, what their memories were. Last year they succeeded for the first time. They found a way to replay and record what the mind of the mammoth had seen when it was alive. You are only the second human being we have tried the same technique on. We didn't expect to succeed so spectacularly in your case.

Caius's brow furrows, he flexes his arms and legs, looks at his fingers as he waggles them. *But my body is alive, not just my head.*

To get blood to your brain we had to engineer a kind of man-made blood that we could regulate the temperature and purity of. We only did this, I should be ashamed to admit, in order to access your brain. We never thought the rest of you would come back to life. We might never have known such a thing was possible if those bungling tomb-robbers hadn't smashed their way through all our equipment at a critical moment.

I killed one of them... Caius sighs gloomily.

We know. And in a way he was your god, if you want one. The person who truly brought you back to life.

Then I am an accident.

So, what of it? Perhaps we all are. There is a very strong argument that all of life, on this world and every other one, is just an accident.

Then the gods are mad. They play with us.

Here the priestess intervenes again: *No, Caius. They, he or she, tests us. To make us better. To try harder to rise up towards the stars. To make us understand the need to choose good over evil.*

Caius, we can see you're getting sleepy now. Will you let our good Sister and myself remove two things from your person? Your sword and your spear. After that we can be certain of helping you down the hill without the city guards shooting you.

Shoot, arrows?

No, something else, much worse, that would kill you instantly. We need to disarm you, then we can take you to that hospital just across the road, where we will check your blood and make sure you stay alive now for as long as possible. We have so many questions to ask you.

Not as many... as mine. He mumbles before nodding off to sleep.

And so it is that the assembled police stand down as a strange trio of figures emerge from the city's necropolis at nightfall, crossing together over the Bridge Of Sighs from the land of the dead and back into the domain of the living. The figures to either side, one male and one female, one carrying a sword and the other a spear, support the limp body of a Roman Centurion between them, his arms outspread and draped over their shoulders, his feet dragging where they cross over each other in the dust. To the most cultured commentators among the media the next morning, something in the scene will recall some old religious oil painting from some altarpiece or fresco from the annals of medieval European history. But no one will be able to define exactly which one. Perhaps it is a distillation of all of them.

~

IX

An emergency meeting is announced with less than two hours notice. The venue is Breshkov's top floor office in the Edinburgh HQ of Tacitus. Its panoramic glass walls afford breathtaking views over Leith up towards the distant medieval castle and the long spine of the Royal Mile, the ancient Greek echoes of Calton Hill, the wider waters of the Firth of Forth to the north and the iconic bridges that cross it to the west.

Ailee and Trevor arrive together in the same air car on the roof, but Ailee stays behind for a few minutes to avoid confirming the impression that they are romantically linked, the newspaper stories having made her increasingly self-conscious. *What am I even doing here? –*she exclaims at Breshkov as she enters the room. Trevor, Ed Strang and Breshkov spin around to look at her from where they have been drinking coffee and admiring the view. *Caius could wake up again at any moment and I... and Trevor as well for that matter, we need to be there to talk to him and mediate between our world and his. Do you realise the moral responsibility we have, you have, Val, for what we've done to this man? Can you imagine what he's been going through since we, since we...*

Resurrected him? An unfamiliar voice rings out behind Ailee and she spins around to see President Drest enter the room, flanked by a quartet of sombre-looking men in black suits. *You must be Ailee Kenzie I presume?*

Ailee struggles not to appear taken aback. *Professor Kenzie, yes, pleased to meet you, Mrs President.*

Likewise... Drest casually responds, turning to introduce her advisors: *this is Doctor James Wallace, Scottish Surgeon General who will be taking over care of the centurion and this is Professor Sandra Lumsdaine, leading specialist in genetics at Edinburgh University. I think I overheard you voicing concern about when your subject wakes up, well I can assure you that subordinates of these venerable specialists are already in place back at the hospital ward in Glasgow you just left and are monitoring his progress carefully. They will keep us informed if he wakes up.*

If? Surely you mean when?

Ahh... Breshkov clears her throat from the window wall, *...Now, about that...*

What? Ailee turns her head, oscillating repeatedly between the two sides of the room.

It might not be that simple, Ailee. —Breshkov continues as Drest gestures with an open hand for her to resume. *You have to understand that this was never meant to happen. The Smart Blood was just designed to mine the brain's last traces of neural activity, not bring a man back to life...*

But he is alive! She turns to Trevor raising her hand... *Trevor and several others spoke with him, and half of Glasgow must have seen him riding a horse like an athlete, what do you mean..?*

It is temporary, Ailee. Breshkov winces, head in her hands. *There is nothing we can do about that. He was preserved under that bog, but now he is exposed to the air, obviously, he is breathing it in and out, and therefore his tissues will be rapidly deteriorating, he has got two thousand years of decomposition to catch up on...*

Drest raises her hand, her eyebrows raised. *If I may... can we convene this meeting properly? — All please sit down together on comfortable chairs with some coffee and tea and discuss all this slowly and calmly?*

Ailee splutters, amazed to find the extremist Drest sounding like the most grounded person in the room: *But.. but.. if time is short then shouldn't we be back there waiting on him..?* Ailee feels her right arm being nudged by Trevor who leans in close to her ear and whispers: *What she said wasn't a question, Ailee.* For a moment their fingers touch and both long to hold hands in this moment of stress, but refrain. Trevor places his hand briefly on her shoulder and the group all move to the meeting table while drinks are summoned by Breshkov.

Trevor Watling... Drest addresses Trevor's back as he crosses the room, forcing him to turn around. *I'm told you were rather brave yesterday in talking our Roman down, and that your command of Latin proved very useful. Where did you pick it up, Roma or Londinium?*

York High School, Mrs President.

Drest laughs. *Very good, Trevor. Before Oxford that is?*

You've researched me then, know everything there is to know already... Trevor answers nervously, not daring to meet her eyes for more than a second, fearful of a slight involuntary shake in his voice.

I've learned a lot in the last twenty four hours, I think we all have. –Drest continues as they reach the table. *But you will have learned what the Latin language was actually like two thousand years ago in Britain. Am I right?*

Trevor nods his head as they all sit down in a circle.

And were there some surprises?

Definitely, yes.

Drest claps her hands, looks around. *Right, all present, this meeting is convened. Audio recordings are being made purely for the stenographers, whose minutes will be sent to all of you for your approval before they are validated, so no one will be misrepresented. Firstly, let's start with you, Valentina. Thank you for allowing us use of your offices this morning. We've all seen the news and I watch the news like anyone else, but sometimes reporters get the wrong end of the stick. Ha! Tell me about it, as they say. So for the benefit for the meeting can you please run us through again exactly what you believe happened yesterday, by which I mean what, how and why?*

Breshkov takes a deep breath. *An accident, a bizarre unforeseen epoch-defining accident. We believe there may have been some foul-play. Something akin to ancient Egyptian grave robbers. Contemporary archaeological thieves who broke into the Balmore archaeopod and got a lot more than they bargained for. The police are already involved of course, and this gentleman seated with us here is the head of Police Scotland...*

Yes, Drest nods, *Chief Inspector Charles Doohan, I should have introduced him earlier.* Charlie smiles to everyone around the room and nods knowingly towards Breshkov.

Then... Breshkov continues, *Then, incredibly, a world-first, indeed a first in world history, the centurion came back to life in response to a chaotic surge in the SHG and nutrient feed to his brain. Accidentally triggered probably by someone colliding with the tubes and wires connected to him. The biological and philosophical implications of that... well...* She takes a deep breath. *We haven't had enough time to even begin understanding. He then killed one of the... I nearly said grave-robbers, but you know what I mean, thieves. Then he fled the scene, found a horse he could ride, in a nearby field, and duly rode it west to Bearsden in search of the fort he was once stationed at on the Antonine wall, hoping, I would imagine, to report back to his legion commander like a good soldier. There he became confused by what he found of course, entered a Catholic church where he was able to communicate in Latin, after a fashion, with a female priest. He then fled again as the police arrived, attacked another man, an innocent golfer I believe, before riding his horse again into the centre of Glasgow pursued by police vans, helicopters... hence all the rest of the stuff you will doubtless all have seen on television by now unless you've been living under a rock. He was finally taken into custody without offering resistance, in no small way thanks to our own professor Watling who we recommended to the police as interlocutor, along with the Catholic priest he met earlier, both of whom seemed able to have some kind of pacifying effect on him. Unfortunately however, he killed someone else, a vagrant, on his way through the graveyard where he surrendered. So as well as being the first man ever-resurrected after two thousand years, he's also now a double, perhaps triple, murderer. Since we're told the golfer's condition is touch and go.*

I'm sure he killed a lot more people than that as a Roman soldier. –Trevor ventures.

Quite. Charlie Doohan answers. *But he's our problem now. In our time, in our jurisdiction.*

But how much of a problem if he never leaves his hospital bed, kept there under guard, as he gradually weakens over coming days? –Strang asks the room.

Now wait a minute... Ailee interjects. *I can see the way this is going. You're all talking about this man as if he is an object, a commodity. He is a human being, he has a name, Caius Flavius. He has a mind, feelings, fears, hopes... We've brought him back to life without his consent.*

But it was an accident... precipitated by criminals.. – Breshkov responds.

That's sheer sophistry, and you know it, with respect, Val. Ailee snaps. *We put the technology in place there, we were the ones playing around with something we didn't fully understand. The moral responsibility rests with us.*

And with me, ultimately don't you think? Drest breaks in. *The Scottish people, with me as their elected leader?*

Tacitus is just the Scottish franchise, Mrs President, Retrovival is an international operation... Breshkov cautions, then breathes in sharply, wondering if she should have held her tongue.

Drest slightly reddens with suppressed anger. *What are you saying? You're not questioning, surely, that this man is a Scottish citizen on Scottish land?*

Actually... Breshkov hesitates, wincing. *I'd say that's highly questionable, if he was born in Italy. But you're taking me up wrong there. All I was saying was that the moral responsibility for all this rests with me as head of Retrovival. Your guilt, if anyone should ever try to apportion any, is merely in having allowed Retrovival to operate within Scotland.*

Drest sighs and thinks for a minute while her suited

cohorts whisper to each other. *I see. Well, that could be construed as some reassurance I suppose.*

I can't believe all this... Ailee exclaims. Trevor puts his hand on her arm to try to restrain her, alarmed by her tone. *You're all just worried about who's to blame, trying to cover your own arses.*

Ailee, that's not fair. —Strang snaps back. *Responsibility is a critical issue to establish, before actions can be agreed. You've got to, I mean **we** have all got to stay rational.*

But what about what Caius Flavius himself wants? Doesn't that even get a look-in here? If he has only a couple of weeks of life left, isn't it his right to tell us how he would like to spend that time? Doesn't he have any human rights? Ailee looks around the room, waiting, then says: *I must say I'm appalled by the silence in this room.*

Can he walk? For how much longer will he be able to walk do we think? —One of Drest's medical advisors speaks up.

What's that got to do with anything? He can be moved around in a wheelchair if need be. Ailee answers.

We can't let him meet people. The Surgeon General Doctor Wallace speaks up. *The bacteria, viruses. He'll have no immunity to them, and his immune system will be weaker every day. He may even carry some potential contagions himself which the wider population might have no immunity to. He could spark a pandemic, in theory.*

He's already met people. Ailee shrugs.

And killed half of them. Strang sighs ruefully.

He was probably frightened... Trevor speaks up, *thought he was under attack. He's a soldier, who from his perspective was engaged in a violent conflict up until a few moments before we woke him up. How would you behave in his... his sandals? You can't imagine, can you? None of us can.*

There are many aspects to this. Drest takes over again. *What about the scientific and archaeological perspective? How do we best further our knowledge at this stage? Does this new situation afford us the opportunity to gain vital new knowledge from this... centurion?*

He has a name! Ailee exclaims in a rasping whisper and hangs her head in despair, running her hands through her hair while Breshkov answers Drest's question:

We had been tapping into his memories intermittently for the last few days, that being after all the purpose of our mission rather than... resurrection, as one might put it. We already have a great many fragments, like pieces of film, of his life story. We were piecing them together like a jigsaw, confident of making sense of it all, when... this... happened. We did not expect to have the subject sit up and tell us himself how to fit all his memories back together, but certainly that would be helpful. There is also the issue of the things that are not part of memories necessarily. Such as his opinions, maybe things he was never asked while alive, or never dared offer honest answers for. Such as what he thought of the emperor or his legion commander or the so-called barbarians facing off across the marsh.

I see. Drest nods her head. *So now that he's alive again, you could ask him a set of questions to try to fill in the gaps in our knowledge of the part of the ancient world he inhabited? Can you organise a list of those questions, perhaps confer with leading historians and archaeologists around the world in order to do so?*

Yes. Breshkov agrees. *That seems like an eminently logical idea. It might take a few days to organise and compile of course. Academics are not noted for their alacrity, generally.*

Ailee snorts at that, and Trevor merely smiles wryly.

We can spare that time, though? You could begin asking your own initial questions in the meantime?

Yes, although I'd say we need to proceed carefully so as not to antagonise him or tire him out. –Breshkov elaborates. *He seems to have developed some kind of rapport with Trevor, Professor Watling here, based on their shared language. I'd suggest we develop that and let Trevor gradually glean information from the centurion and prime him for a more thorough...*

–Interrogation? Ailee proffers.

Question and answer session, I was going to say. Nothing public of course, just a few specialists in the room, nothing to frighten him.

Ailee stands up to leave the table. *Well, I've heard enough I think. I'm sorry. Solitary confinement followed by an interrogation session. Our apology to the man we bring back to life without consent is to torture him back to death again, for our own selfish ends. No compassion, no guilt, no love to be shown. I better get back there and get ready to bring him around to our contemporary entertainment delights such as television and audio books, since that's all he's going to get for the next three weeks.*

I better go with her... after her... Trevor stammers, after the door slams behind her. *I'll try to calm her down on the journey back to Glasgow.*

Very well, Drest nods. *And please make it known to her that we were very grateful for her contribution to the meeting. We don't have to all agree in order to learn something from each other.*

Right, thank you... Mrs President. Trevor responds, almost bowing as he leaves the room.

After a minute's silence one of Drest's advisors speaks up for the first time: *Is he shagging her?*

Drest holds up her hand in rebuke: *That's outrageous, Seoras, we should strike that from the record if we can.*

I mean are they together? The man in the black suit leans over the table, to catch Drest's eye again. *Head over heels in love or something, because I'm getting the feeling that they are not the most reliable people to be left in charge of our revivified Roman.*

They are both highly respected figures in their respective fields, Mister...? Breshkov enquires.

McCechnie, SI7. One of them is married to someone else, I believe. And the newspapers have a hold of it.

Breshkov turns to Drest in disgust: *Really, Mrs President, is this what we are here to discuss? The private lives of my archaeological team?*

Not primarily, no. But I can see that it is a potentially relevant issue. You and I have already had a private conversation about Professor Watling.

Yes. Breshkov's eyes flare. *You asked me that he be removed from the project because of his English accent. For the record.*

Really, Valentina, that is a misrepresentation surely, of what I said? —Drest shifts in her chair uncomfortably. *I merely suggested that he no longer act as a spokesman during the media briefings, that he be kept in the back room where he's probably more at home.*

He should be a national hero now, for the risk he took in calming the centurion down. Too high profile for you to have him fired, I dare say.

Valentina. Drest stiffens with anger. *Let's not be antagonistic like Miss Kenzie, shall we?*

Professor Mrs Ailee Kenzie, you mean, Mrs President. My lead archaeologist.

Drest sighs. *Well I can see we're not going to end up all loving each other in this room. But can we at least agree our actions moving forward? My police and intelligence services will protect the hospital ward and isolate it from media intrusion. You will continue to monitor the centurion's health with the assistance of my chief medical officer. You will gather and compile key lines of questioning from the global archaeological community, to be used on the subject next week.*

Breshkov nods in compliance.

In the meantime your team continue to befriend him and gently coax whatever information they can from him in order to clarify the knowledge you already have. Agreed? Let's not forget that what we have on our hands here is the scientific breakthrough of the millennium, that will reflect well on Scotland for decades and centuries to come, provided we behave with dignity, fairness and morality in the eyes of the world that is watching us.

Drest and her team stand up and turn to leave the building, while Breshkov and Charlie Doohan stay behind to talk.

Doohan waits a few minutes, checks the doors are closed before addressing Breshkov in a quiet voice. *Is this room secure? No bugging, no hidden mikes?* He kneels down and sweeps the underside of the table that Drest's team were sitting at, to answer his own question.

I think so... Breshkov answers. *But it's a reasonably warm day if you'd like to go up to the roof terrace.*

*

Charlie Doohan stands at the parapet edge and marvels at the grey stone patchwork of streets below, the morning light on the distant hills. *That was a bumpy ride, Val. I've never seen anyone be so rude to Drest. How's your face?*

The cuts? Breshkov puts her hand to her cheek. *Wearing make-up has its advantages. Just minor grazes, flesh wounds, I will be fine. The SI7 agent that our centurion put his sword through is beyond repair however. Amazing that they did not mention his presence or identity in the meeting, don't you think?*

No, not at all. Charlie turns around, leans his back against the railing. *That's their style. The Intelligence Services are never talked about, not in front of the minions anyway. They liked your story about grave robbers I suppose, the perfect cover.*

That was supposed to be one of your men coming to meet me. What happened?

Comic book stuff. —Charlie laughs bitterly. *They tied him up in a lay-by with a sock in his mouth then took his place. Now you know what we're up against. I take it you rumbled him before discussing anything sensitive?*

You bet. His failure to quote our agreed password led to a surreal conversation, the height of comedy had it not led on to violence when I asked him to leave.

I think I can imagine. Charlie smiles broadly. *You a black belt in Judo or something?*

I learned how to handle myself from a young age, for a

variety of reasons. And of course, a girl's best friend is a recently resurrected Roman. What's your plan then?

This technology of yours, **revivification** *one of Drest's spooks called it in the meeting there, a pretty phrase. I want you to use it on a dead body I have had recovered.*

Breshkov's shoulders stiffen, taken aback. *How long dead are we talking?*

Six months.

Jesus! –Breshkov spins around and paces to the other parapet, wind blowing through her hair, before returning with blazing eyes: *Charlie. I'm an archaeologist, not a pathologist.*

I think you may have blurred the distinction somewhat of late, don't you?

Breshkov laughs grimly. *The smell, the maggots. A decaying body, the relatives still alive. That is grotesque. Desecration is it not?*

You don't have to tell me. I'm the cop on this roof top. At least you won't have to worry about this one coming back to life, something you'll be having traumatic nightmares about for the rest of your life I would imagine. My assignment will be peaceful compared to that. Look... Charlie locks eyes with her. *Do you want to bring Drest down or not? This body I'm talking about, its brain contains vital information, a confession in effect, of hideous crimes, multiple murders of English refugees, innocent men, women and children. And Drest is complicit.*

Would experiential sequences recovered from such a brain even be admissible in a Scottish court of law? Breshkov wonders aloud, hand to her forehead, looking at her feet.

Uncharted legal territory of course. Charlie answers. *But that means it's not proven inadmissible yet by any legal precedent, a window of opportunity in a sense, and in any case the information will lead us to the other perpetrators still alive, tell us where to find the evidence against them.*

I see. Breshkov nods, looking up at the sky then back at

Charlie. *You are in this deep already. Desecration is the least of it. Treason more like, if you do not succeed, if Drest stays in charge.*

But it wouldn't be treason for you, you're Danish or Ukrainian aren't you?

Breshkov nods again.

And anyway. Charlie shrugs. *If Drest stays in power then Scotland's democracy is over. I am getting on to be an old man now. My kids are all grown up. I have little left to lose, and everything to win. For my country. For all that I believe in and have dedicated my life to. Justice. The rule of law.*

Your country. Freedom. Breshkov reaches out and shakes Charlie's hand, noticing the surprising hint of a tear in a corner of his world-weary eye. *You just said the magic words. I will fight for those things with anyone. Any day of the week.*

*

Travelling back across the Central Belt, Trevor dares to break the silence as Ailee navigates above the hurtling arteries of traffic that connect Scotland's two largest cities. What lies beneath strikes him for a moment as resembling a dissected body, blood running in every direction, the patient supine and anaesthetised. *That wasn't your finest hour, Ailee, if you don't mind me saying...* He flicks through the internet on his phone absentmindedly.

How come? She responds, with a dangerous tone in her voice.

She may be a fascist bitch, but she's President of this country. She could force Breshkov to take us off this project. The next press conference has turned into public explanation of the century.

Not your problem, Trevor.

Why not?

Drest has ordered that you are never allowed to take part in a press conference again.

What? Why? Since when?

Two days ago. Because you're English. Breshkov passed on the news to me after you left to attend to your broken windows.

When were you planning on telling me?

I don't know. I didn't want to upset you. It seems almost trivial now that we have Centurion Frankenstein of the Twentieth Legion on our hands.

Trivial? Overt racism. Ghettos and death camps next. Just seemed trivial when we were shagging away at my house... Trevor mutters.

What did you say? Ailee asks irritably.

Never mind. It doesn't matter. Look at these news stories... He flicks through his phone. *Half the media seem to think our centurion was just a publicity stunt by Tacitus, a man dressed up in Roman garb to get school children excited or impress Breshkov's investors.*

You're kidding. Do you think Drest is covering it up, to stop public panic or press intrusion?

Maybe she doesn't need to. It's like flying saucers or something. Just too mind-blowing for most folks to take on board. The Scottish Government are yet to issue any statement. The few broadsheets speculating anything near the truth are doing it very tentatively, as if they're scared to look like cranks.

People are weird. Ailee sighs as she slows down to allow a convoy of airborne freight, travelling north to south, pass underneath her. *Roman soldier brought back to life. Less important than a pop star's divorce or King George's recipe for pizza.*

It's going to give the international media a bit of a dilemma though.

How so?

Pariah state Scotland, led by neo-fascist maverick president, makes scientific breakthrough of the century while in breach of UN resolutions for illegal occupation of Northern England. Unfortunate timing.

Maybe its not a coincidence then... Ailee reflects slowly, deep in thought as the distant towerblocks of Glasgow come into view.

How do you mean? Trevor asks.

How well do you or I really know Breshkov? Or trust her? What happened to Caius breaks the Rossan convention. What are the chances of Drest doing anything about that?

*

Caius is sitting up in bed by the time Ailee and Trevor walk into his hospital ward. The disconcerting sight of him in an ordinary hospital gown rather than Roman uniform almost stops them in their tracks. He now appears firmly part of the mundane present. He tries to speak to Trevor, then starts to cough before resuming in a lower more hoarse voice, almost a whisper. As if overestimating his own strength, Ailee reflects, thinking he is already looking weaker than yesterday, or do hospital settings do that to everyone? She nudges Trevor's hand for a translation.

He's saying he was horrified and angry to discover himself strapped to the bed when he woke up this morning.

Christ, so would I be. Did they release him?

Trevor talks on further in Latin then translates again. *Only after an hour or so when it was established that he is too weak to harm anyone. Also, he's probably sedated now, although he might not realise it.*

Caius looks on anxiously at their conversation then immediately gesticulates for Trevor to translate back to him. *He thinks you're my wife, by the way, Ailee. I'm keeping things simple for him.*

Ailee snorts. *Whatever. Should we tell him, Trevor, that he's dying? Would that be fair? Do we have the right? Do we have the right not to?*

Well, he wants to know why he's so weak, so if we answer him we either have to lie or tell him the truth. So what do you think?

*The truth of course. Otherwise history will judge us harshly. And we **are** making history, Trev.*

Trevor looks at her, eyebrows raised. *Are you sure? How do you know that we won't be erased from history,*

Ailee? We seem to have changed places recently. You sound like the moralist, the idealist. He turns back to address the patient, asking in Latin: *Caius. We have been discussing your case with our best medical experts, and we have some gravely serious news to tell you. Are you ready for that?*

Caius nods, eyes flicking between Trevor and Ailee, who turns away to hide the tears coming to her eyes, feeling as if Caius is like a newborn child in their care.

Trevor continues: *The science that brought you back to life cannot protect you from all the interaction with the world around you that you have gone through in the last 36 hours. The air going in and out of your lungs, the air and light on your skin. All of it is having an effect on you, wearing you down.*

Caius appears confused, as if not yet understanding, which upsets Ailee so much that she stands and paces to the window back-turned. *Let me put this more bluntly.* Trevor explains. *You know that dead bodies decay and eventually turn to dust? The bog saved your body from that, but only temporarily. The decay of your body was only delayed for 2000 years, but now it must catch up. We can do nothing to stop this.*

Ailee turns around and forces herself to watch Caius' face closely, waiting for Trevor to translate any response.

It is of no consequence... he says after a long sigh. *I expected as much. How long do I have before my death, my second death?*

We currently estimate anything between ten and twenty days, Caius.

Caius closes his eyes and thinks for a long time.

Ailee nudges Trevor. *Can you ask him what he wants to do with the time he has left?*

Is that wise? He asks, looking up at her from where he sits at Caius' bedside.

She sits down and pulls her own seat up close again. *We need to know, even if we can't promise to fulfil any of his wishes. He must be used to that after all, a man of his era and his training. As a soldier I mean, he must be long used to having his requests overruled and getting disappointed. But morally we should know, should ask, what he wants.*

Trevor weighs the logic of this then asks the question. Then translates the answer back to Ailee. *He says he wants to go home. Not to the village in Italy where he grew up, which I have looked for on Google Maps and explained to him no longer exists. He wants to visit Rome, even though he knows it is in ruins now. He wants to visit the ruins and to meet the emperor.*

There is no emperor. Does he mean the Italian prime minister?

Trevor converses again with Caius to clarify then turns back to her. *Don't laugh. Ailee. He says he means the Pontifex Maximus. The Pope, to you and I.*

Ailee's eyes widen, she stands up and paces the room in confusion, leaving Trevor to clarify further. *It must be that female priest he spoke to...* she whispers.

Yes, Trevor answers her, *probably. Her name is Sister Brenda Mullen by the way, the one who joined me on the Necropolis when we took him in. He was asking her questions in the ambulance, and he seems to have reached the conclusion that the Pope is the living descendent of the Roman emperor. He wants to be blessed by the pope and buried in Rome.*

Fuck... Ailee slaps the side of her head. *Careful what we wish for, eh? Don't ask a question if you're not ready for the answer. Let me think... maybe we better get that priest in here. Have you got her number, can we give her a call?*

Sure. Caius has been asking for her. He seems quite religious in his own pagan way. She must have struck a chord with him. I have her details on my phone. But shouldn't we ask Strang or Breshkov first?

Mmmm... now what did we just say about asking a question? Ailee smiles mischievously at Trevor, until she notices that Caius, though unaware of her meaning, is reflexively smiling back at her also.

~

X

Two days later at 3am, Caius' life signs begin behaving erratically, setting off remote warning alarms in the homes of Strang, Breshkov and Drest's chief medical officer. Breshkov rolls out of bed and calls Strang immediately. *What is going on, Ed? You clocking these numbers? We better patch in Doctor Wallace... James, Doctor Wallace? How far away from the secure ward are you at present?*

The doctor's bleary face appears on Breshkov's phone screen, dressed in his pyjamas. *I can be there in twenty minutes I think. I'll get going. Haven't you any of your own people on the ground there?*

Not at present, or they are not answering my calls. I will meet you at the ward as soon as you can get there. Bye for now.

Breshkov stays on the phone to Strang while going to the other room, pulling her clothes on. *Ed, how come neither Ailee or Trevor are answering? What is going on?*

I don't know, Val. The ward staff should have notified us of any emergency, they must be seeing these readings too. I'm on my way there, see you at the hospital. On screen, Strang is already exiting his house and running to his air car.

Breshkov kisses her wife a hurried goodbye, urging her to go back to sleep, then leaves her hotel room to catch the lift up to the roof where her car is waiting. She gets a message from Doctor Wallace just before she reaches the ward: *Hello, Mrs Breshkov? I'm ten minutes away, but just to say that these life signs are perverse. The heart rate, the blood pressure, blood sugar levels. It's as if the patient has suddenly returned to rude health, ready to run a mile. It's impossible, the readings make no sense...*

*

Running into the secure ward, Strang closely followed by Breshkov find nothing untoward, the nurses and doctors unperturbed. The scene inside the centurion's room also appears normal until Strang asks the head nurse to take the subject's temperature. Caius Flavius mumbles something in Latin that none of them understand. When Doctor Wallace arrives and places his hand on Caius' forehead he steps back in astonishment to find brown face paint on his fingers. The centurion's eyes open but they don't appear the dark brown colour everyone remembers them as. He reaches up and wipes more of the make-up off his forehead and addresses them in a strong Yorkshire accent: *Hello folks, I was wondering what was taking you so long. Can't a lad get a cup of coffee in this place?*

Trevor! Strang exclaims. *What the fuck are you playing at? Is this a practical joke?*

No joke... Breshkov frowns. *Where is the centurion? Has Ailee taken him somewhere?*

Damned if I know, Val. Above my pay grade I'm afraid... Trevor sighs cooly.

You stupid bastard, Trevor –Strang rages. *You'll go to jail for decades for this!* –He shouts into Trevor's face. *The Roman needs life support, 24-hour care. If Ailee's absconded with him then she might as well be killing him. This is unspeakable.*

Unspeakable indeed... Breshkov sighs, a hand on Strang's shoulder. *We need a complete media black-out on this until we recover the patient and return him here. How did you pull this off, Trevor? There has been cameras on the whole time...*

Look! Strang reaches up to the CCTV. *There's something over the camera, some kind of bypass device, and that... what's that over there? Nurse! That white box sitting on top of the ECG screen, is that supposed to be there? Show me a neighbouring room, I want to know if that's some kind of add-on to the normal equipment...*

Left alone for a moment, Wallace and Breshkov look at

each other, while Trevor sits up in bed smiling quietly to himself. *This is a sophisticated operation. People with serious computing know-how. Who helped you, Trevor? What kind of plot is this? You are supposed to be a Classics professor, not a mobster or a spy. Who is behind it, the Russians? Chinese?*

Classics, eh? Veni, Vidi, Vici. Carpe diem. Tempus fugit. Nosce te ipsum... Trevor laughs out loud, as Strang returns to the room.

Has the Sassenach gone mad? Strang shouts.

Sassenach, eh? Et tu Brute? –Trevor responds.

I was right... Ed says, turning to Breshkov, *that box is a foreign object, some kind of digital relay or bypass, a microcomputer. Must have run out of battery power or rebooted itself, or we might still be none the wiser. Until the nurses tried to give the bastard a bed bath. Help me prise it off, will you? Have you called the police, Val?*

Do not touch anything, Ed. Forensics will need to dust it all. Better than calling the police, I have paged SI7, as Drest instructed me. They will sort this stupid clown out. Where, Trevor, where? Tell us! Where has Ailee taken the centurion?

*

At Rome's Ciampino airport, Sister Brenda Mullen and Ailee push Caius' wheelchair out of the arrivals lounge towards the taxi rank. Both women are dressed in the white robes of Dominican nuns, while the invalid in their charge is dressed in a black cassock, white clerical collar, and wrap-around dark glasses to protect his eyes from the intense Italian sunlight.

Wait... Ailee hesitates, *before we get within earshot of any driver, Brenda, I think you should call the Italian embassy.*

Back in Scotland? Why?

Because I haven't a clue who to call here. You speak to the Italian ambassador on the phone then he'll get straight through to the top brass in the old country, I guarantee it, with the kind of news we're carrying.

But won't the police here stop us? Brenda hesitates, frowning, fraught with uncertainty.

Not immediately, I don't think. They won't know we're travelling as a three or what we're dressed like. All we need is a couple of hours to show Caius the sights then we'll probably be ready to turn ourselves in anyway. I'd rather we were in the hands of the Carabinieri than vulnerable to Drest's overseas squads, if they exist. It pays to be paranoid, when your country has been taken over by a fascist dictator.

I can also call the Vatican, you know. Brenda smiles.

You can? Ailee responds, wide-eyed.

Yes, I do work for them, ultimately. We could name a location we'll be at in a few hours, and ask them to meet us there. Claim sanctuary, as it were. Asylum.

Caius who has been looking up at the two women speaking in a puzzling tongue, tries to speak.

Wait.. Ailee says, *he's saying something. Put this in your ear...*

What is it?

One of my earphones, so you can get instant translation of Caius' pronunciation of Latin in your head. Trevor developed it for me. I'll load the software on to your own phone later and give you your own earphones. It works, when you get used to it. Shit.

Shit?

Yes, I'm afraid so. He says he needs the toilet. We better turn around and go find one. A disabled one, for all three of us.

*

Brenda, what's the matter? Ailee asks in exasperation. *Can you stop facing the wall and give me a hand please?*

But, he's... he's...

What? Half-naked? Got a penis? Tell me something I don't know. He's practically impotent now, Brenda, thoroughly unthreatening down below. Just think of him like a poor old man who needs our help. Haven't you done stuff like this before as a sister?

I'm not that kind of a sister. Brenda shrugs in embarrassment. *I'm a priest, a cleric, no medical background.*

Well I do have, fortunately. I trained and worked as a nurse to earn the fees to put myself through university. Can you please just come over here, close your eyes or whatever you like, and help me change Caius' nappies? Thank you.

Degrees in archaeology, history, biology, and nursing... Brenda marvels quietly. *You must be some kind of what do they call it? A Savant.*

Ailee sighs, washing her hands. *Would you say that to me if I was a man? Can't I just be a woman of slightly above average intelligence with a penchant for learning?*

I'm sorry. You're calling me old-fashioned now I suppose. Wait, what's he saying now?

He's just saying thanks, like any patient would, and apologising that we have to do this for him.

Aw... he's so sweet, isn't he?

Suave, suave... Caius laughs.

Careful, the translation works both ways. You're starting to communicate fluently with each other now. Neat, isn't it?

I preferred talking to him with his trousers on, or skirt or whatever it was called.

Pteruges is the word, Brenda, Roman military kilt. But you won't need to say it again. He's wearing the trousers now, as we say. That's called a contemporary idiom, Caius, a joke you won't get. It means you're in charge, which I'm afraid you're not. Brenda and I are.

What did he say there? Brenda asks, warming to the novelty of the situation.

That he doesn't mind us being in charge. That we are very kind priestesses making him clean as we prepare him to meet the gods. Not yet, Caius, not yet. You must stay alive for many days, promise us. Otherwise we'll have gone to all this trouble for nothing...

*

The air taxi ride north-west from the airport into the city centre is a source of joy and terror for Caius, as Ailee urges the pilot to swoop down low over monuments of particular interest to him. Then he throws up into a paper bag. His subsequent pall of nausea summarises his reaction to finding The Circus Maximus now scarcely more than a large oblong of empty grass. In disappointment he raves about the many gripping races he watched there as a boy and an adolescent before joining the army. The ruins of the Forum, similarly devastate him, but enough of the Colosseum survives to make him beg for the taxi to land so he can see it from the ground. Before throwing up again.

A modern lift inside the amphitheatre takes the three of them to the first floor level from where Brenda and Ailee help Caius out of his wheelchair and lead him on walking sticks toward the edge of the viewing platform. *Were you here before, Caius?* Ailee asks him softly, as if addressing a child. *What do you remember about it?*

Caius struggles to get the words out: *Wild animals... fabulous beasts... lions, crocodiles... it was astounding. My mother bought me a little painting of some of the animals afterwards, there were people who sold them under the arches outside.*

Did you ever see gladiators fighting? Did you see anyone die? Ailee asks next.

Wounded, but not killed. The fighting was exciting, I remember the roar of the crowd, it was deafening.

He makes it sound like a nice day out at the circus or the theatre. –Brenda muses, almost indignant.

Well, maybe it was, most of the time. Ailee reflects. *People watch horror films now and video nasties, are you really so sure there is a difference?*

Did you ever see Christians put to death in the Colosseum, Caius? Brenda leans in close to ask him.

Who?

Believers in Christ, Jesus of Nazareth?

No, but I heard about it a few times, I think, and other heretics. My father said he disapproved of the killing of unarmed prisoners though or criminals, of anything other than a fair fight. He saw no sport in it.

Wow... there you have it. Ailee marvels. *From the lion's mouth, excuse the pun... sorry, another idiom. Did the wild animals ever kill anyone, Caius?*

He takes a deep breath and thinks for a moment. *Unfortunately not. Mostly it was the poor beasts who died, in vast numbers. Sometimes the beast-masters slipped up, did not run fast enough, and we all applauded because it seemed like the animals deserved their rare victories.*

Has the building changed since you were here, Caius? Ailee turns the wheelchair in an arc to let him see all 360 degrees of the ruins in panorama around them.

Yes, it is so sad to see it in ruins like this. It was so grand, so alive. It was as if every person born into the world at that moment was gathered here all at once. Or so it struck me as a child. I am sorry for you that you never saw it, and never can now. Or will they rebuild it one day?

No, I don't think so. We have other amphitheatres now, Caius, all over the world, but only for harmless sports, like kicking a ball around in teams, and occasionally music by famous bands of minstrels you might say, celebrated virtuosos. There's a thought, what was Roman music like?

How can I describe it to you? I remember it. It was beautiful.

Have you heard anything like it since we brought you back to life?

A little, perhaps, I told Trevor about it, when I heard it on his machine. He said it was 'Evil' music.

Medieval?

That was the term, yes. More space and peace than your music. Most of your music that I hear is so jammed full of panic that it makes me feel sick. You seem to have lost peace in your hearts. What can that mean? Like you have lost touch with your gods.

We've found a single god, Caius... Brenda interjects

while Ailee looks at her disapprovingly, *...and decided that the previous range of them were falsehoods.*

You told me of that before, and I wonder if perhaps all the other gods went away because not enough people worshipped them. I wonder if gods wither without believers. Maybe your one god is a strong one whose strength continues regardless of whether anyone listens to him.

Ailee switches her translator off and reaches over to suspend Brenda's for a moment, who whispers to her wide-eyed: *You don't approve of my preaching to him?*

We mustn't tire him out too much with all this talk. When the right time comes, as in later, you can talk religion to him if it gives him comfort. It won't be a problem. But for now I just don't want us to fill his head with new ideas when we are still trying to understand the ideas of his own he had up until his death. I'm just saying tread carefully, so as not to jeopardise the scientific aspect of this project. And remember that I am recording everything, I mean everything, for posterity.

Brenda nods. *Caius, would you like to visit the one building in Rome that hasn't changed in two thousand years, that is not a ruin? Perhaps you also visited it as a youth?*

*

After the heat of the Roman afternoon, after twenty minutes in a ground-taxi through the dense grid of city streets, the cool of the interior of The Pantheon is a visceral relief. Ailee enjoys the added respect accorded to them by security guards on account of their devoutly religious outfits and the ailing invalid they are tending to. Caius is able to lean back and enjoy the spectacle of the vast coffered dome overhead better than they can, who start to stagger backwards after a few moments. *It's astounding!* Ailee exclaims. *So old, so perfect, so unharmed. You've been here before, Caius?*

I do not remember. There were so many temples back then, hundreds of them. Children were usually barred since they might not show due respect. I recall seeing none quite like this, this circular form.

What about you, Brenda? Ailee asks.

Yes of course, in my late teens as a divinity student. Haven't you?

Somehow it passed me by. But I'm glad I'm here now. I'm starting to feel like you must, Caius, as if human beings have lost their way, as if we were better back then.

Caius tutts, lifting himself out of his chair, as the women rush to help him up, holding an arm each. *Nonsense... he rasps in a hoarse whisper. We could not build metal birds to carry us through the air. Or send moving pictures hundreds of miles in a second. You are better than us now, except...*

Except what? Ailee asks, arm around his waist.

You do not believe in yourselves as we did. You all seem timid and confused. As if you have forgotten something.

What?

Awe, wonder. The majesty of being alive. Bravery. Arrogance. Caius lifts his arms up towards the open oculus 140 feet above, the white clouds sailing across the blue sky like some conquering armada. Then he falls to his knees, his open palms turned upwards and chants something that the translation software struggles to catch.

He's saying something about all the gods, of whom Jupiter is the greatest, asking for mercy for his soul. – Ailee whispers to Brenda then notices something over her shoulder. *Is it just me or is it getting quieter in here?*

Brenda spins around. *Yes, it was crowded when we came in. Those guys in black suits seem to be watching us and ushering people out. One of them is coming over.*

Greetings, sisters, father. English?

*Scottish actually, but we speak English. –*Ailee corrects him.

The handsome young Italian addresses them in perfect English: *The Pantheon is thought to have been constructed in 114 AD, under Emperor Trajan. Today it has been a Catholic church since AD 609. It was built on the site of an earlier temple commissioned by Marcus Agrippa during the reign of Augustus. After that it burnt down, and the present building was ordered by the emperor Hadrian and probably dedicated around AD 126. Even today it has the largest unsupported dome in the world, meaning that there is no metal reinforcement in the dome, only different weights of aggregate ingeniously graded. The bronze entrance doors through which you passed are nearly 7.5 metres high, so well made and balanced that their hinges work perfectly 2000 years later.* He lowers his voice to a more intimate tone: *My name is Marcello. You are Sisters Brenda and Ailee and Father Caius Flavius, yes?*

Yes, although I'm not really a sister, or even her sister I'm afraid. –Ailee answers.

That is quite all right. The young man laughs. *Nor am I a tour guide.*

Caius staggers to his feet from where he has been praying and turns around as the ladies help him back into his chair.

Marcello bows to Caius, kneels and holds out his hand and greets him in Latin. *It is a great honour to meet a true ancient Roman at last. You have travelled far I am told, in time as well as space.*

Who are those other guys over there? Ailee asks.

Marcello looks around and breathes in with a disapproving expression. *Polizia. They shouldn't come in here with guns like that. Disrespectful.*

Are they here for us?

Perhaps. But they should defer to His Holiness if I invoke him. Are you all ready to come with me?

With his dark glasses off, a few spots of rain fall through the open dome and land on Caius' face, starting to dissolve his pale make-up, revealing the much darker skin beneath.

*

Have you heard of The Roman Curia? –Marcello asks in the back of the air-conditioned limousine, in the three kilometre journey through slow-moving traffic to St Peter's basilica. *–The Vatican is a state within a state, with a complex relationship with the nation of Italy.*

Caius, only half interested in this talk, which an earpiece is quietly translating for him, leans to look up through the car windows at the buildings they pass and all the people in the streets, rocking with his hands on his knees like an excited child. He mutters Latin superlatives ceaselessly: *Mirabilis… magnificas… stupendum… infigo…* Sister Brenda clasps his hand and they both smile very broadly, as Marcello continues interminably: *The Curia was created by Pope Urban at the end of the eleventh century. Curia means court as in a royal court, and resembles a monarchy more than a contemporary form of government. His Holiness has been the sovereign and head of state of the Vatican City State since 1929, when the Lateran Pacts were agreed between Prime Minister Benito Mussolini and Pope Pius the Eleventh. Prior to this the Vatican was part of Rome for 200 years. But prior to that, the Papal States were almost one sixth the land mass of all of modern Italy. The Italian state compensated the church to the tune of one billion dollars, in today's money, to purchase this land, leaving only the Vatican its guaranteed independence. Citizens of the Vatican, such as myself, are not citizens of Italy but of the Vatican, as our passports confirm. At just over 44 hectares, the Vatican City is the smallest independent country in the world. Each five years His Holiness appoints a President who is head of government of the Vatican. The president reports all important matters to the Secretariat of State, the Pope's chief everyday advisory body. But over all this, as with a sovereign in the middle ages, His Holiness maintains absolute authority…*

*

After such a daunting potted history, Ailee is somewhat stunned when two hours later Pope Gregory The Seventeenth himself in immaculate white cassock and cape saunters into the splendidly furnished lounge that she and Brenda have been brought to within the Papal apartments. His youthful, almost childlike smile, belies his advanced years and the gravity of his office. He speaks with a soft Hispanic accent, chuckling nervously from time to time. *Did Marcello wear you down with all his extensive litany of facts and statistics? I feared as much. He does like to show off, but in the nicest possible sense you understand.*

Ailee immediately breaks into laughter, giving him all the answer he needs or expects. He shakes her hand, welcomes her to the Vatican and asks if he may take a seat next to her. *The patient is sleeping now, and Sister Brenda is keeping vigil by his bedside. Two of my personal physicians and the Italian Government's chief medical officer will examine him in the morning if that is all right with you?*

Perfectly. Thank you so much, Your Holiness.

Pah! Gregory exclaims. *You don't have to call me that, you know. If you are not a believer. My first name is really Pablo. May I call you Ailee in return?*

Ailee looks back at him wide-eyed for a moment. *Of course, but your secretary, Cardinal Vinales, the Praetorian Guard, they all told me I must address you as Your Holiness.*

Gregory waves his hand and laughs. *All formal nonsense, I apologise for it. It puts a distance between me and ordinary people, and that saddens me sometimes. It interests me greatly that you are of a scientific mind, without faith so Sister Brenda tells me, and yet you have chosen to bring this extraordinary man here to the Vatican.*

Do you hope to convert me?

Again Gregory laughs with quiet delight. *Do you hope to dissuade **me** of my faith?*

Not at all. I respect it greatly, without feeling any need to adopt it or follow it myself. I prefer to think for myself in all matters, without reference to any ancient books.

Gregory is not taken aback or insulted but pleased and intrigued by this candour. *And what of Copernicus,*

Kepler, Newton, Einstein? Aren't they ancient books worth referring to?

Yes of course, but it's not the same.

You are correct, it is not the same. And yet the parallel seems insightful to me. As a scientist you refer to Newton or Einstein, and yet feel free to build your own ideas on top of theirs, even to depart from theirs occasionally if necessary?

Ailee nods.

You might care to consider the ideas of Jesus of Nazareth as of a similar nature, I would suggest. They offer a way to bring peace to the world, that people can choose to learn from. As with science, they can be applied practically and yield tangible results. I have no desire to convert you, Ailee, but I would like if I may to take the opportunity to learn from you, to understand your motivation and perspective. Less than a third of the world's population are Christian. The church cannot help the world without understanding and reaching out to the other two thirds. Perhaps you and I could talk in the same manner as I wish the different factions of the world to talk.

Of course, I would be honoured. What do you want to know?

Gregory smiles with great satisfaction at this response. *You will have seen the media coverage around the world of your remarkable scientific breakthrough, how you brought a dead man back to life?*

It was an accident.

So was Newton's apple I believe, and Becquerel's photographic plates left in a dark cabinet. And many other examples with great moral consequences, penicillin and so on.

Ailee is tongue-tied for a moment, unable to believe that she is having such a conversation with a pope. *Moral consequences, yes. Doesn't it terrify you, didn't it appal you to learn that we had brought a dead man back to life? How can you reconcile that with the idea of a soul going to heaven?*

Gregory smiles. *You almost sound more religious than*

me there, although I suspect you don't find that a compliment. I have learned to accept everything in God's creation. If he has allowed Man, and Woman, to perform such a miracle, then he must have some reason, some design behind it, even one that we are perhaps not yet able to see.

Doesn't Caius' resurrection prove that there is no soul, only electrical impulses in the brain? – That it's all physics, nothing mystical or invisible?

Not at all. And those are just dry words to me. The miracle of life, of you and I and every other creature being able to live and interact like we are doing now... nothing can ever lessen or explain that away. Nothing can ever make it less miraculous. The deeper your science explores, the more it can only deepen the mystery. Look... Gregory stands up and paces over to the window, the lights of the vast city coming on beneath the gathering sunset. *I might say that your experiment brought Caius' soul back from purgatory or paradise because you had re-awoken his body. But what would it matter what I say to you? It happened and therefore it is God's will and we must learn from it.* He turns from the window back to face her. *I, like you, am a seeker after truth, you see. And no true seeker of that kind ever has anything to fear from reality. Reality, which means one thing to you, but to me also means God's manifest will as expressed in the world.*

Ailee reflects deeply. *Your openness surprises me, I must admit. I have long thought of religion as dogma, blindness. The idea that Christ was the son of God, that his birth was from immaculate conception, the idea that he performed miracles and rose from the dead. All of that, forgive me please for saying so, I find absurd and laughable, an insult to logical intelligence. It pains me to see people encouraged to believe such things.*

And yet you yourself have just brought back a man from the dead... Gregory laughs and returns to sit back down beside her, takes her hand for a moment as he gazes anxiously into her eyes. *What you just said. Can you believe that I know what you mean? That I might at times at least partially agree?*

No. Ailee shakes her head vigorously, confused. *That would be too much, surely. You must believe what you preach.*

All I preach, as you call it, is the word of Jesus of Nazareth, his advice on how we should all treat each other. His birth was two thousand years ago, when people also believed in dragons and demons and witches. People did not have cameras and microphones and spectrometers and Geiger counters and what have you, so they did their best, which probably wasn't very good, to record what they thought happened. We cannot test or prove any of it now, except Christ's ideas for how we should live peacefully, and those, I would argue, are what really matter.

Ailee smiles, and throws her head back, laughing with some kind of relief of tension. *You aren't what I thought you would be like at all, you know that?*

Gregory looks at her uncertainly for a few seconds, wondering if she is laughing at him then relaxes again also, and smiles broadly. *Now that, I believe, is a compliment, that I am happy to receive. But I think we have strayed from the central point of our discussion, as I foresaw it. Can you tell me why you felt compelled to bring the centurion here?*

Because my colleagues, my bosses, wanted to keep him chained up like a lab rat, to deny him any freedom or pleasure for his remaining weeks of life, interrogate him and perform experiments on him. When I met him, and from what my colleague Trevor told me, I saw that he was a man, a living human being, a miracle if you like, deserving of dignity and compassion, and that if we didn't treat him humanely then we would be destroying our own humanity.

Imperilling your soul, I might say in religious terms.

I suppose so, whatever you want to call it. A feeling deep inside that made me feel sick with myself, against which I felt compelled to rebel.

Good. Gregory rubs his hands together in satisfaction. *I commend your decision and your actions. They inspire me in fact, confirm to me that good is still a formidable force in the world and inside each of us. You have done well. Taken many risks, jeopardised your career on a moral principle. But what about this man Trevor of which you speak?*

Against all her rationale and self-discipline, to her surprise Ailee finds her eyes suddenly filling up with tears. *He risked everything too, more even than me, but we agreed he would stay behind as a decoy. They'll probably put him in jail now. Once... once Caius has... passed away, I want... I hope that the Scottish government will agree to extradite Trevor to join me here, like a prisoner swap if you like, in return for Caius' body, which they will want back of course.*

Trevor... forgive me. The way you say his name. Gregory tilts his head, as if peering deeply into Ailee's soul. *Do you care for this man?*

Ailee nods her head, once, twice, then repeatedly, biting her lip as tears roll down her face.

You are in love with him, I see. And he with you perhaps?

Yes, I think so, yes, she answers, wiping away her tears, sniffing. Gregory hands her a fresh white handkerchief from within his robes, and reaches a hand to rest on her shoulder. *But he's married...* Ailee adds.

Ah, I see... Gregory sighs, sitting back in his chair. *The complications of modern life. It has happened many times before in the history of the world and will do so again, you know. Does he have children?*

No. But I do, two daughters, both adults now from a previous marriage. My husband and I separated and then he died two years ago.

Does Trevor wish to separate from his wife, do you think?

Yes, very much so I think.

Then the situation is not entirely without hope, is it?

Only if Drest will allow him to leave Scotland to join me. Can you help, do you think?

I am afraid that I really do not know. Gregory frowns, appearing troubled for the first time. *I am not a politician. I have only limited influence on the Prime Ministers of Italy and Scotland. The conversation that you and I have just had may be the greatest help I can offer you. And I will pray for you of course… whether you want me to or not.* Gregory thinks to himself in silence for a further minute. *Although, perhaps I can help Caius in the time he has left. Rome is no place to relax, with all its heat and dust. My summer residence, Castel Gandolfo, I am due to go there next week for the summer months. We can set up a room for him there, with medical assistance to hand, a view over the countryside. You and Sister Brenda would accompany him of course, have rooms of your own. I suspect that Italy will allow you to live here in exile for as long as you wish, years if need be, if your dispute with your own country proves intractable.*

Thank you, thank you, you are so kind. Ailee takes his hand, overcome with emotion. *You look inside me as if I am made of glass. How can I ever repay you?*

Gregory smiles once more, but with eyes this time tinged with wistful sadness. *You have brought a lost Roman home. And I ask only one trivial thing: that you call me His Holiness in front of other people once we leave this room. Although it doesn't matter to you or me, it does to many other people whose expectations I cannot change and on whose support I rely.*

They both laugh and stand up and awkwardly embrace.

Gregory quickly gestures in blessing as Ailee steps back. He pauses at the door. *Now I shall call Marcello who will show you to the rooms we have prepared for you and Sister Brenda. Good night and may God be with you. We shall speak again tomorrow.*

~

XI

When the heat of the day subsides, Ailee and Sister Brenda wheel Caius out onto the terrace of the Castel Gandolfo. Multiple paths, made white in the moonlight, radiate out from the base of the high stone ramparts towards the low terrace wall beyond which Lake Albano glimmers beneath the stars. Ailee points out, and Caius marvels, at how the full moon sails between the treetops. Wind-torn umbrella pines and cypresses, creak and sigh in a light evening breeze. Brenda turns Caius' wheelchair around when they reach the terrace edge and points up towards the two domes of the Papal observatory, explaining that telescopes are held within, with which to observe the stars. *I was showing you the film of men landing on the moon earlier, Caius, do you remember it?*

Pulcherrima! Magnum factum! Caius whispers.

Imagine if the Romans had managed that... Ailee reflects, sitting on a stone balustrade. *Roman rockets, a Roman settlement on the moon... some bath houses, an auditorium.*

A rocket powered by slaves would that be? Brenda asks.

Oh, don't be daft. –Ailee snorts.

But amn't I making a serious point? Brenda insists. *Slavery was intrinsic to everything the Romans did.*

Well I suppose you're right. But also to its failure. Maybe that was the reason why the so-called barbarians resisted it with such force, and turned on it and destroyed it in the end. Ailee stands up and takes off the footbrake on Caius' chair. *Come on, let's take him down to the lower terraces. It's such a lovely night.*

Do you think maybe that social inequality and injustice will, in the end, always destroy any society that relies on them? Brenda asks earnestly, fingering the cross around her neck, hurrying to catch up.

That would be an optimistic thought. Ailee answers as they wind their way down the ramp towards the formal gardens. *Look at America. The civil war was won and yet the failure to properly emancipate, compensate and integrate the slaves and their descendents led to the social division and riots which are still tearing it apart. Maybe populism is a death wish, a death roll, for any society that turns to it.* The road curves down to the bottom of the hill, leading onto the long immaculately pruned avenues of hedges and flower beds, the mazes and fountains.

Well, Scotland's democracy hasn't taken long to die then, has it? Brenda counters, taking over Ailee's position behind the wheelchair to give her a break. Caius rocks his head, taking in the nocturnal scents of flowers.

It is sick, I agree. Ailee answers. *But maybe it's an infantile disease, like measles. That's what Einstein said you know, that nationalism was the measles of mankind. Maybe it can be stronger when it comes out the other side of it and recovers.* Ailee leans down to lift the front of the wheelchair to help Brenda over a marble step.

If it survives at all. Measles used to kill children... Brenda counters.

Ailee talks almost to herself, deep in thought as the trio progress across the moonlit lawns: *Democracy can only survive if it learns the right lessons. One of the most terrifying lessons of history is the dark ages. Rome's culture and technology was largely lost for a thousand years until the Renaissance began. That's from 500 AD to 1500 AD. Just think about that. This is 2089. If a cultural collapse like that were to happen right now then we wouldn't have a recovery until 3089. That's the 31st century. Even Star Trek was only set in the 24th. That human civilisation could regress for that length of time is mind-boggling.*

Should we be frightened by that though, or comforted? Doesn't it show that no matter what goes wrong, no matter how much we lose our way, we will always rebuild and go forward? Brenda ponders as the trio stop, she and

Caius gazing at Ailee who, back turned, stares for a long time into the heart of a hedge maze below them as if it is a puzzle, a knot to be untied.

America... Caius suddenly whispers, surprising them that he has been fully awake and listening with his translator on. *I wish I'd been able to visit there. No time now. New Work you said it was called? Man Hatting? Such tall edifices.*

New York, Manhattan island. Yes, very good, Caius, the Americans. Ailee kneels and pats him on the knee. *They're a bit like the Romans were to the Greeks. To us Europeans, I mean. They grew out of our culture, rebelled and then grew to surpass us. And yet now they are collapsing. Then again the Greeks looked up to the Egyptians who in turn looked up to the Atlanteans... whoever they were, if indeed they ever existed. Because if we could have had a thousand year dark age, who is to say what previous civilisations might have predated even the Egyptians and Mesopotamians... it's probably impossible to know.*

Until time travel is invented... –Brenda laughs. *And then we're bound to go back aren't we? Who could resist it? Nosey little monkeys that we are. And nothing fascinates us more than our own belly buttons.*

I'm surprised to hear a woman of the cloth call humans monkeys, Brenda, I must confess. Ailee feigns astonishment.

Darwin believed in God you know, Ailee, and I believe in Darwin. Well there you go anyway, Caius. Civilisation is a baton race. Thank you for handing it on to us. We dropped it, but we went back eventually to pick it up.

I wish... Caius whispers, *I wish my family were here, I miss them. My mother and father, my brother and sister, and...*

And who, Caius? Ailee kneels down to listen more closely.

I thought her name was Varinia, but it was something else... Dorcla. –Caius whispers.

Dorcla? Who was Dorcla, Caius? Ailee takes his hand

in hers and peers earnestly into Caius' face. *Who was she to you?*

I don't know... Caius' brow furrows, as if struggling with memory. *I knew her as a child. I taught her Latin and mathematics and geometry. I slowly grew to care for her, and she for me, perhaps.*

Where did you know her? On the wall, at Litana? Brenda asks, sitting down at the same level.

Litana, yes... Caius murmurs. *The adopted daughter of Petrovius.*

Who was Petrovius, Caius? Ailee asks.

A renowned scholar.

Caius. Ailee takes both his hands and tries to maintain eye contact. *We scanned your memories before you were woken up, brought back to life, the accident. There was something said about rape. The reason you were meeting a delegation of barbarians was something to do with rape. Can you tell us who was raped and who was the rapist?*

Caius' body becomes visibly tense, his breathing starting to speed up as if in distress. *I don't know. Some native girl. By one of our auxiliaries. It was supposed to be an exchange. We were to hand him over, the rapist, to them, in return for... for...*

For whom, Caius? For whom?

Dorcla... he gasps.

But you said she was Roman, an adopted Roman. We don't understand, Caius. Ailee prompts.

It was a trick, a deception. I was a fool, a fool. Caius shakes his head, breaking out in sweat. The moonlight shadows of trees play across his face as the breeze picks up.

He's distressed, Ailee. Brenda intervenes, standing up to wheel his chair back to the palace. *We need to give him some kind of sedative. It's all right, Caius. Relax, everything is fine. You escaped. We rescued you. Everything is fine. Relax. You can go to sleep again if you like. We're taking you back inside.*

Maybe we can make more sense of that when we play

back the recordings later, Ailee says quietly, taking her turn pushing the wheelchair uphill.

You and your bloody recordings... Brenda hisses. *Our priority should be real life, avoiding suffering. You scientists creep me out sometimes. Where is your respect, your compassion?*

Brenda... Ailee gasps, out of breath, pushing against the hill. *Give me a break. I trashed my career to bring this man here. My compassion shouldn't be in question. But I also want to tell his story.*

*

In the bright light and burning heat of the noonday sun, Valentina Breshkov's air car slowly rotates, coming down to land amid the effulgent greenery of Castel Gandolfo's gardens. Ailee waves from the open shutters of a high window on the palace walls then hurries down through the cool shade of the spiral staircase within. She emerges in a long plain white dress and crosses the parched lawn to embrace Breshkov as she reaches the foot of the steps from the lower terrace.

You've forgiven me then, Val? Ailee looks earnestly into her eyes.

I was going to ask you exactly the same question, actually, Ailee. Of course I have. But for what? We've all done what we agreed. They turn and climb the steps together.

Likewise. I know, of course. How's Trevor?

Well, that is the real tragedy. Haven't you seen on the international news? Drest has leaned on the trial judge and insisted out of spite that he be jailed indefinitely in a high security prison, in with the ruffians, all the worst of the worst.

Oh that's terrible! Ailee nearly collapses, sits down at the top of the steps. *What have we done?*

Breshkov sits and puts her arm around her shoulder. *It's not your fault. It was his choice. What we agreed. Be patient. He will outlast Drest, don't worry. Her days are numbered, Ailee. And once she herself is in jail, then*

Trevor will be released. Like a see-saw, one goes down and the other goes up.

Fortuna Imperatrix Mundi... Ailee mumbles.

What's that?

The Carmina Burana, 12th century. Fortune, empress of the world, to thy cruel pleasure I expose my back. Once I was seated on Fortune's throne, crowned with a garland of prosperity. In the bloom of my success I was struck down and all my glory stolen. As Fortune's wheel turns, one is deposed, another lifted on high to enjoy a brief happiness. Uneasy sits the king —let him beware his ruin, for beneath the axle of the wheel we read the name of Hecuba.

Very good. Breshkov almost feels like applauding. *Always the Classics teacher. Who was Hecuba?*

The wife of the last King of Troy.

Ah... I see. The wooden horse and all that. I get your point then, and it is the same as mine. Drest will fall and Trevor will be freed.

How can you be so sure?

Because I have recently played a major part in her downfall myself, or done my very best to. But it is so hot out here. Can we go inside before we talk more? I am dying for a drink, wine even, after a long flight like that.

*

Did anyone suspect our ruse, Val? Is that why you're here? To evade arrest in Scotland? —Ailee asks once they are indoors and sharing bread and olives on the thick wooden bench in the cool pantry of the castle.

No. Not at all. But that is maybe part of the problem. The deception you and I agreed was contrived to make Trevor and you and Brenda look like sole conspirators. With Ed and Bruce and Sonja left in the dark. Plausible deniability and all that. But it has made things worse for Trevor than if I had been part of the package, as it were. You should have seen Ed's rage at Trevor. I have still not told him the truth. But at least with me still at large I have been free to come here, all as we agreed and planned. I've brought my equipment with me in the air car, you know. A scaled-down version of the Retrovival apparatus, and a few questions for Caius if that is alright? How is he faring? How many days left do the Italian doctors think he has?

Ailee pours them both a cup of coffee. *Perhaps a week or two, Val. His mind is still pretty lucid. It's just his physical body, his limbs which he is being encouraged not to use or strain in the least. The Italians are worried about his bones. They say they are dissolving.*

Of course. That is always the problem with bog bodies. The calcium levels can be boosted I believe, but the human metabolism processes it too slowly to be of any help to Caius in this situation. We would need a few months at least, and anyway that is just his bones. The rest of his tissue will inevitably be failing I would imagine, his epidermis particularly. His skin will be very black by now, am I right? And his internal organs, they will be fighting harder against natural contaminants every day while only losing strength. Not pleasant. Are they giving him painkillers? Morphine? His Glycine levels will be lowering, compromising neurotransmission, which will be causing brain fog soon. You say he is still sharp but not for much longer I would think. Can I see him now? Time may be of the essence.

Drink up and I'll take you there now then. The medical rooms are in the basement of the south wing. We can talk as we go. The building is closed to tourists this month so we'll have it all to ourselves.

As they walk the corridors they pass open doors onto lavish state rooms with polished marble floors, occasionally pausing to marvel at the threshold. *Did they ever identify who the grave robbers were, Val? –Who caused Caius to come back to life?* Ailee asks.

Ahh... about that, Ailee. Breshkov looks at her feet in shame. *I am sorry to confess that was just a story I told. The truth is that one of them was me, and that the other one was an SI7 agent who got Caius' gladius thrust through his gastrointestinal tract for his trouble.*

What? Why? Ailee halts in amazement. *What were you doing there? Surely you're not saying you resurrected Caius on purpose?*

No. Most certainly not, Ailee. That bit of the story was true. There was a fight, during which the apparatus was knocked over and uncontrolled quantities of Smart Blood and Glycine were unleashed on the patient. The SI7 agent was supposed to be a plain clothes policeman sent to recruit me into helping gather evidence against Drest. But I knew he was a fraud when he did not know the password we had agreed. SI7 are loyal to Drest while the police are not. Black Forest Gateau. It was a phrase I heard you or Trevor come out with once and I liked it and remembered it. So I asked him what kind of cake he'd like with his coffee and he started havering about Red Velvet, then I knew I had a cuckoo on my hands. I asked him to leave then he attacked me, demanding information. So... how do you say in Glasgow... Breshkov looks around and lowers her voice. *I beat the fucking shit out of him. Or was doing so, when Caius woke up.*

Wow, Val. Wow. Ailee marvels as they resume walking.

I got a few flesh wounds for my trouble, but I was smart enough to get the hell out the way of Caius once I saw he was on the rampage. You do realise I was born a man, don't you?

What, sorry?

I am trans. Born Valentin, not Valentina. In a very tough area of Kyiv. I became a good fighter to stop all the kids mocking me for my perceived femininity. They called me a sissy. Sestrychka. And a Russian, which hurt much more.

I see. Wow again, Val. I really had no idea. You've had quite a life. From street kid to millionaire archaeo-biologist.

To international pariah in breach of the Rossan convention. But don't worry about me. I still have my liberty, unlike poor Trevor. I will try to help him, I promise. I am working on a plan.

Retrovival

*

Ailee assists Breshkov in rigging up the Retrovival equipment next to Caius' bed in the Papal hospital in the palace basement, connecting wires to his head so as to be able to see his memories in response to the prompts that they give him. Breshkov sits down next to Caius when he wakes up, introduces herself and asks him a series of questions: *Caius. What can you tell us about the Damnonii tribe? How often did you interact with them? What did they dress like? Were you or any of your fellow soldiers able to understand their language? How much trade went on between you and the tribe? How often did they attack the wall and what triggered this aggression? Did they resist right from the start of the wall's construction or only later on, in which case why? What were their villages like? What were their buildings made of and what form did they follow?*

The first third of these Caius answers verbally, albeit in a slow weakening voice, while only a few flickering visual images appear on screen recorded from his occipital lobe. The next third he loses consciousness during, and his answers come only as intermittent fragments of visual sequences in response to the stimuli. His responses to the final third become more intermittent and seem to relate only tangentially to Breshkov's stimuli. *He's dreaming now, basically...* she concludes.

Astonishing... Ailee gasps, *has this ever been done before? Dreams recorded?*

With normal living subjects? Yes it has. In several research projects in America and France I believe. The same principle as disabled people accessing the internet directly from their brains, but in reverse. It's very interesting but unfortunately unlikely to give us any information that is useful in terms of reliably answering our specific historical questions.

Look... Ailee returns to the Retrovival monitor to point at the screen, *what is that he's dreaming about?*

Looks like a deep blue ocean... Breshkov peers over

her shoulder, *an abstracted memory of one he crossed perhaps. And a galleon on it, painted red as if covered in blood. Freud or Jung might have been interested I suppose, but we're not psychoanalysts.*

Look! Ailee points at her screen, *what or who is that inside the boat?*

A blue woman. How peculiar. Breshkov whispers.

Symbolic of some of the tribespeople, do you think? What is she calling out to him? Can we translate that?

Probably not. I'll get the computer onto it. It's not even Latin. Being a dream it could simply be gibberish of course.

Now the boat is sinking, and his pulse is speeding up slightly, do you see that?

That means he will probably wake in a moment, even partially, Breshkov notes.

Caius mumbles in his sleep, tries to turn over, then falls back into deep sleep again, his breathing returning to normal.

Breshkov nods her head. *Usually one like that every hour or so in the average human. REM sleep cycle.*

*

Ailee and Breshkov retire to the lounge of Ailee's apartment within the Castel Gandolfo, to talk over a glass of wine, occasionally nodding off to sleep on their respective sofas. The architecture is modest compared to the state rooms, white plaster walls and simple cornices, dark oak beams and shutters, faded tapestries and fabrics. *You haven't told me yet...* Ailee asks Breshkov, *about this thing you were recruited to do for the Scottish Police, to help bring Drest down, as you put it.*

Probably because it's not a pleasant memory, Ailee. Horrible in fact, utterly horrible. But I did it for a good cause. This stays between the two of us, right? Doohan, the head of Police Scotland, he got a dead body disinterred in secret, of a guy who only died six months ago. He asked me to use Retrovival in order to try to recover his memories.

My god... Ailee gasps, hand over her mouth. *How did he die?*

Hanging. Suicide. Brain tissue intact, you see?

But not in a peat bog, so decayed?

Yes, which is why it was so vile. I had a special mask and goggles, but I've woken up every morning since remembering the smell and shouting out in horror. The brain was not irredeemably decayed as it happens. The process worked.

What information did you retrieve?

Him talking to his fellow murderers, his co-conspirators. They're border guards who've been killing English refugees, for years. Shallow graves all over the remote moors. It turns out that guilt does a cerebral investigator's job for them. The things that linger longest in the chambers of a dead brain are the memories that bothered us the most, our sins, our shame, our terrible misdemeanours.

Ailee shivers so hard that she nearly spills her wine. *Jesus, that creeps the hell out of me, Val. Was it worth it do you think? Will this lead to convictions?*

Doohan seems to think so. He's made several arrests already in fact. But his real prize is Drest. He says she and her Justice Secretary knew all about it and tried to suppress any investigation. Grounds for impeachment.

Here's hoping... Ailee raises her glass in a toast with Breshkov.

*

The following evening, after a similar late night discussion in which she and Ailee have both nodded off, Breshkov is a woken by a loud alarm on her phone. *Bozhe miy! Proklyattya!* – She leaps up, shouting.

What? What? Ailee staggers over to put her hands on her shoulders to restrain her from spinning on the spot as she reads her phone. *Val! Speak English! What is it?*

Caius! Caius! He's died... prematurely. Doctor Russo is paging me. How can this happen? They said they thought he still had several days left. We better get back over to the ward.

Oh no. Oh no. Ailee runs to get her shoes on. *We better wake up Sister Brenda as well. I'm not sure if she'd even given him the last rites yet.*

The last what? Breshkov shouts over her shoulder as they make for the door.

Last rites. Mumbo jumbo to us I know. But it matters to her, and it mattered to Caius apparently. She claims he converted to Christianity last week after talking to the Pope. Ailee locks the apartment door behind them.

You met the Pope? The actual Pope? When were you going to tell me about that? —Breshkov asks, out of breath as they run along the corridors together.

I thought you knew. That's why we're here. This is his personal holiday gaff, as it were.

Of course. What is he like?

Really nice actually. Although not enough to convert me...

Did you convert him?

That's funny. He made that joke too.

When they storm through the ward doors they can see Caius' flat-lined ECG traces on two monitors over his bed. Sister Brenda is already present and crying hysterically as she tries to disconnect the wires from Caius' head, as the doctors try to restrain her..

What are you doing, Brenda? Ailee calls out to her. *It's too late, he's gone. Right, Doctor Russo? Il paziente è morto, morto, si?*

I know... Brenda sobs, *but have you see what this obscene machine of yours is doing? Take a look at your screen things. It's disrespectful, you should be ashamed. Help me to stop this and get him free!* —she shrieks.

Brenda, Brenda... calm down, Ailee urges, placing her hand over Brenda's where it rests on Caius' shoulders. *He's gone. Please, just leave the wires. Don't touch anything until Val says so.*

Ailee... Breshkov's voice rings out behind them both in a strange tone. *I think you better come over here and watch this. You too actually, Brenda. You're the one who believes in life after death after all. I mean it. Please just leave the wires and step over here...*

In his sleep Caius finds that he is falling deeper and deeper into a dark tangled wood towards sunset. The many criss-crossing branches form a texture like woven fabric that rubs across his face, his eyes. This texture seems to fuse with the sound of his own breathing, which is slowing the deeper he walks into a deep dell within this strange forest. Gradually his eyes adjust and he sees that at the foot of the wooded dell is a rock outcrop with the entrance to a large cave. He walks down the steep glade until he finds himself at the entrance to the cave. It forms a ragged semi-circle, like a gaping maw of stone. He can see a dim red light emanating from somewhere deep within it, and hears a distant sound, perhaps like the ocean, perhaps like many human voices. He now notices that two torches have been left burning at the cave entrance and by picking one up he is able to make out writing carved into the surface of the rock arch above. It is in Greek and he struggles to decipher its meaning.

Just then, the sound of a dog barking echoes from within the caves, rattling the chains which restrain it. Drawn irrevocably into the cave out of curiosity, Caius soon finds that in avoiding the reach of the chained dog he has begun a descent into the caves towards the mysterious light and sound. The hound's fur is pitch-black, its eyes burning red lights that illumine anything in front of it. It watches him as he walks away, serenading him with a low growl. A gradual sense of profound foreboding comes over him as he proceeds, and yet somehow he is unable to halt his advance or force himself to retreat backwards. The cave is vast, endlessly unfolding in scale and depth. Its paths wind down, deeper and wider, forming a natural amphitheatre at the depths of which he begins to see there is a body of water flowing. He looks over his shoulder in fear and desperation but sees that he has already lost sight of any possible way back. His legs keep bearing him downwards, terrace after terrace. He starts to see that what he at first thinks are some kind of woods on the bank of the river are in fact large crowds of figures, each dressed in dark cloaks and hoods. All of them are weeping and lamenting, mourning, muttering to themselves, milling around, aimlessly pacing back and forward. His sense of terror is intense as they each turn to look at him as he approaches. Some of them have faces reminiscent of people he knew in childhood, forgotten friends or relatives. Some of them seem to have no faces at all, as if erased with dust and ash.

The mourning crowd parts as he approaches, revealing the way to the shore of what he now sees is a wide slow-moving river which curves away from him in both directions. He sees that a single wooden boat is pulled up on the shore, in which stands a boatman also cloaked and hooded, but whose face seems different, his eyes blazing bright, his gaze fixed unwaveringly on Caius as if willing him on. This figure makes the boat ready, begins to push it out, and holds out his hand to help Caius step aboard. The boatman brings his face up close to that of Caius and makes him open his mouth, whereupon he reaches in his fingers and withdraws a single coin that Caius has been keeping there. He drops the coin into the dark folds of his cloak. The boatman slowly rows them out into the river as Caius sits down and looks back towards the crowds on shore who gaze after him longingly.

On the other side of the wide waters, Caius eventually alights and once again is alarmed to discover that what he thought was vegetation or undergrowth is in fact more living human bodies in shades of dejection. He walks through crowds of despairing souls, and crying children, each unable to console themselves or each other. He hides his face from them in shame, finds that he himself has also been wearing the same dark cloak and hood. Beyond these crowds he finds a flat wide wasteland into which many pits have been dug, each glowing with red fire. From these he catches fragments of terrible cries of pain and torment as he passes. Afraid, he hurries up, longing to reach the other side of this expanse safely. The only vegetation in this desert are occasional burnt-black stumps of trees, the blasted and twisted arms snaking upwards to where no sky draws them on. He senses there are other souls on the far side waiting for him, waving to him in the dim light, urging him on to join them.

He looks to his left and catches sight of something in the far distance that makes him shiver: a king and queen shrouded in darkness, their faces obscured, seated on huge stone thrones at the foot of a cliff face. Judging by the heights of the crowds of mourners standing at their feet, he estimates these gloomy monarchs to be over a hundred feet high. Red fire glimmers around their crowns and shoulders. He sees their heads nod slightly, and fear grips him that they can see him from even this distance, that they can see everything.

But as he forces himself to look straight ahead and keep walking, his mood finally, gradually lifts. The next set of figures he sees emerging out of darkness are in better spirits. Many of them raise their hands and greet him, some even smile. Some are dressed athletically, others in something approaching finery, scholarly wreaths and robes, although all colours remain muted, as if everything down here in this domain is always coated in black dust. As these figures part before him, he sees that they stand on another shore and the river behind them is much brighter than the last one. On its far shore, although surely still underground, he sees a glorious expanse of lush green fields, long grasses waving in a breeze. From the figures around him, among the heroes and sportsmen, warriors and statesmen, he now recognises the faces of his aunt, his uncles, his brother and sister, and finally his beloved mother and father. They all embrace him, and tears begin running down his face. He sees that their flesh is cold and smooth like the marble of white statues, but that his tears are altering them, bringing back to life some living substance held within. They gradually become more vivid and sanguine as they take his hands and lead him towards a boat on the shore. The small family group take up the white birchwood oars and set out across the bright river as the crowds left behind cheer them on optimistically.

Somehow some subterranean sun is rising over the glorious green meadows as their boat approaches the further shore. He hears joyous singing from groups of white-clad men and women emerging from between the tall sheaves of grass to bring their vases to the shore and draw water from it. As he and his family disembark an amphora of water is handed to him by a tall woman with braided blonde hair whose smile shines through him like the morning sun. He drinks from the jug and its splendidly refreshing essence flows down into every inch of his body, slowly erasing all discomfort, all regret, all memory. The whispering grasses of the eternal fields enter his heart and soul, scouring him, wiping him clean. Like the amphora itself, made of clay, he is at last emptied of everything, ready to be filled again. He comes to realise that he has been hearing a deep distant drumbeat under everything, throughout his entire journey from the entrance of the cave. And that now it has stopped.

~

XII

What is Hell? Does it exist, on earth or in an afterlife? Sometimes it may come disguised as something that looks like Heaven. Unable to return to Scotland, Ailee requests a new identity and passport from the Italian government, a new job even. In the Umbrian hill town of Perugia she appears before her first class in the quaintly named *University for Foreigners of Perugia*. She is relieved that nobody recognises her. She has dyed her hair black, grown it long and almost perpetually wears dark glasses. She endeavours to be known as little as possible to as few people as possible, despite striving to master a new language. In the evenings after classes she strolls through the maze of winding cobbled streets and alleyways, picking up a few items of groceries before returning to her modest apartment in the Piazza Giordana Bruno. – A little triangular square in front of the archaeological museum, which occupies a 13th century former convent. Ailee teaches History and English now, maintaining her cover, but finds herself gazing enviously at the archaeology lecturers, craves museums and digs.

Perugia is an ancient Etruscan settlement, mentioned by the Roman historian Pictor in 300 BC. She likes to wander down the Corsa Petro Vanucci to sit in the Giardini Carducci and gaze out over the white marble balustrading. From here she gets a sense of the whole town tumbling down from this height towards the undulating plains of Umbria sizzling in the warm evening light, rolling wooded hills punctuated by church steeples, cypress trees and red-tiled roofs.

Ailee, or Signora Connelly as she is now known, keeps herself to herself, becomes introspective, brooding. She is troubled by the memory of Caius' visions after death. The celebrated 14th century text of Dante's *Divine Comedy* has come to fascinate her. Perhaps it is her students who have sparked her interest in it, but she is also haunted by her memory of Trevor talking about it, how he said he felt that Caius' life, but all of their lives also, were some kind of enactment of its narrative or moral message. She wants to understand what he meant by that, but reading the dense text and copious notes and commentaries doesn't seem to shed light on its central mystery for her. It strikes her at times as little more than Dante filling Hell with all the people he hated and showing hideous punishments being meted out to them. She has asked Breshkov to pass on her secret address to Trevor in prison in Scotland, and month after month passes as she awaits any letter from him.

*

Time doesn't slow down in prison. It stops. Trevor seems to remember witnessing his own trial as if it was happening to someone else. As if it was six weeks of an obscure political pageant of no relevance to him or anything he had known in his life up to that point. The jeers of the spectating crowd echo in his memory from time to time, not so much as taunting or humiliation but as signifiers of estrangement, like the sound the hull of some ancient ship makes as it weighs anchor and creaks against a quay it's departing from. The journey in prison vans, down endless corridors, being examined and fingerprinted, struck him as if setting out for a holiday in Hell. The sound of his own private hollow laughter at jokes like these come to fill his own head. Until he begins to hear real laughter in the world around him, fellow inmates whispering, taunting him, calling him English, Sassenach. The guards don't seem to take any action to prevent this. Some grin, others chuckle, all are complicit. Everything is grey: walls, floors, clothes, food, skies. This, in every sense grey environment progressively seeps into his soul, begins to assert itself as who and what he now is. Complete numbness and cognitive denial become his daily bread.

At first he shares his cell with a six-and-a-half-foot

human bear who playfully attempts to strangle him on his second night. He finds he can subdue 'Bear' by telling him stories about Rome, galley slaves who escaped. Bear wants to hear about chariot races and gladiator fights in the colosseum. Greater physical strength and capacity for violence than his are commonplace in prison, and so by default Trevor begins to find that his intellect is his best weapon, his understanding of history, which is after all merely the psychology of human interaction made manifest, a tool by which to be more savvy than he has hitherto considered himself. Know thyself, as the ancient Greeks inscribed on the Temple of Apollo at Delphi. *Gnothi seauton.* Maybe contemporary prisons should carry the maxim. Maybe all our houses also.

*

Ailee goes to visit Sister Brenda at the Convent of Frati Minori Cappuccini Montemalbe, which she has been accepted into, a few kilometres north-west of Perugia. It is a foreboding building, of medieval towers and castellated high walls. Somewhat milder and more modern buildings are hidden within the complex, however. Long colonnades and courtyards of white render and timber shutters, gentle curves of brick arches forming cloisters, their rhythm like music.

Ailee and Brenda walk side by side in the convent grounds after a Spartan lunch together in the refectory. *Brenda, I keep thinking about Caius' death. You were there when he passed, before me and Breshkov were paged. Can I ask... what was it like at the actual moment of his death?*

For the second time you mean? –Brenda looks at Ailee ruefully.

This time more peacefully, hopefully? Ailee adds.

Yes, it was very sad. I felt an immense responsibility and loss, as if I had become his second mother or something. The day before he had said to me that our world was beautiful, that we were the true inheritors of the Roman empire. People reaching the moon certainly impressed him, as did everything we've found out about astronomy, how vast the cosmos is. He said he was sorry for killing three people after he was revived.

A thief, a golfer and a tramp?

Yes, it sounds like a joke doesn't it, an Englishman, an Irishman and a Scotsman. But seriously, it was important to him to repent I think. He spent quite a bit of time with Pope Gregory before we left Rome, who persuaded him of the power of Christianity. He was anxious that his soul be saved and he be treated sympathetically in the afterlife.

His old religion bleeding into the new I suppose. Ailee reflects. *The Elysian fields transmuting into Heaven guarded by St.Peter. What we did to him by bringing him back must have seemed like an afterlife of sorts to him. Heaven or Hell?*

Purgatory, more like, Brenda corrects her. *A test, a trial, a long wait, a weighing of his soul.*

Purgatory... the word stops Ailee in her tracks and she stares towards the gushing waters of a fountain at the end of the colonnade they have just entered, lost in thought. *A word I've scarcely given thought to in my life, not being Catholic. I suppose it's what poor Trevor is going through.*

You blame yourself? Brenda touches Ailee on the sleeve, full of sympathy for her friend. *Guilt is universal. We're all born with it, the human condition. What's important is to face it, to open ourselves to God. From atonement comes humility then grace. I will pray for you.*

Ailee wipes a tear from her eye, turning to embrace Brenda. *You can do something else for me maybe, crazy though it sounds. Have you read Dante? The Divine Comedy?*

I'm aware of it, have read about it certainly. It's important to Catholicism.

I have a copy with me, from the library in Perugia, in English translation of course. Will you read it for me so that we can discuss it when we next meet?

Of course... Brenda almost bows in pleasure, delighted by Ailee's interest in theology.

Retrovival

*

Dear Ailee. As I write in prison I have no
way of knowing when you will get to read
this, if at all. Correspondence to and from
these places is heavily censored so its
content may even end up depleted or
scrambled. I am hoping that a letter I've
sent to Breshkov will get through and that
she with her international connections can
become a conduit between us. You will have
seen on the news some time ago that I was
convicted of aiding and abetting a
kidnapping, conspiracy to sell state secrets
and espionage. All trumped-up nonsense of
course, laughable were it not so serious for
me.

   Things are bad here, I won't pretend
otherwise. I wonder how many ordinary people
out there really know that prisoners can be
locked in their cells for 22 hours a day.
That a cell can be shared with 2 other
strangers, who all have to piss and shit into
the same bucket overnight, then carry it out
ourselves to 'slop out' at the end of the
corridor in the morning? - Or know that
prisoners who misbehave are taken into
isolation cells and kicked and punched
senseless on the floor by guards? And this is
Scotland in the 21st century. Being English
doesn't help me, to say the least. This makes
me a constant target for intimidation and
ridicule by the least intelligent and most
bigoted amongst my fellow inmates. I really
shouldn't be in here along with murderers,
thieves and rapists. I am a political
prisoner, basically. But I am not the only
one it seems. Last night during our dinner
hour I was introduced to a young man called
Ben Woolf, a reporter for the Scottish Mail
who has been jailed for refusing to reveal
his sources for a story on Drest suppressing
evidence of border atrocities. He said he is
optimistic that several major scandals are
going to bring her premiership to a premature
end soon. This kind of news and solidarity

gives me hope, which is very hard to come by
in here.
    Inevitably enough, Judith left me and
returned to England shortly after my arrest.
The house has been sold, and the proceeds
halved between her and myself. With my half I
instructed my lawyer to purchase a plot of
land up north for you and I to build a house
on when I get out. If anything happens to me,
if I never make it out alive from this
nightmare, then my will now instructs that my
money and this land will pass into your sole
ownership. I have no other family really to
leave things to anyway. I hope you are doing
well wherever you are. Please send me news if
you can, as often as you can, about how you
are getting on. Letters are like a vital
lifeline to everyone here in prison. Like
water to plants, we slowly wither away
without them. Whatever happens, Ailee, know
that I truly love you, and never regretted
even for a second the decisions that we took
and the time we had together. Be happy
always, wherever life leads you.
    Yours forever, Trevor.

*

Trevor is surprised when he receives an official note
under the door of his cell to tell him that he has a visitor
coming to see him the next day. Isolation wears away all
sense of perspective and reality. Despite him knowing it
was inconceivable that it would be Ailee, still his whole
mind and spirit rise like a bird in flight towards this
fantastical thought. He walks lighter during his exercise
hour in the yard, as if lifted by invisible wings. He
struggles to sleep for excitement, his head buzzing with
frenetic hopes that most of his being knows must
inevitably be dashed.

When the guards lead him in to the visiting hall, Trevor
is profoundly deflated to see that his visitor is Valentina
Breshkov, but in the thirty second walk to reach the booth
he regains his composure enough to reason that Breshkov

is very much the second-best thing and his potential lifeline to the outside world. *Val...* he presses his hand to the toughened glass. *Thanks for coming. Boy, am I glad to see you? What news?*

Breshkov flicks her eyes up to the guard hovering behind Trevor within earshot, in an exaggerated way that she knows Trevor will take meaning from. *I'm sorry I've not come sooner. We have to be careful what we say, Trevor.*

Why? I've been banged up for twelve years. What have I got left to lose?

Trevor... Breshkov lowers her voice, *you know what we agreed. If Ailee is ever to get back into the country then I need to remain a neutral figure in all this, someone who can vouch for her. I don't know how much they censor your news coverage in here, but there are various trials ongoing now that are threatening Drest. She's at her most dangerous when cornered, like most wounded predators. If she rescinds my visa or arrests me on some spurious pretext then I won't be able to take your letters to Ailee, or vice versa.*

You've seen her? Trevor's knuckles whiten as he clutches the desk.

Yes, only last week. I've brought you her letters, but the censor will have to go through them before he issues them to you. Could take a day or two they told me.

How is she? His eyes bore into Breshkov's.

She's well, Trevor, but missing you and consumed with guilt.

Trevor winces, clutches his fists, looks down at the table as his eyes fill with tears.

Time is limited, Trevor, so I'll just tell you what you need to know right now. She loves you very much, and you need to stay strong and get through all this. Me and others are working in the background to sort out the bigger political picture, because until that changes your prospects for early release are not good. Not good at present but they will improve. Stay strong.

*

Kirsty Denholm is brought to trial at the High Court in Edinburgh, accused in much the same way as Ben Woolf, of publishing classified government documents in her newspaper. The council for the prosecution, Grant Chisolm Esq cross-examines her.

You will be aware, Miss Denholm, that your fellow journalist Ben Woolf was convicted last year of the theft of state secrets, for his failure to reveal his sources in the Border Refugee Atrocities story which his newspaper ran?

Yes I am.

Are you also aware that he cited in his prosecution that he had stolen some of his information from yourself by using his mobile phone to photograph typewritten notes in your handbag without your knowledge? Was that allegation in your view true or false?

True.

The court gasps in suppressed astonishment, this claim having been emphatically rejected by the judge in Ben's trial. *May we ask then...* the prosecutor continues, recovering his composure, *–where it was that you in turn obtained your copies of highly sensitive and classified state documents?*

From the head of police Scotland, Charles Doohan.

The sitting judge, Lord President of the Court of Session, Francis Mackintosh, intervenes at this point. *Are you aware, Miss Denholm, of the gravity of the allegation you have just made, and that if you do not have convincing evidence to support it then you may be harming your own case?*

Yes, I am, my Lord, perfectly aware.

Then... Grant Chisolm rises to his feet. *We would respectfully ask, My Lord, that this session be adjourned while the prosecution reviews its case and prepares to call Charles Doohan as a witness.*

*

Sister Brenda comes to visit Ailee in Perugia and they go for coffee together on a hot August day, then wander through the intense shadows of the maze of streets, drifting in and out of churches that they pass, savouring their coolness.

I have been writing a lot recently... Ailee relates.

Oh really? A memoir, fiction? Brenda enquires.

Letters. Letters to Trevor, over and over, even though I don't know yet if he will receive any of them.

Such devotion is admirable. I pray for you both, Ailee.

Ailee pauses and watches as Brenda lights a votive candle to place on a church altar. *I suppose you like this kind of long-distance thing. Like Hildegard of Bingen longing after God.*

Why mock it, Ailee? Brenda asks as they return to the heat outside. *In writing letters you get closer to an understanding of spiritual transcendence, sublimation, if you will.*

And will you? Explain, I mean?

It might seem insensitive of me to spell it out at a time like this in light of what you're going through. But since you like plain talking I'll put it simply: is any fellow mortal really worthy of our love? – Of all the things we project onto them when we're in love? Isn't it always like an endlessly receding horizon? Isn't the deep wisdom that we finally might come to in middle age this: that it was love itself that we loved, more than the endless succession of persons we mapped this feeling on to?

You're going to use the phrase carnal love any moment now, I can feel it. –Ailee sighs.

And why not? Brenda asks.

Because I find it reductive, dismissive. As if we're talking about animals rutting. I've always found something spiritual in it, at its best, two souls trying to find a way to get closer through their bodies, to unify, even.

Whatever you think you see, or find, that is spiritual in it, to me that is God. –Brenda says as they walk down a narrow alleyway.

But how do you know what you're even talking about? –Ailee blurts out before thinking carefully enough.

Brenda's eyes flare with an anger Ailee has never seen before as she turns and brings her face close to hers, as if peering deeply into her soul for something that she finally finds, then smiles bitterly. *Ahh... I see it now, you pity me don't you? – You look at me and my faith and are flooded with pity.*

Isn't pity a good Christian emotion? –Ailee stumbles, running after her, increasingly unsure of herself.

Not if it's in error, Ailee. Not if it's misplaced.

Is it?

Brenda spins around again to face her. *Do you want to know the truth, Ailee, the real truth?*

Of course.

*I pity **you**. I've always pitied you since I first met you. Look into my eyes and tell me that what I say isn't true.*

Ailee returns her gaze for a minute, then goes to sit down on the steps of a church doorway, deeply shaken. *How is that possible, Brenda?* –she whispers, reaching out to take her hand as she sits down beside her.

You refer to sex as if I've never experienced it. Brenda speaks more softly now. *It doesn't enter your head for a moment that I have done, but have since found something much more satisfying. Carnal love is inferior to spiritual love, all forms of which are shadows of God's love. Carnal love is selfish, hence all the trouble it causes in society. Spiritual love opens you up to all other human beings, and there's nothing like it. Sex is like blowing your nose compared to it.*

Ailee laughs so loud and with such strange and unexpected relief that paradoxically they both feel obliged to walk away from the church steps to continue the conversation. *We have both pitied each other equally then, Brenda, each unknown to the other. That makes me both laugh and cry. What a basis for a friendship.*

Maybe it's the basis for all of love, when you really think about it. You asked me to read Dante's divine comedy and explain it to you, Ailee, and maybe it's highly relevant to what we just said.

Go on... Ailee says, wiping her eyes. *I'm hooked.*

*Beatrice died when she was only 24. Dante only met her twice, and simply admired her from afar. This chaste object of desire and her premature death made her a divine being to Dante, who in the Divine Comedy he uses as the spiritual guide who leads the pilgrim Dante through hell and purgatory towards paradise and God. Beatrice is long dead. Only her death could make her divine. An earthly, living Beatrice, could only have disappointed Dante. Her death must have been a physical loss to her family, but to Dante her death was like a door opening onto another world, a glimpse of the divine and of the sublime purpose of God. Death has to mean something, Dante is saying, such a young pointless death as Beatrice's just **has** to mean something, must have purpose. This is what Christ teaches us: that sacrifice gives life, that death is not the end, but a gateway to paradise.*

Ailee reflects in silence, as they emerge from the maze of streets onto parkland at the edge of the old town. *I see the beauty in it, Brenda, I really do. But is it enough for me? I am a humanitarian. Involved with mankind. No man is an island, and all that. This world is too beautiful in itself, despite its cruelties, for me to forego its pleasures in favour of a mythical sequel.*

You are talking about sex of course, Brenda counters, *but are such pleasures really pleasures, or terrors and torments in disguise? You see, all experience carries with it the charge of memory and regret. To lose a lover and thereby to suffer jealousy and grief, or simply to catch syphilis or to become debauched and depraved by memory; all these are the other side of the coin of carnal love. You cannot separate one from the other.*

It's okay, Ailee responds, *I don't think I need to, personally. To stretch the metaphor to breaking point: I'd say I'm just happy to have used the currency, and still have some spare change in my pocket.*

*

Chief Constable Charles Doohan, head of Police Scotland is called to the witness stand in the trial of Kirsty Denholm. The council for the defence, Dale Cunningham Esq cross-examines him: *The defendant, the journalist Kirsty Denholm, has alleged that you passed confidential documents to her pertaining to an ongoing investigation into alleged extra judicial killings by Scottish border guards. Is this true or false?*

True. –Charlie answers.

Can you expand on that please? As in, why did you see fit to give out this classified information?

I chose to do so as the only means at my disposal to bring the crimes in question to the attention of the public at large, given that the Justice Secretary and his staff had made it known to me that they had no intention of allowing the Scottish State to bring a case against the accused.

Are you saying, Chief Constable, that you believed a cover-up to be under way by the Scottish government to bury all evidence of these crimes?

Yes, that is what I am saying.

How far up did you believe this cover-up to go, and what evidence did you have for that?

All the way to the top, since the Justice Secretary Roderick Allan is the husband of President Drest. My evidence is numerous emails and more importantly telephone conversations, online meetings, video calls, all of which I made recordings of.

Are you saying, Chief Constable, that you took it upon yourself to instigate a surveillance operation against your own employers?

I suppose you could look at it like that.

Did you feel any conflict of interest in this? – Any sense in which you were violating the terms of your office which require absolute loyalty to the Scottish State?

I felt, it, yes. But my sense of justice and fair-play outweighed it. I felt that my highest loyalty was to the Scottish people, rather than to any particular government administration which may come and go according to the vagaries of politics.

Were you concerned for the reputation and safety of Miss Denholm when you chose to draw her into this plot of yours?

Charlie nearly laughs. *She was, and is, an experienced journalist, well-versed in the risks of disclosure of classified data. I made sure to explain to her at great length the extent of the risks she would be taking on board in this instance.*

And did the extent of your wildcat surveillance operation, as it were, Chief Constable, extend to include Miss Denholm? That is to say, did you record all your conversations with her, and do you still have them now?

Yes I do. But my conversations with Roderick Allan and President Drest are much more interesting, I think you'll find.

Objection, your honour. Grant Chisolm, Esq, council for the prosecution stands up.

Objection upheld. –The judge answers testily. *Council for the defence, will you please note that the Justice Secretary and the President are not on trial here?*

Certainly, your honour, but I venture to suggest that they shall be, very soon...

*

D Wing at Provanmill High Security Institution is unofficially ruled by one inmate, known as Big Vern. Even the prison guards defer to him nervously, mysteriously keeping their distance. On paper his behaviour is impeccable, thus he is granted numerous privileges that other prisoners are never offered. In reality he has numerous henchmen among his fellow inmates who will commit any atrocity he requests of them, on pain of death at the hands of other henchmen. What Vern says goes. Rumour has it he is gay and not above taking it out on new arrivals, which is not a figure of speech.

Trevor is picked on by one particular inmate, Cammy, a loudmouth bully-boy who is unfortunately afforded invisible protection as one of Vern's henchmen. *English poofter*, the thug repeatedly calls him to make his friends laugh, mimicking his Yorkshire accent. In woodwork class, Trevor watches the movements of the guards carefully and chooses his moment with pinpoint accuracy. The thug expects Trevor to respond, if at all, in anger at the moment when he is being abused, the latest being a tub of sawdust emptied over his head. That Trevor might respond an hour later with complete calmness does not occur to him. As the nearest guard turns his back, Trevor leaps over to Cammy's bench and breaks his nose with a sheet of plywood, stabs a pilfered Stanley blade into his stomach then trips him so as to fall face-first onto the floor. The codes of ethics between prisoners of which he has become acutely aware over the last eight months means that he can be confident no one will tell the guards what they saw happen. Cammy writhes on the ground in pain, wailing at the sight of his own blood while the guards rush to restrain him. When one of Cammy's friends pulls a sharpened screwdriver from his pocket at lunch the next day, Trevor kicks it from his hands with such force that it lodges into the soffit of the metal walkway overhead.

Trevor fully expects the worst the next evening when the door of his isolation cell is mysteriously unlocked by guards out of normal hours and Big Vern saunters in to talk to him. He even carries a folding chair with him that the guards have seemingly provided him with. *Don't get up noo, Trev. I thought ah'd just droap by and pay youz a wee hoos call while yur oan solitary efter that nasty wee incident in woodwork. Who'd have thought you wur sae handy wi' yer fists and feet, an academic like you. Where did you grow up, mate?*

The roughest part of York. My father was a butcher.

Forgive me, Trev, but I didnae even ken York hud a rough bit but ah'll tak yer wurd fur it. Last I heard yer whole shitty country was fucked. Butcher sounds grand though. Do you ken hoo tae divvy up a coo then, mak it intae sirloin steaks?

With the right equipment I could probably still give it a go. You getting one delivered soon?

Vern laughs like a drain, head thrown back. *I like you, Trev, you know that? I didnae ken you took all the anti-English ribbing sae hard. Ribbing, that's what English folks call it, intit? We call it slagging up here, not sure if that's worse or better. Were you tryin' oot yer rusty butcher skills on oor Cammy then? You know whit, dinnae even answer that withoot yer lawyer present, as we say in oor line of work. He's a fat wanker, let's face it, a silly cunt. I hate him too. But he huz his uses sometimes. We all huv oor uses in here, Trev. The screws like tae talk aboot reform and rehabilitation but it's nothin' o' the kind maist o' the time. It's a criminality factory, you know that? Maist o' the guys in here grew up in sae-callt sink estates and huv been in an' oot ae borstal and YOIs since they were weans. They re-offend within a few fuckin' milliseconds o' leaving an' are right back in again. In here ye pick up a loat ae contacts and a loat ae tips. It's a britherhood. People look oot fur each other an' oan the ootside there's a network who'll dae the same. Whit ah'm trying tae tell you, Trev', to cut a long life sentence short, is that maist criminals are thick as shit, pig ignorant. But you've goat brains and balls. I could dae wi' men like that, on the ootside as well as in.*

Well, thank you, Vern, I appreciate that. Trevor manages a smile, despite his whole body being on edge, ready to defend himself.

Ah'm glad yae dae, Trev. I've hurd stories aboot your stories, all the stuff you ken aboot ancient Rome and Greece. The guys love that soart ae thing, every cunt does. Entertainment is hard tae come by in here. Ye should tell stories mair, educate us all aboot history. Military history particularly, Trev', if you ken whit ah mean.

I'm not sure that I do, actually.

Vern stands up and leans his head towards the door then lowers his voice as he sits back down. *Ah mean, wid ye like to get oot ae this place? The quick way ah mean.*

What quick way?

Well, see thing is, ah wiz kinda hopin' ye could tell me,

Trev, a man like you wi' all that knowledge and cunning. The art o' war and all that. I mean like the Trojan Horse, Icarus wi' his fucking balsa wood wings or whatever the fuck they wur. Those Romans with yon tortoise thing wi' their shields, I saw it once on telly, you ken, Tetsudo or something.

Testudo, you mean. Tetsudo is a martial art I think.

Wouldnae surprise me if yur a black belt in that too, Trev. So what dae ye say?

To what?

Will ye come up wi' something for me? A plan? The best strategy ye can devise. An analysis o' the weak-points in this shitty wall o' steel the screws have around us. I want oot. Lots o' the lifers do. And you shouldnae even be in here. Any cunt can see that. So ye want to protest, draw attention to yer cause. Tae oor cause tae. Overcrowding, slopping oot, lack o' staff tae supervise work detail. A nice big banner unfurled oan the roof. Trevor Whatsit is innocent or some shit. Even a riot wid dae, ah dare say. A quality piece o' mayhem. Huv a wee think aboot it wull ye?

Vern folds up his chair and prepares to go, when Trevor laughs to himself before realising the danger of such a reaction.

Somethin' funny ma friend? –Vern turns back, leans in closer, threateningly.

I was just remembering something... Trevor improvises, *as a matter of fact I have spotted a weakness. These big empty pitched roofs above us, they must need maintenance access and I've been trying to work out where the ceiling hatches are. Inside the attics there'll be skylights out onto the roofs themselves. The parapets are little flat roofs wide enough to walk along, from what I can see from below from the exercise yard. Find those ceiling hatches and we might be onto something.*

Vern nods his head, his smile broadening. *Nice work already, Trev. Ah'll get some o' the boys tae start keepin' an eye oot. Could be hid in the screws' offices or something. Ah kennt ye wur a smart cookie. Anyone calls you an English cunt from noo oan ye send him tae me, right?*

Sure thing, Vern. Trevor answers with his best macho voice, waits for the door to close then runs over to his bucket to enjoy a long piss of relief.

*

One night Ailee is eating alone in a small trattoria near her apartment that she often frequents after work. A handsome young man bumps into her table by accident and apologises profusely. Catching her accent he immediately draws her into a conversation in English. He is charming and amusing and asks surprisingly little about her life before, asking only about the university and what she teaches there. Before she knows it he has sat down to eat with her and they talk for several hours. As they leave the trattoria together and he asks if they will meet again she simply indicates that she tends to go there every second or third night.

They begin to meet regularly, twice a week. His name is Carlo and he claims to be a tour guide keen to improve his conversational English. He laments how slow business is in the off-season, how oppressive Perugia can be in Winter when darkness comes early and cold winds whistle through the hilltop streets. Clara Connelly born in Glasgow, Carlo Esposito born in Milan. Flattered, she begins to feel a slight flutter of some romantic impulse, but all of it reminds her of Trevor, about whom she can never speak. She mentions her husband and grown-up children instead, safer territory. He tells her about his childhood growing up in a poor suburb of Milan. They take walks around the old town in which he points out hidden attractions, historical sites off the usual tourist itineraries.

Finally she asks him back to her place for coffee one night and leaves him in her living room for a few moments. Ailee comes back from the toilet sooner than he expects and catches him rifling through her belongings. Startled he flees, taking with him photographs and documents, some of which might prove who she is. She pursues him through a maze of narrow alleyways then down the impossibly long flight of stairs of the Via Appia under a full moon, calling after him: *Aiuti! Fermalo! Torna Qui!* then: *Vaffanculo, testa di cazzo!* as she finally runs out of breath. He escapes along the Via dell'Acquedotto. Was he just a common thief and conman, or something else? A reporter sent to try to track her down? – To unearth the false identity of the once briefly-famous archaeologist who betrayed her own country? Ailee worries that her cover may be blown, but knows she can't return to Scotland while Drest remains in power.

*

What is Hell? Does it exist, on earth or in the afterlife? The murderous Border guards Hugh McDaid and Geordie Armstrong, colleagues of the late Lachlan Graham, have now been convicted and handed down life sentences, in no small part due to the evidence uncovered by Charlie Doohan and Val Breshkov. Ben Woolf has been pardoned and released. Now in turn, President Fiona Drest is at last asked to stand in the dock as the Judge reads out the charges against her: *Conspiracy to defeat the ends of justice. Violation of the oaths of honour pertaining to the role of commander and chief. Unlawful destruction of state records. Witness tampering. Conspiracy to misappropriate state funds to administer a private army. Sedition and Treason by virtue of seeking to circumvent the terms of the Scottish constitution with regard to election law and to defeat the ends of democracy. Do you understand the charges brought against you? How do you plead?*

Drest looks down at her feet, takes a deep breath and pictures her two children, her husband now also in custody. She is filled with hatred for all her political rivals who have contrived and collaborated with each other to bring her to this pass. Already she sees herself as some kind of tragic hero to be admired by future generations. Someone who expanded her country's borders and made it feel proud of itself again. How like the Scots to turn on one of their own like this, she tells herself. She won't go quietly. The trial will last month after month as she takes her pound of flesh from every knave with their knife in her.

Outside: the world's press wait to gloat and catch fleeting images of her taken away each day in the police van. It has been agreed in advance that they will spare her the handcuffs. No one wants the unsavoury image of a Scottish leader reduced to a common criminal. Likewise they shall doubtless spare her jail, her lawyers reassure her. Although there may be The Hague, the International Court of Justice, to contend with. The wolves of justice are only just getting started.

*

What is Hell? Does it exist, on earth or in the afterlife? Perhaps Hell must always be our ultimate fear come true. On the roof of Provanmill HSI, with the riot police climbing up and out to apprehend him, Trevor finds his only route of escape is to leap across a chasm onto a neighbouring building, as one of his fellow ring-leaders has just done, as another one behind expects him to do also. Trevor decides not to even look over the parapet, but to take a few steps back and then run at maximum speed towards the leap. At first he is confident that he will be able to make it, but time alters as he approaches the edge, seconds telescope into hours in which he sees his fate unfolding and yet is unable to escape it. In these endless moments he remembers his childhood fear, his recurring nightmare of falling, recalls telling Ailee about it in one of their conversations together, naked in bed. But everything is too late. It is dark, but the full moon is emerging as he reaches the edge and leaps out, out into the abyss, arms and legs flailing, hoping that he will reach the other roof but realising that his trajectory has been too weak, too stumbling, that he has failed, that he will fall, that his life will now end. To his surprise, once he sees that his fingers will not even scrape the opposite parapet, that he will have no struggle or dilemma, he feels a tremendous sense of relaxation, of giving up. It is akin to the mysterious sensation he felt across the years every time he sat on a passenger aeroplane as it lifted off from the runway. The knowledge that responsibility for your own life has momentarily, finally, been taken out of your own hands. A merciful, magnificent, release. All he hopes for is that there will be no pain.

~

XIII

It takes six months of Socialist Party government in Scotland for Ailee to finally have her extradition order rescinded and be able to return to her homeland with a new identity. She and her lawyer visit the public reception wing of Provanmill prison in order to claim Trevor's personal effects. She presents various proofs of her true ID and signs the relevant forms, only briefly taking off her dark glasses to allow the clerk to compare her to her passport photo. Within the box handed to Ailee are the deeds for the plot of land Trevor bought for her in the far north. The paperwork notes that there is a small cottage on the land in not irretrievably derelict condition. They are led out to a small graveyard for those prisoners who died in custody without any relatives to claim their remains. Trevor's place is marked by a simple white cross and silver name plate, beneath which Ailee leaves a bouquet of flowers.

*

It takes another two months before Val Breshkov decides to leave her air-car in Inverness and hire a land car for the rest of the way north, anxious not to draw any attention to Ailee's new location. She enjoys travelling through terrain at eye-level for a change, experiencing the drama of Scotland's Highlands, the snow-capped peaks soaring above placid blue lochs along whose edge passenger trains crawl like caterpillars, or worms in the carcass of some vast brown beast awakening slowly from the last chill of winter.

The site is spectacular, on a hillside above Bonar Bridge, with a sweeping view down towards where the Kyle of Sutherland and the Dornoch Firth meet and the river Carron snakes away south like festival bunting celebrating their union. An auspicious confluence of three water bodies, no doubt of great significance to prehistoric peoples. The cottage on the other hand, is a somewhat dismal prospect, clearly badly needing many years work and thousands of Euros to bring it back to an acceptable contemporary standard of accommodation. But as Breshkov trudges up the dirt track towards it, she smiles to see that Ailee is labouring away outside with her hair tied-up, repainting the white render, while several joiners work at installing a delivery of new windows. One of them spots Breshkov and nudges his employer to tell her that she has a visitor arriving. Ailee almost drops her paintbrush, before wrapping it in a rag, laying it down then running to embrace Breshkov.

I'm so sorry about Trevor, Ailee. Breshkov says over her shoulder as they embrace. *I know I've said that already in messages, but I wanted to say it again in person, face to face.*

Let's not talk about it, Val. It's just too painful, to be honest, even still. Come on into the house, the back room is good now, the place will be brand new by the end of this summer. He bought this piece of land for both of us you know, to build a house on together, but I decided I rather like this old wreck. The stone must hold so many memories of past generations. Folks who had a harder time of it than any of us. It seems disrespectful just to pull places like this down.

Seated at the kitchen table with a steaming mug of coffee, Breshkov can't help but return to the subject of absent friends. *If only our original idea had worked out that Trevor would join you in Italy. If only Drest had released him in return for Caius Flavius' body coming back to Scotland.*

Yes, but the vengeful bitch wouldn't have any of it.

And the Italians became rather reluctant to part with their archaeological windfall once the reality sunk in.

Pope Gregory promised otherwise.

So you were shafted by the Pope? That's a perverse claim to fame… Breshkov chuckles.

Not that unusual, as it happens, if you know your medieval history, Ailee sighs.

Negotiations are still ongoing though, aren't they?

Like the negotiations to return the Elgin Marbles to Greece, or Northumberland to the English, eh? Funny, how the Socialist post-Drest government has denounced her policies while hanging on to her ill-gotten gains, isn't it?

Breshkov stands up and goes to the window to enjoy the view up the hill to the windblown Scots Pines and gorse and heather. *Politics, bargaining chips, facts on the ground. Nothing changes, Ailee. The Romans would recognise themselves in all of us. Caius would confirm as much, no doubt, if he were with us today.*

Do you think anyone, any bog body, will ever be brought back to life again, Val? Ailee asks, pouring them both more coffee.

Not now that it's firmly against the new international laws. Therefore not legally at least. A body as well-preserved as Caius' was an extremely rare find. I suppose some rogue lunatics might attempt it at some point in future decades, like the Isaiah Cult human cloning incident in 2053, that sort of thing. But the fanaticism of such people usually also leads to them being easily found out, it's intrinsic to the paradigm, as they say.

Weren't we fanatics, in our own way, Val? Looking back on it?

Breshkov returns to the table to lock eyes with Ailee. *Funny you should say that, Ailee. There's something I've been wanting to ask you. Weren't they great days? Don't you look back on them with joy? What I'm trying to say, is to ask you to consider coming back, coming out of retirement, to return to the field.*

Oh no. No. Not a chance, Val. I did enough harm as it was. I want no more part of all that moral morass again. No more grave robbing for me.

Wait. All I ask is wait. Don't say definitively no, until you've heard me out, because I have some confidential news that may interest you a great deal.

Really? Well, I'm all ears.

We've finally located a third bog body. The Celtic warrior girl who was leading the pursuit against Caius and his party. I had to purchase that house near the site and get planning permission to demolish it first. These things take time. Her location had drifted over the centuries. Even bogs have currents apparently, very slow ones, that can pull in unexpected directions.

Ailee shrugs. *Is Drest still in prison? She will be so pleased. Just what she was always hoping for. A window into our gloriously heroic Pictish past.*

You're sounding cynical and dismissive, Ailee, but you don't fool me. I've known you for too long.

Knew me, Val. Knew me, past tense. I've changed and moved on. Got my fingers burnt, if you want to look at it that way.

It doesn't fascinate you? Breshkov stands and paces the room. *That chance to explore and unravel the mind of one of your ancestors? A so-called savage barbarian, who had the balls to take on the might of the Roman empire? And a woman to boot, in stark contrast to the Roman patriarchy, a product of a matrilinear society in which women held equal status to men, were trained to be just as good fighters? Don't even answer me, Ailee. Do me the favour of silence for now. Just think about it for a couple of weeks.*

Ailee laughs. *Silence, eh? Not much of an ask or a gift. But one I've come to regard as golden. What do you think of my new house, by the way? I've still got some painting to do upstairs, and I've got big plans for the garden. Maybe even a vegetable patch, some poly-tunnels. Although the winters are pretty harsh here, but this is a good south-facing hillside. There are iron-age hut circles up the hill there you know, buried remnants of them, further up among the moorland. So our ancestors must have thought it was good fertile spot too I suppose.*

Ahh... you see? Always the archaeologist at heart really, aren't you?

Heart... but my heart was broken, Val. I'll never forget

that I was supposed to share all this with... well, you know who.

Maybe in time you might meet someone again, Ailee. You're still on the young side to be a retiree by today's standards.

I don't think so. I enjoy the peace and quiet here. And I feel sometimes as if I carry him around with me like a parrot on my shoulder. I hear him talk to me, inside my head.

I was divorced last year you know, single again, but I'm planning to remarry later this year. It's not good for anyone to be alone too long, in my humble opinion.

Congratulations. Who's the lucky girl?

Guy. It's a guy this time, Ailee.

Oh really? I've no idea how all that works I'm afraid, but I'm glad for you, although I don't understand.

No need to, it's okay. You just need to understand love, and clearly you do. It's about the person, not the gender.

I've said it before I know, but you should write a book, Val, you must have had one hell of an interesting life so far.

Well, you're working on a book yourself aren't you?

That's strange, I don't remember mentioning that to you...

Ahh... I still have my contacts on the ground here and there, Ailee. I look forward to reading it. And hoping you're not too hard on me.

How are the old crew these days, do you stay in touch? Strang, Bruce, Sonja?

Bruce served time for his involvement with you and Trevor of course, for providing technical expertise. Served eighteen months I think. But he's gone to ground since his release. Maybe a new identity, like the one you have, I don't know. He could find me if he wanted to, so I presume he doesn't. Ed runs my European operation now, although he talks a lot about retirement. Sonja is a television presenter, a celebrity almost these days, who'd have thought it? We exchange the occasional email, talk of meeting up but never do.

Will you ever retire do you think, Val?

Ha! Like you, do you mean? Run away and hide from the world? Fat chance.

You'll die on the job then I suppose, as it were. Ever wonder if someone will revive you in a thousand years?

Breshkov visibly shivers for effect. *Cremation for me, mate, the will's got it covered. Oh, before I forget, do you know we discovered something really strange when we were going over the memory tapes of Caius and the auxiliary after you left.*

What?

There were reports along the wall of soldiers seeing strange lights and objects at night, what we'd call UFOs or UAPs today, flying saucers basically. The auxiliary we dug up even saw one first hand and we analysed it carefully. Guess what?

No guesses please, Val.

I reckon it was us, the archaeopod. It was as if they could somehow see us from back in time, as if our dipping into their minds sent back a ghost of us into their consciousness. Isn't that a mind-blowing idea?

Very. But hard to scientifically prove, surely? But I see where you're going with that. Like Schrödinger's cat, as if the observer changes the scene by virtue of the observation. But if that was true... oh wait a minute, you think...?

I don't know what to think. But just imagine if people from the future have been coming back to look at us, or are probing some of our dead brains right now.

An astonishing theory... Ailee involuntarily shudders. *But I hope you're wrong. I don't like that idea one bit. I might go for the cremation myself come to think about it. But you've reminded me of something else... about the events that led up to Caius' death, his first death. He tried to talk about it every so often, but always became agitated, upset. It was something about the adopted native girl that he was asked to teach, and a female leader of the Damnonii whose name he kept saying: Dorcla. It was like a password, it seemed to unlock some kind of unresolved longing and panic. He said we should look for her, whatever that meant. Could this possibly be connected with your discovery, the third body?*

It's possible, yes. We've still to lift the body, but we expect it to be Damnonii from all the scans and clues we have so far.

*

As Breshkov is leaving the next morning, Ailee asks her: *Val, why were you asking me that stuff about my being single, looking for love again?*

Breshkov smiles enigmatically. *Oh, just curious, on behalf of a friend.*

Who?

Oh, you'll see. Soon I hope.

After Breshkov leaves, Ailee feels confused and unsettled, haunted by the past. She goes for a long walk in the woods above her land. After half a mile she chances upon a configuration of puddles in the rough dirt track that catch her eye. Something odd happens in the sky overhead, perhaps a sudden darkening of clouds or a rain squall, but when she looks back down again she seems to see something strange in the water. She rubs her eyes and asks herself what it was. Faces, two of them. Caius and Trevor. Impossible. Hallucination. Living alone for too long in introspection. She returns to the third puddle and peers down into it and there is her own face, or is it? She seems changed, as if some other face is looking through her. She tries to look closer, but the wind picks up and disturbs the surface, returning all three portals to the usual vista of surly Scottish skies.

*

In the evening of that same day, while sitting at her desk writing her journal, Ailee receives a video call from her daughter Onya in Australia. *Mum, is that you? Can you hear me?*

Onya! Perfectly dear, what are you doing in that white gown? Are you in hospital? Are you hurt or something?

No, Mum. I am hurting, but only for good healthy reasons. Take a look at this... She swings a tiny newborn baby into view. *This is your granddaughter, born two hours ago. We're both doing well. She's perfect.*

Oh my god. That's marvellous. Look at her lovely little face. Her wiggling her toes. What is her name?

Shona, we're calling her Shona. It means gracious and merciful, apparently. Onya smiles very broadly.

You look exhausted you poor thing. Are you alright? Was the birth difficult?

Not at all. It all went like clockwork the doctors said. She started coming about six o' clock this morning. It's nine o' clock here now. Vincent is here too, I'll let him wave to you.

The boyfriend waves politely but stays diplomatically in the background. *Do you forgive me, Mum?* Onya asks, when she's alone again.

Forgive you for what? Ailee gasps, tears of joy on her cheeks.

You know, all the stuff. What I said about that bloke of yours, what was he called? English name, began with a T...

Ailee looks up from her desk to see a beautiful white crescent moon sailing amid the pink and gold cirrostratus clouds above the ancient twin peaks of Carn Bhrain and Carn Salachaidh, noble native faces sculpted by glaciers. For a moment she wants to tell Onya that Trevor died and how, but then realises she doesn't even want to say his name. That somehow even that is her property now. Just as some north American native tribes believed: perhaps even to speak the name of the dead is to risk disturbing their rest.

Mum?

There's nothing to forgive, Onya, nothing at all. When there's nothing left to learn from the past, we need to learn to leave it alone.

Sure, Mum. But I was sure it began with a T.

Tacitus... Ailee smiles sadly, wiping her eye. *It's Latin. It means he who is silent. And now he is.*

*

The next morning, Ailee is woken by a gentle knocking at her front door. She assumes it is one of her helpful neighbours on the hillside, come to offer her free eggs or retrieve their sheep from her fields. When she opens the door, a tall middle-aged man with shoulder-length white hair is standing there with his back turned, gazing out over her land towards the twin peaks across the Kyle of Sutherland. He turns around, and as he does so, the world drops into slow motion, Ailee hearing only her own heartbeat, the blood beating in her ears. His smile is like the dawn sun breaking through clouds after a long cold night. She lets out a small involuntary scream before their embrace envelops her like a tidal wave, both of their chests heaving with sobs. All the pain the world has done to them can be confronted at last, the indignation faced up to. Life, whatever that is or means, knows better than either of them. They prise each other apart to paw each other's faces in disbelief. *This is impossible, how can it be you, Trevor? Are we dreaming?*

One good resurrection deserves another... he laughs. *Breshkov sure pulls some strings in high places. My coffin is empty and long may it remain so. You can call me Terrence Wilson now, by the way, miss Clara Connelly I believe?*

Let's drink to that, shall we? She takes his hand as he closes the door behind them then kisses his fingers, running them under her nose, breathing deep to take in his smell, the glorious evidence of flesh in animation.

*

Through the telephoto lens of her camera, Kirsty Denholm watches Trevor and Ailee embracing on the threshold of her house before vanishing inside.

I do like a story with a happy ending... Ben Woolf says, seated next to her in his air car, skilfully concealed behind a copse of Scots Pines at a safe distance from Ailee's land. *When we going to run this story then?*

We're not, I'm afraid, not yet anyway. –Kirsty answers.

What? Why not? Not even interview Kenzie? Scoop of the century. What the hell have we come here for then?

I thought you enjoyed your chat with your ex jailbird chum, Ben. You and he seemed to have a good old laugh all the way up from Stirling.

True. Shit like that binds men together. Although I was only in his wing for a couple of weeks, truth be told. His wing man, as it were. Shall we head back south then, you strapped in?

As Ben takes the air car up and they hurtle south over mountains and lochs, ridges and estuaries, Kirsty begins talking with increasing nervousness, rambling, puzzling Ben with her tone: *They looked so sweet and happy there, the pair of them, didn't they? Back from the dead. A new identity, a fresh start, starting over, a blank slate. It's what we all want in a way, isn't it? Life accumulates so much baggage. I agreed we'd take him up as a favour to Charlie Doohan. He didn't think dropping Lazarus off in a Panda wagon was going to be the done thing.*

What do you owe Charlie Doohan, Kirsty? Ben looks askance at her.

Everything, if you must know, absolutely everything.

Oh yeah? How so?

It was him that gave me the Border atrocities story, as you know, me out of a hundred other journalists he could have gone to.

Such as me, for instance.

Well, actually, in a way he did give it you, through me, Ben.

My own stupid fault for raiding your handbag, Kirsty. You forgiven me for that yet?

Actually, Ben... her voice starts to shake. *It's you who I should be asking to forgive me.*

What? Ben feels confused. *What are you saying?* He looks sideways at her for so long that he swerves the air car's controls for a moment.

To his amazement and disquiet Kirsty begins to cry, her

chest rising and falling in sobs of sorrow, her hands dabbing at her eyes but unable to stem the flow.

Disturbed and distraught at this spectacle, Ben brings the air car down to an emergency landing on the nearest mountain top, his wing even clipping a tree. He turns round to face her, reaching out his hand to touch her cheek. *What the hell's wrong, Kirsty? Talk to me, will you? Explain.*

I put you in prison, Ben... She blurts out. *It was my fault. Charlie and I agreed that we would set you up to use the story first so that you could take any heat for us, as a decoy while we went on digging up more facts. We knew you'd look at those notes I left within your reach. I'm so, so sorry...*

I see... Ben says slowly, as her weeping continues, feeling like his head is about to explode with indigestible facts. He thinks for a minute, rubbing his eyes. *You ruined my life then... I served nine months for you. Not as long as Trevor right enough, but still pretty bad. And at least he did it voluntarily, in a way. Nine months. I still have nightmares, probably always will. You brought me here to confess. I really ought... ought... to really hate you. If I had any sense.*

Kirsty keeps crying for another minute before Ben continues his train of thought aloud: *...If I had any sense. Except that I don't. Hey don't be daft, come here.* He embraces her and she lays her head on his shoulder, burying her sobs in his flight jacket. The scent of her hair, the feeling of her body against his provokes a revelation in him, as he sits and reflects. It occurs to him that he stands at a crossroads in his life, a dangerous one. *I don't regret any of it...* he finally adds *...because I helped bring down a tyrant and... it brought you and me together.*

I'm so sorry... is all the words Kirsty can find to repeat.

Let's get some fresh air for a moment, Ben says after a further minute, stepping out of the vehicle. He looks back at the broken tree they have collided with, inspects the minor damage to the car, then gazes up at the April morning sky, the wisps of thin white cloud up above, finely whisked by high-altitude winds. He experiences some kind of flash-forward, the momentary insight that he will come this way on foot in some future year and see this tree here again. He can see the tourist path leading here. They have alighted on a mountain top, some minor peak, not even a Munro. Will he come here with his wife and remember to himself with a romantic twinge this moment and a path not taken, an avenue of possibility with Kirsty? Or will he come here with Kirsty herself to this unlikely monument to when they first kissed and threw in their lot together? What is he even doing here after all, on a day out like this in his free time with Kirsty, while Rachel knows nothing about it?

What are you thinking about? –Kirsty asks, emerging from the car and coming to join him.

Oh, I don't know… he sighs, still staring at the broken half of the tree, as if struck by lightning, except it has been struck by them. *Maybe how we think we have choices in life, when actually we probably don't. How maybe it's all decided by fate or some obscure creative force up there or down below or whatever the hell you believe in.*

What choices? Kirsty asks, but he is still so deep in thought that he ceases to hear her. To be alone or in company. To be with one lover or another. To hurt one person or another. To stand up for what you feel or believe in, or spend the rest of your life as a regretful coward. The dilemma never grows old.

~

XIV

We see what Caius sees. On clear summer days surveying the western half of the wall of Antoninus Pius under construction. He squints through brass dodecahedra on oak tripods at the snaking line over green hills and glens. To mark out each milestone for the sweating legionaries to carve and celebrate their progress.

One evening he is on watch on the parapet near the fort at Medio. He asks Marcus Claudius, a fellow centurion from Etruria, about the barbarian tribes that have been increasingly harrying them with nocturnal raids. *The ones directly to our north here are called the Damnonii I believe...* Marcus explains, *...which supposedly means those who dwell in the deep. Although Jupiter knows why, since they seem to live on the high ground on the opposite side of this valley. I half wonder if they hail from the underworld itself. They are insidious, cunning, cowardly by Roman standards. By day they play innocent, even trade with us sometimes but...*

Marcus never finishes his sentence on account of a barbarian spear lodged in his neck. All Hades breaks loose as soldiers run to and fro with fire balls incoming overhead and droves of savages rushing the defences. By morning twenty soldiers have been killed, a dozen wounded. A bathhouse and barracks burnt down, a well poisoned.

*

In retribution the next day Caius is ordered to lead a cohort out into Damnonii territory, to burn their crops and salt their fields, raze any village within three miles radius, kill or take prisoner any foolish enough not to flee. As he approaches they mysteriously disappear before his men can gain the high plain on which their settlement sits. He sends lookouts to climb the surrounding ridges who are unable to see evidence of them escaping on horseback, even when they set fire to each surrounding wood. He wonders if they have vanished into the boglands and swum for it, where his men might be unable to follow with their armour and cavalry.

Content with having despoiled the settlement and its fields, they have begun the march home to the wall when something very curious happens. Entering a clearing at the head of his infantry Caius finds a young Damnonii girl, not more than five years old, who has dismounted from a little white pony and is playing with a fox cub in her arms. Halting his men, he approaches her alone, looking around, uncertain how to proceed. Before he can address her in Latin or her own tongue two adults emerge suddenly from the undergrowth as if guarding her, raising their spears. He draws his sword and orders them to surrender, pointing to the soldiers behind him, how vastly they outnumber them. But to his amazement the men run at him undeterred, as if suicidal. He raises his shield to deflect both spear throws. One man he slays himself with a gladius thrust to the stomach, the other falls with a Roman arrow through his neck before he is even within reach. The little girl appears startled but sits down rather than runs, cradling her fox cub. Her white pony neighs in alarm but is unable to break its skilful tether. His men find two other ponies nearby, take the girl and the three mounts and one fox cub back to the wall. He presents them to his legion commander at the fort at Litana, who gently mocks him, having expected slaves and the heads of a few chieftains. There is something haunting about the little girl, otherworldly. She neither cries nor speaks, makes only the slightest attempt to resist capture.

*

Time passes. Strange areas of darkness erased by monotony in Caius' memory. Until he is summoned one spring day, to meet his legion commander Valerius Messallinus at his villa in the rising shadow of the new wall, almost at final completion.

Retrovival

Salve, Caius. I want you to meet Commodus Petrovius, a venerable scholar who has been resident here these last two years in our new town of Litana. All the way from Rome, a man who has spent time in the company of great men such as Tacitus and Agricola, and wishes to study life on our northern frontier.

Caius notes Petrovius' startlingly white robes with gold and crimson lines and trims. *Perhaps you have heard, Centurion, rumours no doubt, that my wife Silvana was somewhat smitten at first sight at the little barbarian girl that you and your men brought back here a year or two ago?*

Caius bows then straightens his back, clicking his heels together. *I did hear something to that effect, sir, and I wondered what noble house could have been so benevolent as to take her in.*

Not just taken in, we have adopted her formally these last six months. She will live not as a slave but as a free woman. She is as bright as a polished aureus, has learned the Latin tongue in a remarkably short time. We are anxious that she should learn to write it also, and we wondered if you might be willing to help?

Me? Forgive my impertinence, sir, but have you not slaves who could teach her better than a soldier like me?

You are too modest I fear, centurion. I gather you are somewhat more than just a soldier. Half of the men under you cannot read at all, while you hail from an old patrician family I am told, and are adept at mathematics and geometry, both of which I would also like my adopted daughter to learn. I believe my great grandfather may even have been an associate of your great uncle back in the glory days of the republic. Strabo Marcellus of Vulci?

That is remarkable, sir, I had no idea that my family history had preceded me to this far flung corner of the empire.

You mentioned slaves... Petrovius continues, *and in a way you have hit on one of the main issues at the heart of this, Caius. I trust slaves to wash my children and my animals, to prepare my meals, but Varinia's education strikes me as another matter. She is an intensely inquisitive girl, and she would doubtless question any educated slave when I was not within earshot on all the details of barbarian life they had left behind them... and winkle it out of them. She has already a knack for that, a trait of her blossoming personality, and this I do not wish. Do you get the drift of my argument?*

I think I do, sir. I would be able to tell her only very little of her tribe since I know little myself. All I would talk of is Rome, my fond memories of it and my admiration for the glories of its civilisation. Such might keep her eyes turned towards the future rather than the past.

Precisely, precisely, Caius Flavius, I see my intuition was correct then, that you may indeed be the perfect man for this role. You are too valuable to be wasted on the frontline, pacing the battlements all day long. At any rate, things have been quiet between us and the Damnonii your good commander reassures me, these last six months. – That they have returned to their recovered land and sought to open diplomatic channels with us, pleading that they were unjustly punished for the attack on the wall, which they claim was actually perpetrated by their eastern neighbours; the Votadini, on a passing raid. We are investigating the possible veracity of that. But should this current peace cease to be the case then you may return to soldiering of course at a minute's notice in any emergency. But until then I would wish to place my daughter's education in your charge.

I am greatly surprised, sir, but greatly honoured.

Good. It is agreed then. Oh and one further thing, Caius. If the child ever asks for details of the circumstances in which you and your men captured her, will you hold your tongue until discussing the matter with me? I am uncertain whether she remembers a thing of that day or its aftermath, which is probably for the best. But if she is to learn anything of it then I fancy that the knowledge must be imparted only gently and guardedly. We are making a little Roman of her, and I would hate to squander our progress with a few rash words that might enflame whatever traces of the savage still persist within her.

*

Caius is teaching Varinia Latin declensions: *Singular: aqua, aquae, aquae, aquam, aqua... Now Plural: aquae, aquarum, aquis, aquas, aquis...*

Desinamus nunc, quaeso, quaeso! —She begs and breaks into tears. *It is so boring and long-winded, master Caius. It tires me out. Why is it so complicated? My own language was not like this.*

Caius frowns, then softens, takes down a scroll of pictures from her father's shelves to show her. He unrolls it and points to drawings of Roman viaducts and theatres, paintings of sophisticated aristocrats in impressive robes. *Complicated language is required for complicated ideas and great inventions. I am forbidden to speak to you of your people, but suffice to say that they will never build wonders like those of Rome while they are inhibited by primitive language and backward superstitions.*

She looks at him wide-eyed for a moment. *You know something of my people? How do you know that their gods are not more powerful than yours?*

Because they have no inventions, no machines. Look at this room for instance, glass in the windows, hot air rising through the floor in the depths of winter, hot water available any time you want to bathe. The written wisdom of great scholars a thousand years dead for you to read and learn from.

Varinia stands and goes to the window and runs her fingers across the glass. *It is a wonder to behold, I must confess. Like ice that never melts. How is this miracle achieved, can you explain it?*

Sand heated to very high temperature in a mould I believe, so that it loses all its colour, then allowed to cool into a sheet.

And you give this knowledge out freely? —Don't seek to conceal it as a sacred rite?

No, why should we?

In case your enemies use it?

They lack our organisation and industry, the power and experience to make use of the formula. They lack Latin, and thereby mathematics and geometry, as I am trying to tell you.

Varinia smiles to herself then turns away from the window. *And what if I told you that my people have other secrets and other powers, bestowed on them by their gods, things that Romans will never understand?*

How would you know? You were only five summers old when you came here to Litana.

You were there? You remember me? —She suddenly asks him urgently, locking eyes with him.

Caius nods, wary that he has been drawn into forbidden territory by her curiosity, just as he was warned. To his discomfort she moves closer to him and leans down to sniff his arms and his neck, before he recoils in alarm. *Please...* he rasps... *I am forbidden to discuss that with you. You must forget your barbarian past, miss.*

Her green eyes flare. *I remember you. Your smell. It was you who first lifted me up and carried me as a child, was it not?*

He says nothing, but she laughs at what she sees clearly in his eyes. *At this very moment I think you would love to be able to use one of the powers my people have, master. That of invisibility. The power to disappear at will and reappear whenever and wherever they wish. You did not know about that did you?*

Caius sighs and taps his hand on the slate and chalk and bids her sit down again at the table with him. *Those are the fantasies of a child I think, just as Roman children have, and all children everywhere have had since the dawn of time, miss. You are no different. Unless you study and learn now. When you go to Rome one day you will be something then, the wife of a great statesman or general perhaps, with a hundred slaves, a hundred dresses in finest silk and ermine.*

She laughs and looks at him sceptically. *The Chinese*

have kept their secret of silk-making from you, I am told. And as for an ermine, I would rather have one alive to play with as my pet.

*

One evening at Petrovius' villa, Caius hesitates before knocking on the door of the tablinum, and hears Petrovius inside talking heatedly to someone. Before retreating he can't help eavesdropping part of their conversation which both disturbs and fascinates him:

Perhaps this wall should never have been built, if it is only to be abandoned so soon. What damned fool ordered it be raised in wood and turf rather than stone anyway?

Who do you think? If you hang around the senate long enough, you learn that this epithet of 'Pius' he goes by is a joke against him which he is too fool to understand.

Careful, Sextus, treasonous talk does not befit you.

But it is true. He is weak, no warrior at heart. He thought his wall would impress the natives into surrender, can you believe it? Would impress them with our technology. You would almost think he was a Christian, the way he goes on. Peace makes a man soft, and no less so an emperor.

*

Varinia's affinity with animals has become her most notable quirk, which the household slaves often pause to wonder and laugh about. When her fox puppy grew old and died she begged for others to be brought to her until two wolfhound puppies were given to Petrovius by a visiting senator. Then a kitten was forwarded from the fort commander at Credigone, which she taught to bring her mice alive that she could play with, much to the horror of Silvana, the mother of the household. She found a way to tame wood doves and blackbirds landing on the parapets of the Petrovius villa, with caraway seeds. Until they would eat from her hands, let her carry them about on her shoulders.

One morning arriving early to speak with Petrovius

before Varinia's lesson, Caius finds his pupil kneeling down among a circle of wood doves in the courtyard. He walks quietly up behind her to see what she is doing. He notices her unwinding some sort of scroll from around the leg of a particularly white dove. She suddenly becomes aware of him and is startled, standing up and scattering the birds in panic as she conceals something behind her back.

What is it? Caius asks, intrigued by her blushing. He holds out his hand. *Let me see. You write Latin poems to your beloved pigeons?* He has to hold her hand and prise her fingers open in order to obtain the piece of vellum. But all she has written is a series of strange lines and ticks such as a prisoner might leave on a prison wall to count the days. He snorts. *Next you will be telling me that your have mastered the language of the birds!*

She laughs and snatches the script away in seeming relief. *But I have, I have! Watch this! Ad me volare, ave!*

The white dove hesitates for only an instant from where it has been watching from the roof tiles, then swoops down to land in her hand.

In Latin. You have taught them Latin! –Caius exclaims.

She smiles very broadly and he is melted by her blossoming beauty in the morning sun. *You approve?*

I approve... Caius chuckles. *They were more obedient pupils than you I would wager.*

*

Caius wakes the next morning at his barracks, troubled by the memory of the strange marks on the vellum scroll. Feeling unable to ask Petrovius himself, he rides east instead, along the wall to the fort at Pexa, where he has heard that another scholar is stationed, a specialist in languages. The man lives modestly in a wooden shack close to the fort, and they take to each other immediately. After exchanging pleasantries over bread and olives, Caius raises his question: *Do the barbarians have a written language here?*

Some of them perhaps, we believe, although it is not certain. –Felix Decidius answers.

You have found examples of their script then, where?

Carved on monument stones, commemorating ancient battles we suspect, or perhaps honouring ancestors.

Do you have any examples you could show me?

Felix stands and begins to rummage through his shelves of wicker baskets. *No original stones, no, they are all too cumbersome to move, but I have rubbings, and a few drawings by others. Look, here...*

Caius reaches his hand out, tracing the distinctive lines in the air over the scroll Felix unwinds. *What is it called?*

Ogham, we believe, the written word of the Celtic tongue. But few of them know it. We suspect it is only their priest class who are taught how to make it and decipher it.

Druids you mean?

Perhaps, sometimes they look a little different from the commoner stock.

How so?

Paler, smoother skin. They leave the physical toil to others, their concerns are all spiritual and ceremonial, although they do not hesitate to cut throats and stomachs for sacrifices, and not just those of animals so the rumours go.

Could I make a copy of this?

Of course.

Has any Roman decoded this language yet?

Felix shakes his head. *Sadly not. We have so many other more pressing priorities on this frontier. Their priests would never divulge such a thing, if that is what you are wondering. Sacred knowledge, forbidden to us, the crimson plumes.* Felix laughs bitterly. *They would die to a man before they told you stuff like that. Death means nothing to them it seems, their lives are cheap.*

Yes... so I have noticed. –Caius mumbles dejectedly, before thanking the scholar and turning to go, then pauses at the door. *Oh, could I ask you a favour, brother? That you speak no word of our conversation on this matter after today?*

Drop by again some time! Felix smiles in bemusement then gestures with his index finger twice: one swipe across his mouth, followed by another across his throat.

*

At a pause in her next lesson, Varinia speaks boldly to Caius. *My father said last night that I have long since come of age, whatever that means. That he plans to take me to Gaul next year then on to Rome to find me a husband among the patrician classes. What do you make of that, master Caius?*

Caius shrugs. *It is normal and healthy. Rome will amaze you. I hope your father and mother choose well in terms of finding you a fine husband.*

Damnonii women... she begins slowly.

Caius winces involuntarily. She has never before dared to use the name of the tribe in his presence.

She continues: *...may chose their husband, or several, have children by several. They may also become leaders, warriors, queens. They are not considered inferior in any way to their menfolk. Quite the reverse, because they can give birth to new life.*

Caius reddens with anger. *You read this somewhere?*

Yes. I have a free run of my father's library. Perhaps I am even becoming better read than you, master.

Caius shrugs again. *That would be no great achievement, I am only a soldier after all.*

To his astonishment she reaches out and touches his hand. *No, you are much more than that. And do you have a wife back in Rome? A childhood sweetheart who awaits you perhaps?*

Caius turns sideways in his chair and gazes out the window, somewhat discombobulated by this shift in their permitted areas of conversation, the nature of their relationship. *How could I? I have been here fifteen long years now, labouring on this god-forsaken wall and teaching you. Doubtless I will be recalled to Europe soon. One more campaign then I shall probably be ripe for retirement. Retired soldiers are much in demand among the young ladies I am told, for their pensions. I might raise a family of my own yet, if a barbarian spear does not catch me.*

Distracted by this rare interval of self-reflection, he finds himself absentmindedly drawing on the slate in front of him. Both he and Varinia seem to notice at the same moment that it is an Ogham inscription, the one he learned last week. With a sharp intake of breath she leaps up from her chair and storms out of the room in tears. Pursuing her a few minutes later, her slaves block the way and tell him she is taken ill and will not return to her lessons today.

*

We see what Varinia sees. For such was the name her Roman captors gave her, meaning virgin and pure, as befits a blonde child on a white pony. But that is not who she truly is. That is a thing she pretends to have forgotten but in fact guards closely, hidden deep down inside herself, a buried treasure.

Leaping from the wall at the pre-arranged location, Varinia rolls down the embankment, scales the ditch and finds the pony her people have left there for her at the agreed hour. She leaps onto its back and rides north hard and fast, leaving the wall behind in the darkness. As the first light of dawn breaks she rides not to the rebuilt Damnonii hamlet with its circle of stone roundhouses and thatched conical roofs, but further on to the thickly-wooded gorge a mile east. Within that a tortuous footpath leads down to a secret waterfall which in turn contains another secret. Behind the waterfall is the mouth of an ancient cave system carved out even before her father or grandfather's time. Tying her horse up at the edge of the gorge, she walks towards the waterfall, but before she has even had time to call out to him, her father emerges sideways from behind the screen of white water. They both break into uncertain smiles, half of pain, half of unbearable joy. The long ordeal of separation is over. They embrace and she hears him speak her true name again for the first time in twelve years: *Dorcla.* She gazes up at the blue sky and thanks all the gods for their benevolence, this proof that their lives mean something, that the stories they weave against the red-crests will be the basis of legend told by many generations to come.

I dreamed of you, father, every night, that you would come back for me. I dreamed you sent yourself in the form of an eagle to visit each window under which I slept.

I saw that you saw this, my daughter. Sometimes I was the raven with his wizened voice to call out news, other times I was the blackbird to soothe you with the beauty of his morning song. I put my soul into the eyes of many creatures that would reach you, and they brought me back news of your heart. I saw that you blossomed. I saw all.

My loneliness, father, my confusion and shame? How they tried to bleed the memory of you and our people out of my body and mind. How they wiped our language from my tongue. You saw all of this? Then you are still the greatest of wizards the Damnonii have ever known.

I saw all this and more, thanks be to you, for the messages you entrusted to the feathered breasts of wood doves. We see through your eyes the plans and schemes of the red-crests, we and our allies, all the tribes. And we draw our own plans against them that will soon be acted upon now that you are safely away from their fold. He sighs and pulls away from her for a moment, sits down on a boulder at the water's edge. She sits next to him and takes his hand before he continues: *But time is growing thin for me now, my child, I have grown older and sicker from the pain of our long separation. I am tired. You know the laws of our people, or may remember some echo of them at least. Soon my successor must take over, and your brother has been lost in the east these last five summers. The sequences of the moon portent of a time of women, in the wave of the great awakening that is to come. The power of the red-crests is weakening, their tide will soon ebb and we will drive them from this land like vermin. I will show you soon in the vision pools at the sacred place. But first you must follow me back into the heart of the hill where all of the family await your joyous homecoming. The invaders will doubtless seek us out in anger when they learn of your escape, but they will find only an empty village as before. Therefore must we retreat and renew our power in the sacred caves. Now take my hand and follow me, child, behind the curtain of immortal water.*

*

Craelmadrus, leader of the Damnonii, primes the altar with fresh bull's blood and sets the three ritual vision pools in motion. Then he lights a sheen of oil on their surface: three ancient circular depressions carved into the flat top of the enormous seer stone. As his hand passes over each they clear one by one, red dissolving to blue and white, reflected sky then moving vignettes of distant times and places. He muses aloud to his daughter: *Past, present and future: the three pools, men, women and the spirits; who are both gods and dead ancestors rolled into one, a great ocean of strength and knowing. Living people in touch with such voices have no fear of death, understand that their bodies are just the fingers of a great invisible hand that dips into the world in order to stir its waters. The Damnonii know they cannot die since the greater part of them always exists outside of the visible world in the reservoir of the spirit.*

Dorcla remembers her awe when watching this ceremony of her father's as a child. Soon it will be her role too and she must learn and master all his powers of prayer and divination. With the bull's blood she mixes the blood of a Roman soldier, recently captured, his entrails spread-eagled on the sacrifice stone behind them, long red tubes like tree roots teased out towards each of the four compass points. In the first pool she sees armies marching, their feet shaking the water's surface; in the second: fire and confusion followed by flight; in the third: the wild hunt as the old gods resume their mastery and the people their sacred lands.

*

Legate Valerius Messallinus summons Caius in the aftermath of the suspected abduction of Varinia, and addresses him: *You will have heard some rumours I imagine, Caius, regarding the disappearance of the adopted daughter of Petrovius last month, that she may have been abducted and so forth. I have to tell you, just between you and I, that all of that is pigswill unfortunately. Word has since been sent to us from the Damnonii to inform us that she fled to them of her own accord. What intelligence we have on the ground suggests that this may well be true. Furthermore the Damnonii have offered us some kind of negotiation, a deal if you will. That they will return Varinia to us in exchange for one of our soldiers. I would not normally entertain such nonsense of course, we could wipe out their entire race like rats if we set but half a legion loose on them. But Petrovius is a very influential intellectual, brother to a senator who can pull strings in Rome and is related to... well, as you know, I need not go on. We are obliged to try and get the little vixen back for him because the man is half mad with paternal love for her. Misplaced I would argue. Once a savage always a savage, it takes a couple of generations to civilise these people no matter how early you catch them. But that is just me, a military man and veteran of thirteen campaigns so what do I know? Will you do it, Caius? Do this thing for me, for Petrovius? You will be highly thought of for it, again, I should not wonder, in high places.*

Do what, sir? I suspect I have little choice despite your courtesy in citing some.

To ride out with a small delegation to meet an equal number of theirs on neutral territory and negotiate the exchange of one of our auxiliaries, a miserable little thug called Titus Britannicus, yes it does not even sound like his real name does it? He has been accused of raping a

Damnonii girl he encountered during a patrol. And while normally I would discount such accusations thrown around by natives, this man has a record of similar previous charges, and frankly getting him off our hands would probably suit me. They are promising not to kill him, but to make him marry the woman in question according to their laws. The height of black comedy, is it not? Except that it harms our reputation for discipline if we are not careful. Again in strictest confidence, Caius, I even foresee a chance this lout could prove a useful spy for us in future years if he settles in and the savages accept him. The Damnonii are a puzzle to us in many ways, and maybe another ear on the ground could unlock their mysterious machinations, their knack of appearing and disappearing like phantoms. Anyway, you know this girl Varinia well by now with having tutored her, perhaps she will be more at peace in returning to us under your guardianship. What do you say?

*

We see what Caius sees. He is riding out north again from the wall, a much smaller party this time, just himself as envoy, one fellow legionary and three milites. He has his doubts but must follow orders. He fears for his life, but finds himself vaguely uplifted nonetheless, at the prospect of seeing Varinia again. To be returned to her Roman father supposedly, although he wonders how that prospect strikes her. The agreed meeting place is in a circular clearing in the woods on the Damnonii side of the valley, within sight of both the wall and the barbarian's village. Both parties arrive as the sun reaches its zenith, the Romans on horses, the Damnonii on ponies. His fellow centurion, Quintus Amata, has been chosen because he has met the Damnonii leader before and identifies him at first sight to Caius. A tall elderly man with long white hair and beard, he reaches his hand out to the female rider at his side who Caius fails to recognise at first. Her hair has been cut and braided in the elaborate native style and her skin covered in numerous blue tattoos. Caius' milites bring forward their prisoner and push him into the centre of the circle, hands tied behind his back. Caius calls out to the rival party in Latin: *Rape is a crime in our culture just as it is in yours. By order of my legion commander, I offer you this soldier, so long as you spare his life, in return for Varinia, adopted daughter of a Roman scholar. Please bring forward the girl...*

The old man replies to them in pidgin Latin: *I, Craelmadrus, would give the order to comply with this bargain were I still leader of our people, Centurion, but I no longer am.* At this a dozen Damnonii men with spears appear from the undergrowth in the circle around the clearing and the Roman horses neigh and rear up in fear.

Impossible! –Quintus hisses, *I rode through that scrub a minute ago and beat it all clear.* As Caius turns he sees at last the key to all his puzzling: a Damnonii warrior carefully replacing a bundle of gorse over a rocky opening in the ground.

Caves... Caius replies to him. *Of course, a network of subterranean caves. No wonder they fight to the death. Ever tried to hunt a fox back to its lair?*

Look! Quintus bids him turn back around... *is the female in command?* Caius sees that the men halt where they stand, obeying the slightest hand signal from Varinia.

Varinia! Caius addresses her, calming his horse. *What madness is this? You must know that if we do not return unharmed then Rome will send a legion against you from the wall, slaughter every man, woman and child before sunset.*

Craelmadrus laughs. *You do not think that we might have legions too? Allies ready to fight with us? I am pleased to see that you address my daughter as leader, rather than myself, for such is her role now, her birthright. We thank you for taking care of her.*

You must know that such thanks ring hollow, if I am to return to the wall without her now. My masters will not settle for such an insult. If they spare my life it will only be if I promise to take scores of your lives in retribution.

Quintus whispers urgently at Caius' side: *We are*

doomed unless we skirmish now, flight is our best chance against these odds, if we make for the marsh.

Stay with us then... Varinia shouts back. *I offer you our hospitality and protection from the punishment of your own people, if you surrender your arms and come with us. I speak not as Varinia, for that name is dead now, but as Dorcla, leader of the Damnonii. We have armies massed in readiness behind these hills, so you need not worry for us, only for yourselves.*

Now! –Quintus shouts, and fires off an arrow then another as he gallops against the circle of warriors. Caius rides at the prisoner Titus and cuts his bonds with one swipe of his gladius and throws him a shield and dagger. The remaining milites also spring into action as they have been trained, attempting to sow panic with their horses and spears. Breaking through the startled Damnonii, all but one of the four horsemen escape, while the Damnonii take up their own mounts in pursuit.

*

We feel what Dorcla feels. She and her entourage ride hard to catch up with the fleeing Romans. Many others of her warriors have appeared on each side, blocking the fugitives' escape. She was so sure this was what she wanted, but now something unexpected is giving way inside her, something she imagines that her father could never guess or understand. The purpose of breaking the deal was to keep Caius prisoner, to make him part of the tribe *because...* her pony's hooves thunder under her as she races downhill over bracken and gorse. She finds it hard to face down the turmoil of feelings inside her now. *Because...* her heels dig into her pony's sides, as they leap over a burn. *Because...* she does not want Caius to escape, but she does not want him to die either, as he doubtless will if he continues to ride on the same course into the heart of the marshland. *No!* She cries out to her archers and spearmen. *Their spokesman must be spared. We take him alive only. Only the others may be killed.* She knows those not yet wounded will be claimed by the marsh.

But then she shrieks in dismay, seeing that it is already too late. Caius himself and his horse are floundering, beginning to sink into the treacherous mud of the bog. Every Damnonii child knows the stories, the dangers, but what is this thing rising up inside her now, her horror at the thought of Caius' death, of his blood on her hands. She cares for him… it must be, the only shameful explanation. Or maybe even something more. Her tutor and guardian for the formative years of her life. Who probably guessed at her treacherous intentions, but let her go anyway, who wanted her to be free. She knows in a terrible moment of calm logic that she must try to save him.

She calls her men off, to wait on the dry land, even as they reach out their hands, begging her to desist and not go any further. But she tells herself she is lighter than the armoured soldiers and their horses. What momentary dreams flash through her head? Some childlike fantasy of a future in an unimaginable Rome? –or of a simpler life in exile in some other wilderness where the shackles of their two worlds might finally fall away under the hammer blow of the heart? She falls to her knees then moves forward on all-fours, then on her stomach, a Damnonii queen in her white robes brought down to this. What is this folly, this indignity that would risk all decorum and wisdom in front of all these appalled onlookers? She calls out his name, and he hers, even as the mud grows closer to his gasping mouth. She reaches out her hand, he reaches out his to hers. But they never quite touch. Instead the ancient cold of the peat bog reaches both of them with its eternally remorseless grip, then clutches and drags down. Redemption for the mortal comes too late it seems, in every culture. The mud knows no differences, knows no human tongue, neither Latin nor barbarian. Only that they are a man and a woman, and how to preserve their dead bodies as a message to the future, for the next two thousand years.

~~~
~~~

ACKNOWLEDGEMENTS

Thanks as ever to all encouragers and inspirers, including but not limited to: Peter and Alison at Elsewhen, Margaret Elphinstone for close reading, suggestions and wisdom, and to C M Muller for publishing in America the first and last chapters (in earlier versions) in his anthologies *Nightscript* Volume 7 and *Tenebrous Antiquities* respectively.

AFTERWORD

By Margaret Elphinstone

What can 'Retrovival' possibly mean? Could it mean the resurrection of the two-thousand year-old body of a Roman centurion once stationed on the Antonine Wall? It takes a veritable tour de force on the part of an author for the reader willingly to suspend disbelief and accept not only the proposition but all its disruptive consequences. Douglas Thompson entices us into a world of possibilities, and keeps us there through empathy with his bewildered characters and a wildly spinning plot. The spinning, however, is carefully controlled by thematic unities. All the threads come together, showing an intriguing, multi-faceted pattern. The whole is an interrogation of Scotland: its past, its present (by implication) and possibilities for what its future could look like, ranging from the inspiring to the horrific.

Retrovival means much more than infusing one dead body with artificially induced life. We don't call it crazy fantasy to try, often obsessively, to revive the past. Enlightened study of history is all about revising narratives of the past based on recovered evidence, intellectual rigour and, of course, the zeitgeist of the changing present. But anyone – politicians, artists, fiction writers, demagogues – can re-write the past according to their current visions. Any individual, family or nation can create a narrative of the past that mirrors their need for a perceived identity.

The novel is all about links between the Scottish past and its future, created by narratives spun in the ever-changing present. In the Prologue, two of the protagonists, separated – or not – by a space of two thousand years, confront one another. "They both approach the glass wall from different sides and test it with their weapons, trying to find weaknesses, some way through". But no one can actually cross the glass wall of time, however much they have in common, because the body is corruptible, and flesh can only live and breathe for its own brief lifetime.

As the plot unfolds, modern international political tropes are transposed to a Scottish situation. Drest the woman fascist dictator (shades of Thatcher darkly marked), the cruelties enacted at the Border wall, the invasion of Northumberland… this dystopic fantasy reflects all too realistically Israel/Palestine, Russia/Ukraine, Northern Ireland and many more conflicts of our own times. In the last two centuries fascist appropriations of history are legion. On chillingly recognisable Scottish ground – the geography of the novel is at all times as precise as any geopositioning – we see the all-too-familiar sequence of repression giving rise to new forms of authoritarianism and Neo-imperialism. What happens, for example, to the character Trevor is truly terrifying because the seeds are latent in our present. This is political analysis expressed through futuristic fantasy, set in a real, recognisable country. Prophetic fantasy is an ideal way of revealing possibilities without getting drawn into entrenched argument.

The plot may be fantastic, but it's founded in solid ground. The topography of both Scotland and Italy, also the ubiquitous symbolic buildings, reveal a meticulous architectural approach which gives classical substance even to the most Gothic flights of plot. In any case, the breathless suspense will carry readers anywhere the author wants to take us. The archaeological thread leads us literally underground, as we follow the grave robbers on their equivocal journey. Throughout the book the past is constantly dug up, and abused, consciously or unconsciously, by different agendas. It's not only Caius who is resurrected. Other characters are re-instated, or deliberately take on new identities. The archaeologists themselves, although engaging, are not exempt from critical interrogation. Just how far will academic imperialism, in any field, carry one into very debatable lands?

The book ends with an epilogue that occurs, literally, in these same debatable lands. A moving story in its own right, the past is re-written once again. All through the novel the Border has been a lethal place. In the Prologue, the instinct of the two soldiers meeting across the impregnable wall of time, is immediately to attack one another. From the very first chapter the Border has been a place of malevolent derangement, separation and violent death. But in the final chapter another possibility emerges. Caius and Dorcla each had their own vision of how oppositions might be reconciled. Two thousand years ago such dreams could only fail. But the dream existed, and still does. Could the future, even now, be different?

'Retrovival' is Thompson's most engaging and hard-hitting book since 'The Brahan Seer'. It shares with the earlier novel the re-structuring of past and future into a single imagined present, embodied in individual lives. One could call the plot-line of both books fantasy, but isn't this precarious balance between reimagined pasts and speculative futures also the reality which we all inhabit, always?

– Margaret Elphinstone, September 2024.

Elsewhen Press

delivering outstanding new talents in speculative fiction

Visit the Elsewhen Press website at elsewhen.press for the latest information on all of our titles, authors and events; to read our blog; find out where to buy our books and ebooks; or to place an order.

Sign up for the Elsewhen Press InFlight Newsletter at elsewhen.press/newsletter

About Douglas Thompson

Glasgow writer Douglas Thompson won the Herald/Grolsch Question Of Style Award 1989, 2nd prize in the Neil Gunn Writing Competition 2007, and the Faith/Unbelief Poetry Prize 2016. His short stories and poems have appeared in a wide range of magazines and anthologies, including *Ambit, Albedo One, Chapman* and *New Writing Scotland*. Variously classed as a Weird, Horror, Sci Fi, Literary, or Historical novelist, he has published more than 17 novels and collections of short stories and poetry since 2009, from various publishers in Britain, Europe and America.

https://douglasthompson.wordpress.com/